THE CLINCH

Visit us at www.boldstrokesbooks.com

By the Author

Hers to Protect

Secrets on the Clock

Shadows of a Dream

The Clinch

THE CLINCH

by

Nicole Disney

2021

THE CLINCH

ISBN 13: 978-1-63555-820-3

This Trade Paperback Original Is Published By
Bold Strokes Books, Inc.
P.O. Box 249
Valley Falls, NY 12185

First Edition: January 2021

CREDITS
Editor: Cindy Cresap
Production Design: Susan Ramundo
Cover Design By Tammy Seidick

Acknowledgments

First, I want to thank Bold Strokes Books. I am so honored and happy to be part of this group of incredibly talented and kind people. Thank you to Radclyffe for building this beautiful community and giving our stories a home.

To my awesome editor, Cindy Cresap, thank you so much for all of your work, patience, advice, kindness, and for seeing the things I can't. You always take me up a level.

And, of course, to the love of my life, Cassandra. Always my first reader, my guidance when I'm stuck, my reassurance when I'm full of doubt, my fellow dreamer, and my best friend no matter what. I love you.

Dedication

For all of the incredible instructors and coaches
who brought the beauty of martial arts into my life,
especially Kancho Joko Ninomiya, who was of
particular influence in life and in this story.

Chapter One

The last few moments in the twilight of class are enchanting. At the start, students are humming with extra energy, blitzing through the warmup and first techniques with haphazard enthusiasm and overextended motions. By the middle, they're winded and cherry faced. Technique tapers as they become afraid exerting full effort will render them too exhausted to protect themselves. The end creeping into the room gives them permission to use their final reserves. They're deep in the mental space of the art now. They're strained, fatigued, but focused. All awareness of cell phones and emails and squabbles drains, and there is only breath, the next movement, the resonance of a roundhouse landing on a body shield.

I circle the room, watching, feeling my weight sink into the red mats that shape a large rectangle, enclosing the blue mats that make up the center and majority of the dojang. The design mimics a large fighting ring, the colors reflecting those of the Korean flag that hangs at the front of class next to an American one and a row of the different color belts. The dojang is relatively small, fitting only fifteen students at a time comfortably, though in my morning classes I often have as few as five.

Today, I have a handful of my most dedicated, a blue belt named Mateo who was only recently promoted to his rank and is still trying to prove he belongs in this much harder and older class; my serious regulars Josh, Mariana, and Cael. And last, Laila. She's the first student I ever took all the way from white to black belt and will always hold a special place in my heart. She's also the membership manager, and these days, only jumps in for class when it's slow enough to allow.

On the far side of the dojang, Josh's strong and relaxed energy highlights Mateo's frantic effort to flank him using much longer steps than he ever should. On the closer side, Laila whips a spinning back kick right in front of Cael's face.

I want to stretch this moment and give them a few more seconds of this peace where all their worldly problems are suspended, but ending class late is a privilege I reserve for only the most extreme circumstances. It's typically punishment for a heinous lack of respect, a problem I haven't faced once since winning the UFC featherweight championship. Would-be students flooded in when that happened, but most of them filter right back out in confusion and agitation when they realize I teach traditional Taekwondo, not the modern mixed martial arts of the UFC. What I teach is only a slice of what it takes to compete in the Ultimate Fighting Championship.

"Jonglee." I project the Korean word in my deep, assertive instructor voice that comes second nature these days. They follow the command to line up, sprinting to their places designated by rank, high to low with equal space in between each of them. I stand at the head of the room facing them and give a slight nod to Laila.

"Cha ryuht," she commands, calling the students to attention, the position I've already assumed. "Recite the tenets."

The class chants in unison, filling the dojang with just a few voices, "Courtesy, integrity, perseverance, self-control, and indomitable spirit."

I indicate for them to continue with the student oath, and each of them recites one line starting at Laila and ending with Mateo.

"I shall observe the tenets of Taekwondo. I shall respect the instructors and seniors. I shall never misuse Taekwondo. I shall be a champion of freedom and justice. I shall build a more peaceful world."

Laila issues the command for them to return to their previous position, "Bah ro." Then sit. "Ahnjoe." When they've settled, I nod at Laila, and she says, "Mukyum." Meditate. It used to feel strange to meditate for such a short duration and on sudden command, but I find the miniature reprieves comforting now. After just thirty seconds or so, Laila claps twice to end meditation. I rise, and Laila tells the class to face me and bow. "Sah bum nim keh. Kyung nae."

Cael, as the second ranked student, instructs the class to bow to Laila for guiding them through the beginning and end of class. "Sun bae nim keh. Kyung nae."

"Hai sahn," Cael says to officially end the lesson. The entire class thanks him and bows. Mateo's posture slumps the moment he's relieved of the command to stand at attention, and he heads for his gym bag at a crawl. I catch up to him easily before he can bow off the mat and put my hand on his shoulder.

"Hey, that's not how you usually look after class. What's the matter?"

Mateo is easily one of my favorite students. He listens with all of his energy, always tries his hardest, and is just plain sweet. He looks at the floor and shrugs. I kneel, which makes me shorter than he is but improves my chances of real eye contact.

"You know Josh has been training a lot longer than you, right? It's okay if he got the best of you sparring today. You'll be just as good before you know it."

He nods, but somehow, he looks even more upset. Before I can ask again, he covers it with a smile that almost looks genuine.

"I'm okay, Master Bauer, but I have to go."

My first instinct is to press more, but the way he's already backing away tells me not to, so I let him join the others, hoping he'll tell them whatever he can't tell me.

It takes a few minutes for all of them to change their clothes and wrap up their chitchat. It always fills me with affection when I see students become friends. Living in Highbridge isn't easy, and before the influx of students my career in the UFC brought, the kids who showed up at the dojang were ones who grew up just like I did, broke and equally terrified of home and the streets. Learning to fight certainly helped me walk the neighborhood with more confidence, but what really changed everything was having a community, people who waved at you when you passed by, people who would help if you were being mugged or harassed.

The room falls to silence abruptly with the clang of a bell as they leave. I jump a little when I turn and see Mariana right next to me.

"Sorry," she says with a slight jolt of her own.

"It's okay," I say. "I thought you all went out at once. Wasn't expecting you to be there."

"I know, sorry. I'm such a creep." Mariana rakes her sweaty black bangs out of her eyes.

"Not at all. What's up?" I've been teaching Mariana for three years now. She was a fifteen-year-old kid walking around Highbridge on the fast track to become a problem the first time I saw her stalling in front of the dojang. I invited her to a class, much like the way Jin, the founder of the dojang, scooped me out of the jaws of the street years before that. She's changed so much since then.

"Nothing, never mind," she says.

"Are you sure? We could go to the office—"

"No." She backs away. "Nothing, there's no thing."

"Mariana."

"See you next class, Master Bauer." She backs out the door before I can stop her. Damn, strike two. I churn over the interaction as I inch over to where Laila is typing away at the computer. She's still flushed from class and wearing uniform pants and a tank top now.

"Is it just me or was that kind of—"

"Awkward as a chicken on ice?" she says without looking up. "Yep."

"You think she's okay?"

Laila makes eye contact for a long second. "You're adorable."

"What?"

She smiles, mostly to herself. "She's enamored with you, UFC goddess. Duh."

"Oh, stop." The thought is mortifying in one way and a relief in another. I thought she was in trouble. Enamored is a word that wouldn't have come to me in a million years.

Laila plucks a paper out of the stack in front of her and looks it over. "Yes, long live your denial bubble. What I need to know is, does the end of class really need to have eight thousand steps? Attention, bow, attention, down, up, meditate, bow to the person who told you to bow to the other person, thank that person for thanking the other one, do the macarena. For fuck's sake."

I shake my head and smile. "That's how Taekwondo classes work, Laila. Don't let the students hear you crying about it, either."

She cracks a wry smile and tries to spike up her Halle Berry hairstyle again, reviving it from its sweaty, flattened condition. "Please, I would never. I just like harassing you. You know part of you wants to lose the uniform, blast some Metallica, and just punch people in the face."

"That's what I have you for."

"Mateo didn't pay his dues again."

I sigh. "So *that's* why he was upset."

She hands me the paper she's been studying, his membership agreement. I take it because it feels rude not to, but there's not much I don't already know about Mateo. He's only twelve and trying to pay for his own membership on a dishwashing job while also putting food on the table for two siblings and his father, who seems to be equal parts addict and dealer.

"Just charge it to my card."

Laila cocks her head. "You can't do that for all of them, Eden."

"Of course I can. If you ask him about it he'll either quit or find an illegal way to come up with it. I don't want either of those things."

"Neither do I, but this isn't sustainable. You're paying full or partial tuition for almost half of our students. Does the grandmaster know that?"

"No, and don't you tell him. I'm fine with it. Really."

"I know you are, Mother Teresa, but it doesn't change the fact that the dojang isn't profitable. Hasn't been for a long time."

"Yes, it is. Everyone's dues are paid, just by me."

The corner of Laila's mouth tugs into a half smile, and she shakes her head. "You know what I mean. If it weren't for you,

Emerald Tiger would go under in less than a year. What happens when you don't have this kind of cash to burn? No one fights forever."

"I'm smart with my money."

"Anyone watching you do this would beg to differ."

"Yikes." I chuckle. "Really going in on me today, huh?"

"No." She sighs. "People who are always watching out for others just tend to forget themselves. This place is your post competition plan, which means at some point it needs to give you money. And besides that, what about Grandmaster Suhmoon? It would kill him to have the dojang go out of business."

Just the thought of letting Jin down is unbearable. "Is it that bad?"

"We're ignoring a failing business model because you're stable enough to keep it afloat, and yes, that's risky. But no, it's not *that* bad. We both know how you could fix it."

"I'm not turning it into an MMA gym."

"Do you have any idea what up-and-coming fighters would pay a world champion to coach them?"

"No, and it doesn't matter. That's the same as losing the dojang. Grandmaster Suhmoon wouldn't let us do it anyway. You act like it's my place."

"He would too, if you asked," she says. "He trusts you."

"That's because I would never ask him something like that. He's a Taekwondo grandmaster, Laila. To tell him his dojang is failing and ask him if I can take over, strip it of all its tradition, and turn it into a sport fighting gym?" It's uncomfortable to even picture it. "It would be so profoundly disrespectful."

"Do you think he would've helped you train for MMA fights if he thought it was so awful? You're representing his teachings in the biggest, most challenging competition in the world."

"Not if this becomes like every other MMA gym." I hand back Mateo's membership agreement. "Look, I promise to take the problem seriously, but there has to be another way. In the meantime, I don't care if I have to spend every penny to my name. The dojang stays open, and the membership for every single Highbridge kid stays current."

"You're the boss." Laila tosses the paper into the extra space of the filing cabinet, not bothering to file it correctly. "All right, are we done with dojang business?"

"You tell me."

"Girl, I am done, and I am switching hats to your so-excited-I-might-pee MMA friend. Let's hit the road and go see these fights!"

"You know Atlantic City is only two and a half hours away and the main card isn't until ten, right?"

Laila cocks her head and shoots an incredulous scowl at me. "Please don't tell me you think I'm only interested in the main card. Eden, I know this is business as usual for you, but I thought you understood that I'm going to need you to use your champion superpowers to get me into the main card, the prelims, the early prelims, the locker rooms, the octagon, preferably introduce me to all the martial artists, Dana White, Joe Rogan. I want to meet the ref. I want to meet people I don't even know exist yet. And I'm going to need pictures of all of this. Not to mention we have recon to do."

"Recon?"

"Reconnaissance…" She pauses. "On Brooklyn Shaw. Isn't that why we're going to this?" She pauses again. "Because everyone's saying she's going to take your belt?"

"They're what?" I hear my own voice go up an octave and wish it wouldn't do that. "Wha…Who said…She's been competing for two seconds! We're going to this because it's close and you've been begging me to take you to an event for months."

"Okay." Laila holds up her hands innocently.

I want to pretend the talk is too far beneath me to worry about, but I've already blown that. "No one's told me anything like that."

"Of course not," Laila says. "Who the hell would say that to you? I just thought you probably saw it in *Combat Zone*."

"They're talking about it in *Combat Zone*?" There goes my voice again. I have that stupid newsletter sitting in my email but haven't gotten to it yet.

"Okay, I'm not talking anymore," Laila says.

I try to shake off the jolt. "Forget it. I would have seen it in a day or two anyway. It's no big deal. That's what they do, right?"

"Right," she says in a peppy voice that doesn't quite balance out her slightly scared expression.

"Seriously, don't worry about it," I say. "Just caught me off guard. I'll go change, and we'll head out. I'll take a video of you doing a walkout to the octagon and we'll put some music to it later."

The rest of her apprehension melts, and she flexes and grins. I let myself through a locked door that leads to a hallway that then splits off to four tiny live-in student rooms, one of which is home.

I play around with Laila like her obsession with the UFC is obnoxious, but being able to make someone as happy as she is now is new to me. It's my favorite thing about the fame that still fits like I'm wearing someone else's coat even after four years as the champion.

Brooklyn Shaw. I take off my dobok, or uniform, and fold it with the same methodical motions Jin taught me so many years ago, eyeing my laptop as I do. I mean to just grab a T-shirt and jeans and go meet Laila out front, but I can't help it. I open my *Combat Zone* email, an MMA news source I suddenly find repulsive, and scroll down until I see it. I've heard her name before. I even saw the highlights from her debut, including the haymaker of a punch that knocked her opponent out and garnered her an early buzz.

Even so, seeing a clear still of her where she's facing the camera, I realize I never had a great look at her. She's built differently from me, three inches shorter and even more shy on her reach according to her stats, but visibly stronger. Her skin is warm ochre brown and traced with tattoos over a good portion of her arms, but the angle doesn't allow for a clear read of them other than the cross on her left forearm. The sides of her head are shaved and feature some simple stenciling while the top is a few inches long and curly.

Certain fighters just inherently own an intimidating quality. It could be the strength of her jawline, the prominence of her cheeks, the obvious musculature of her arms, or the intensity in her deep brown eyes. Whatever it is, she's the type of fighter people who know nothing about martial arts assume will win. I've never had that myself. I'm tall, but naturally lean, and though I'm strong and toned, you wouldn't call me jacked. Chopping off my long hair or inking up more could probably help my cause, but I've never been one to concern myself with impressing the public.

I scan the article for the goods and land on a few simple lines. "Brooklyn Shaw may just have the answer to reigning champ, Eden Bauer. Bauer's precision striking has been too overwhelming and technical for her former opponents, but Shaw brings insane power, heart, and an iron jaw to the fight. I won't be surprised to see her walk right through Bauer's best and take her to the ground. Once that happens, there's little to debate about what happens next. Everything you need to know about Shaw's Brazilian Jiu-Jitsu is right there in her name. She's Samson Shaw's daughter and the youngest in a family line that has produced nothing but BJJ brilliance. Her skill on the ground is miles beyond what Bauer can handle."

I'm not too big to admit the words send a jolt through me, a mixture of bruised ego, resentment, and yes, if you must know, a twinge of, let's call it uneasiness. I scroll back up to look at her one more time. A rush tingles through my arms and plummets into my stomach. It's not a reaction I was prepared for and is so off topic it's disorienting, but there it is. Besides being shredded, inked, and an apparent grappling prodigy, the woman is also crushingly sexy. Jesus, that's annoying.

I slap my laptop shut, finding my way back into reality. I take a deep breath and remind myself these *Combat Zone* writers have similarly extolled other new fighters who were subsequently run over by the established talent. It's way too early to get worked up. Even if everything goes perfectly for her, she's at least a year away from being my problem. She's only had two professional MMA fights, and I'll get to see her third tonight. Recon may not be the worst idea after all.

CHAPTER TWO

Laila acts like she needs me to get her into behind the scenes conversations, but really, I just get her past the door and she's off like a firecracker. I've barely shaken the drive out of my legs before she's in the back corridors of Boardwalk Hall bumping into the athletes, coaches, and unknown people she chats up just in case she's failing to recognize someone important. I keep an eye on her in case someone starts to look like a hostage, but they all seem more than happy to break down all the matchups and swap theories with her. Even though she comes off bubbly and flirty, she both has her ego magnificently in check and knows her stuff.

She goes to a top MMA gym almost an hour from the dojang. It's definitely not a compliment to have an employee who has the benefit of a free membership drive across town and pay exorbitant fees to attend another school, but it doesn't offend me. Laila is a pro hopeful, and she's not delusional to reach that high. As much as I credit my success to Jin's Taekwondo, Laila isn't wrong to want training in a full range of skills. I'm not any better about it. I go with her to her gym a few nights a week to get in some Brazilian Jiu-Jitsu training, not to mention the third gym I go to every morning for Muay Thai training, but then, it's basically my entire job to train. The fact that Laila damn near keeps up is impressive.

On top of all that, we still throw on gloves and get after it between classes, and she's always there to spar and hold pads for the eight weeks of fight camp, the intense training immediately leading up to a professional bout. I couldn't ask for a better friend or be happier to put her around people who could change her life.

"What's good, Bauer?"

I turn to find Arlo Ruiz on my right, a casual friend I don't see much of since he moved to Canada to train with a coach who seems custom made for him. His hands are already wrapped even though he's the second to last fight of the night, going up against a tank of a Russian named Rodion Kuznetsov. I slap hands with him and wrap my arm around him.

"You look good, bud. I can't wait to see you slap a triangle on this guy." Arlo is a Jiu-Jitsu specialist, like so many now. He took risky fights out of the gate and has a record that doesn't do him justice because of it.

"Oh yeah? You like my triangle?"

"Thing of beauty."

"All right, girl. Triangle it is, just for you. Hey, you let me know if you ever want me to show you how I lock it in. It's not as fancy as it looks."

It shouldn't mean anything to me. Just Arlo being friendly like he always is, but I can't help but wonder if he read the *Combat Zone* article too, if he's gently suggesting I get better at Jiu-Jitsu before it's too late.

"And you can show me that patented Eden Bauer wheel kick," he adds.

"Any time." I slap his shoulder to end the conversation. The buzz in the arena is getting louder, which means the prelims are starting soon. I gesture at Laila to wrangle her in. I half expect to have to drag her away from the coach she's talking to, but she wraps it up without further prodding and joins me again.

"I cannot believe I'm here," she says. "I can't believe this is your life every day."

I laugh. "It's not every day." It's not even a lot of them, really. Everything I do is read as completely odd and a bit standoffish to the community. I train in a Taekwondo gym with a handful of mostly non-pro sparring partners, have no MMA coach or nutritionist, and almost never socialize. People think I'm insane. Laila already fits in better.

"Let's get to our seats."

"Are they ringside?" she asks. "Er, octagon-side? Boy, that doesn't roll off the tongue, does it?"

"Hell yes, they are." I guide her out of the back corridor and onto the main floor. Once we pass through the thick door, it's like someone turned up the volume on life. The arena is about half full, fairly normal for the prelims.

"Eden! What do you think about the Corelle vs. Shaw fight? Who do you like to win?"

I can't even place the reporter, and I don't particularly want to. Security is flanking both our sides like magic, helping us get down to our seats. One "Eden" turns into three, then five, then the whole arena starts to cheer, and I look up to verify I'm on the big screen. I smile and wave. Laila looks flummoxed to be on camera. Her lack of recovery makes me laugh. I grab her wrist and keep her moving. It always feels like it takes five seconds too long for the cameras to move on to someone else. When it finally changes to another fighter in the house, Laila faces me and grabs my shoulders.

"That was horrifying."

"Better get used to it, future contender."

"Do you get used to it? Tell me you get used to it."

"Not really. Kind of?" I shrug, pull her to our seats, and thank security before they go. "They'll probably do it again by the end of the night."

Laila looks mortified and starts running her fingers through her hair. She only gets through a couple of mad swipes before the lights go out. Red lights circle overhead while the announcer's voice booms through a welcome and moves into the first introductions of the night. The first fighter, Smith, bounds down the aisle in a bouncy jog to an extra twangy country song. The second comes out slow and smooth to Snoop Dogg.

"Okay." Laila leans in. "So, I thought this kid, Smith, was going to win," she says. "But Randall, the supercoach, just told me in back it'll never happen. I'm such shit at predicting winners."

"Everyone is shit. It's guesswork."

"Bastard."

"All they're doing is looking at the fighter's history, which is the exact same thing their opponent is doing. Anything we see, both of the martial artists have seen and prepared for too."

"Thank you, wise one."

I bump her with my shoulder. "Shut up."

The ref points at each fighter, asking if they're ready, then signals for the start of the fight. Smith and Crowler dance around the octagon, throwing sharp jabs that don't come close to landing, trying to loosen up and find their range. There's no sport's crowd more intolerant of down time than MMA's, and soon they're urging the fighters to engage with incoherent yells. The guys start throwing punches, their arms tangling as they battle for position. As preliminary fights often do, the fight goes all three rounds, finally ending in a decision by the judges to award the victory to Smith.

"Hey, you were right." I nudge Laila with my elbow.

The arena seems to warm up as the prelims march on and more people trickle in. I do my best to enjoy the matchups with Laila, but I can't pretend I'm not distracted. The main card consists of five fights, the first of which will be Brooklyn Shaw and Jada Corelle, and it's all I can think about. The fact that Brooklyn is on the main card at all with only two fights to her name may indicate the impression she's made on the UFC brass. Then again, it could also simply mean some other scheduled fight fell through as they quite often do.

There's an unspoken tension between Laila and me as Brooklyn's fight creeps closer. I don't want to give Brooklyn more power than she's earned, but I'm not sure anymore what takes that power back, admitting the *Combat Zone* article got under my skin, or denying the words the right to exist in real discussion.

The break between the prelims and main card feels ungodly long, longer than usual, though I know that's unlikely. Jesus, how many times will I have to defend my title to stop feeling like some kind of fraud? Will it ever happen? Or is there something deep inside me that's too broken to ever feel that kind of confidence?

Just as the arena is in the full buzz of idle chatter, the lights snuff out and the crowd roars back to life. The octagon floor is painted in glowing blue light and the overheads are a dazzling display of red, blue, and yellow. The start of these events always tickles the same giddiness I felt the first time I ever saw one. It awakens the other half of my soul, the piece that's so different from the quiet stillness I find in the tranquil wisdom of the dojang. This is where instinct emerges, where discipline is tested at its most animal and desperate. It's where you find out who you are in a fight to the death without actual death.

Brooklyn's walkout song blasts into the arena, much louder than the ones from the prelims. The apocalyptic chorale masterpiece, "Carmina Burana: O Fortuna." I can't help but crack a smile at the entirely unexpected choice. It's like Brooklyn is walking to the octagon accompanied by an armada of angels at her back. I watch her on the big screen. There's nothing unusual about walking to the octagon with her hood up and an expression like she's entering the colosseum, but there's something uniquely convincing about her.

She stops at the steps to the octagon, just twenty feet from us now. She strips down to her fight clothes, blue knee-length shorts and a crop tank top, which is really just a sports bra. She hands her hoodie and sweats to one of the men at her side, then turns to the one who's presumably her coach. He has model features, a strong jawline and prominent cheeks. I'm so focused on how much he looks like her it takes me a second to realize he's Théo freakin' Shaw, the accepted greatest BJJ phenom of all time, though his career ended prematurely from a series of brutal injuries. Brooklyn's lineage snaps to vivid reality.

"Eden, that's—"

"I know."

Brooklyn hugs the other two men who comprise her team. By their appearance, I assume they're relatives too. Besides Théo, I don't know them by name, but I do know the Shaw line has others, and now I wish I followed Jiu-Jitsu more closely. Brooklyn kneels at the steps to the octagon and bows her head in prayer. It surprises me at first, but as I look closer at the tattoos I couldn't make out in her picture, I realize most of them are religious, ranging from angels to saints to what I'm fairly confident must be scripture. Brooklyn takes her time with her prayer before finally crossing herself, slamming the mat with her palms, and launching into the octagon.

She looks out at the crowd as she does a lap around the mat, pointing and hitting her own sculpted arms and chest to hype herself up. Her muscle mass is even more impressive in person. She's hit the absolute maximum a person can achieve before it ceases to be functional in martial arts. It's strangely comforting. Picking apart martial artists who are used to winning with sheer athleticism rather than technique is my specialty.

As she circles to our side of the octagon, she locks eyes with me. A surge of adrenaline shoots through me as she holds the contact. It's like everything there is to know about her is right there, open and daringly accessible. She smiles and winks. My stomach roils like a constricting snake, but I don't react, mostly because I have no idea how to. She settles into her corner as Jada Corelle's intro begins.

Jada bounds down the aisle in a near sprint. She's leaner, longer, more experienced, and well rounded. The fight should be ideal for information gathering.

Bruce Buffer's classic announcer voice thunders through the crowd as he announces Brooklyn, sounding off her height, weight, and record before building up to her name and shouting in his way that never gets old, "Bruuuutalllll Brooklyn Shawwww!"

She may be new, but the crowd has taken notice and rumbles for her.

"Fighting out of the red corner, she's a mixed martial artist with a professional record of sixteen wins and four losses. Standing five feet, eight inches tall, one hundred forty-four and one-half pounds, Jadaaaa, the Executioner, Cooorellllle."

Young and hungry or not, Brooklyn has her hands full. It's almost not even fair to match her with Jada when she's still so new.

The referee puts his hand in the air between them, asks for a nod from each fighter, then pulls his hand away like it may get snapped up. "Fight!"

They bound to the center, bump gloves as a show of respect, and step back into neutral space. Jada has a bouncy style, always moving, always on her toes. She circles to Brooklyn's right, throwing a series of punches from too far out. Brooklyn evades them by pulling her head back. It's not wrong, but a better striker wouldn't waste the movement on shots that have no chance to land.

Jada pivots into her next punch, committing to her jab. Brooklyn eats it on the chin without reacting and fires back with a windmill overhand right. Jada covers up to block, but even though she manages to put her glove between Brooklyn's strike and her head, the force still knocks her way off center, and she backs away with a series of quick steps. Brooklyn pursues her, taking control of the center of the octagon, one of the categories fights are scored on.

Jada circles the outside of the octagon in what's more a shuffle than a fighting stance. Brooklyn comes after her in methodical forward steps, but Jada circles back the other direction, staying out of range.

"Damn, she didn't like that," Laila says.

"No, she did not."

Jada bends her knees to drop levels and shoots for Brooklyn's legs. She wraps her arms around Brooklyn's thighs, way too high, and Brooklyn sprawls, shooting her feet backward to break the grip. She hooks under Jada's arms and yanks her back to a standing position, then fires off a quick jab cross combo. Jada dodges enough to avoid full impact but looks thoroughly rattled.

"Why is she keeping it standing? Doesn't she want to go to the ground?" I mutter it mostly to myself, but I see Laila shaking her head in answer. Jada tries to back away again, but Brooklyn isn't having it. She launches after her in long strides, throwing punches trying to get back into range. Jada is a skilled boxer but seems to have forgotten everything as she all but runs from Brooklyn's high-pressure attack. The crowd heats up, cheering and yelling things at both martial artists, all mixing together in an indiscernible rumble.

Every single time Brooklyn strikes, she's swinging for the rafters. If Jada can keep her catching air, she's sure to tire by the end of round two at the latest, but nothing about this exchange suggests it will last that long.

Jada throws a front kick in an effort to get Brooklyn off of her. It lands right in Brooklyn's gut, and I search her for a reaction. I don't expect her to wear it on her face, but it ought to get her to reconsider the danger of setting up camp in striking range against a world class kickboxer. Brooklyn launches forward, slamming chest to chest with Jada and shoving her up against the fence in a rock-solid clinch with her hands locked behind Jada's neck, controlling her head. Jada tries to push back, but Brooklyn is so solid Jada's hands just slip off of her. I sit forward in my chair before I can stop myself.

The clinch is a position in which the fighters are holding on to one another and one of, if not the only, positions that can be good for either the striker *or* the grappler. It offers a striker the potential for devastating elbows and knees while also giving a grappler the chance to control the body and convert to a takedown. It's an equalizer.

I'm positive Brooklyn is about to make her move to take Jada to the ground and go for the finish, but still she doesn't. She slams an elbow into the side of Jada's head, then pulls back and does it again two more times before Jada realizes Brooklyn has no intention of stopping. Jada steps around Brooklyn's front leg and tries to pull her over, but Brooklyn steps out of the trip effortlessly and throws another elbow before finally pushing out of the clinch and firing off absolute bombs of punches clearly intended to end the fight.

"Oh shit!" Laila says.

Jada has both arms over her head now trying to shield herself, but Brooklyn's so powerful it doesn't matter. Finally, one slips through the center and catches Jada in the jaw. Her knees buckle, and she goes down. Brooklyn follows her to the ground, throwing hammerfist after hammerfist until the ref shoves an arm in between them, ending the fight.

Brooklyn springs away from Jada and yells a victory cry. She pumps her fist and circles the octagon like a pacing tiger. Théo bursts into the octagon and lifts Brooklyn up as she celebrates while Jada is in a crouch against the cage shaking her head. I wish I could crawl into her mind and see what she's thinking. Brooklyn pounds back to the canvas when Théo lets her go. She runs back to our side of the octagon, locks eyes with me, and raises her arm to point at me, holding the pose and staring me down with the intensity of someone hell-bent on avenging a death. It's more than determination. It's almost hatred. The crowd screams their approval. I smile and shake my head at first at the surprising antic, but she isn't stopping. Thousands of eyes burn into me waiting for a reaction, and heat crawls up my body.

It's like an eternity passes with her standing there pointing at me. She won't look away. What the hell is her problem? Who does she think she is? A jolt of anger takes over my body and before I can think about it, I'm on my feet with my arms held wide. The crowd freaks out. I don't know if I've ever heard them so loud. It jolts me into awareness. What am I doing? This isn't me. I've never in my life participated in this kind of literal posturing. It's like an out-of-body experience, but we're suspended in a faceoff I know I can't stop, not now.

The commentary legend, Joe Rogan, appears at Brooklyn's side for the post fight interview, and she finally drops her arm but keeps staring at me. I drop mine too and sit, waiting for whatever she's about to say to me.

"Brooklyn, congratulations on an incredible win. Take us through your thoughts on the fight."

Brooklyn takes the mic from him and promptly ignores his question. "What's up, Bauer?" She yells into the mic, filling the arena with a jarring but crystal-clear volume. "You got my belt. I'm coming for you, baby. Get ready." The crowd roars to life again. "Your reign is over. I'm going to crush you."

I roll my eyes and shake my head. Rogan takes the mic back. I can see security exchanging glances and discreetly positioning themselves in case this turns into something.

"Brooklyn, what an amazing performance. I know you have your eyes on a title shot. Can you tell me if you've been working on your striking a lot? I think we all expected you to take this to the ground going up against a boxing specialist like Jada Corelle."

"Everyone already knows about my Brazilian Jiu-Jitsu. Tonight was about showing the world I can rock anyone any way I want. You think you're safe on your feet I'm going to knock you out. You try to take me down, I'll rip you up. I'm the next champion."

"We're all looking forward to seeing you again, Brooklyn. Congratulations on your impressive victory."

Someone pats me on the shoulder. When I turn, there's a twenty-something-year-old guy way too close for comfort. "She's going to fucking kill you, Bauer."

Another guy who's watching leans in. "Pack your bags and run!"

"Hey, back up!" Security inches closer.

"Fuck her up, Eden!" a man screams from a couple of rows back. "Shaws are just thugs!"

The first guy turns around and snaps back. "Thugs win fights! Brooklyn, baby!" He's approaching the aisle with his chest out, apparently with the intention to go up to the other guy. More and more people are getting involved. Security rushes to intervene while one of them leans down to me.

"I'm sorry, but it would be best if we escort you out at this time."

"That's fine, let's go," I say it half to him and half to Laila. She springs to her feet and we file out, making our way into the staff halls where viewers can't access. We're surrounded on all sides by security now, and I can't decide if it makes me look cool or weak, not that it matters.

"Eden! Eden, what do you think of Shaw's callout? Are you going to fight her?"

I glance over my shoulder at the reporter and realize there're actually five of them. Shit.

"Are you worried about her striking now that she knocked out Corelle?"

"What do you think of the matchup, Eden?"

"Just one question, Eden!"

They sound off in a desperate squabble that blends together like a flock of geese. I stop abruptly, irritated beyond reason.

"You want to know what I think of the matchup? I think it's ridiculous. She came in hot and overwhelmed Jada. That doesn't mean she became a striking expert overnight. Her footwork was a mess. You can see her punches a mile away. Her defense is to bite her mouthguard and march into shots. She's not ready for me. She's had three fights. I don't care that she got a couple of wins. You don't get to fight for the title just because you want to. You have to earn it. If she does, of course I'll fight her."

"Eden—"

"That's it, guys. No more questions."

I blast through the back door into the private lot where we parked my Acura. I jump into the driver's seat, relieved and appreciative Laila is right there in step even though I'm hauling ass. They open the fence to let us out, and I pull onto the street. I lean into my seat and sigh, letting the exhale melt through all my muscles.

"You did so good," Laila says. "I know that kind of thing disgusts you, but you held your own. That statement is going to destroy her when she sees it."

"Shit, I didn't even think about that. I can't believe I let that get away from me so bad."

"You did perfect. She left you no choice."

CHAPTER THREE

I thought teaching class would give me the mental break I need from the eruption of attention that's been vomited all over me through articles, podcasts, videos, and social media following my little faceoff with Brooklyn. Turns out my students, even the seven- to nine-year-old class, are just as determined to talk about the possibility of a fight with Brooklyn as everyone else. They're wiggly and distracted and talking out of turn on a rotating basis.

"We should all be facing our partners in a fighting stance," I say. I pause to give the ones who aren't a moment to realize it on their own. Two do. The third is a boy named Jason who's still standing with his feet parallel and his top half tilted over his left side.

"Right foot back, Jason," I say. He shoots his hand in the air. In an older class I wouldn't allow another interruption, but in the younger classes you never know when one desperately needs to use the bathroom, so you can't ignore them.

"Yes, Jason?"

"Sah Bum Nim, when are you going to fight Brooklyn Shaw?"

"Class is for your training, Jason, not conversations. Fighting stance, please." Jason looks deflated but does as asked. No sooner than he pulls his foot back, Elaine's hand goes up.

"Elaine?"

"Will you tell us after class?"

"Focus on your teachings, Elaine. We're doing front kicks, ahp chagi. Trading off, begin. Seijak."

"Why won't you answer us?" Elaine turns into Silly Putty and starts drooping, bending her knees and collapsing into a puddle of defiance.

"Yeah! Tell us, Master Bauer! Are you going to fight her?" AJ pipes up now.

"Are you afraid?" Shanae asks.

This kind of behavior is not only inexcusable, but contagious. I'm about to swap my nice voice for the strict one and give them a rude awakening, but Jin beats me to it.

"Jonglee!" His voice is so deep and powerful it thunders through the dojang, yet he's not yelling. The students, not having realized he'd entered the room, jump, then sprint to line up. Jin, or Grandmaster Suhmoon, as he should be called in most situations, doesn't teach often anymore. He's not responsible for any classes whatsoever on the schedule and instead chooses to involve himself mostly in testing, tournament preparation, judging, and special training, which has mostly consisted of readying me for fights for years now.

I handle most of the classes, and we have one other instructor for the rest, an incredibly impressive martial artist named Corey who I almost never see because he only takes the hours I'm too busy to take. When I'm preparing for a fight, Corey will handle more and more. Even though Jin doesn't use the right often, being the grandmaster means any class he decides to take over becomes his the moment he sets foot on the mat.

I go to the front of the room and come to attention, leaving room for Jin in the highest-ranking space even though he doesn't move to fill it. Jin walks up and down each line of students. He doesn't have to move to correct their stance. They simply make the adjustments as they become hyper aware of his proximity.

"Jon gyung," he says. Respect. "When you are in my dojang, everything you do will be with respect. You will walk with respect. You will bow with respect. You will spar with respect. You will speak with respect. You will be silent with respect. Do you understand?"

"Ahlge seoyo," the class acknowledges in unison, or I understand.

"It is an honor to learn martial arts," he says. "In this dojang, you are taught techniques that can injure others. You are taught techniques that can kill others. As your grandmaster, I am responsible for you and what you do when you are here and when you are not. Students who cannot control themselves cannot be trusted with martial arts. Do you understand?"

"Ahlge seoyo."

"You will apologize to Master Bauer for your disrespect."

They apologize as a class, yelling even louder. "Choesong hamnida, Master Bauer."

Jin takes his place next to me at the front of the class and issues a warning that means he's about to put them through it. "If you leave before you are dismissed, you will not have shown the character required to continue your training. Do you understand?"

"Ahlge seoyo."

"Juchoom sohgi." Horse stance. It's a position most students have trouble properly reaching at all, and it becomes difficult to hold in a matter of seconds. Think of it as a plank for your legs. Jin will have them holding it and punching for the rest of our time.

When I was younger, I loved this style of class. It was torture, but it made everything feel so much more ancient and mystical. I felt like a Shaolin Monk learning from a great Sifu. Real warriors are made through extreme intensity and discipline, not automatic rank progression and fun. Maybe in trying to be understanding with the students I've sacrificed strength. For the first time in years, having Jin take over my class feels like I've been sidelined not for his enjoyment or as a treat for the students, but because I've failed.

When he dismisses class, the students bow out and gather their things, still quiet. Several of them apologize to me again before they go. They don't seem angry or upset, just, well, respectful. The door closes after the last one, and the dojang is silent again. Laila is in the supply closet doing inventory. Seeing her organizing all the different color belts reminds me testing is coming up in about a month. I sit at the computer and start clicking through students to evaluate who's ready, who isn't, and who I may be able to nudge along in time.

"You okay?" Jin asks. He's standing on the other side of the desk. His eyes are kind and soft, his face wrinkled but handsome. He's as tall as I am and maintains good muscle mass and posture, which makes him look young. When I first walked into Emerald Tiger seventeen years ago, he had a much heavier accent and spoke almost entirely in Korean. There were so many times I had no idea what he was saying. He would demonstrate a technique over and over again, stomping the ground or slapping his thigh trying to communicate what I was doing wrong. Now his English is close to perfect.

"Yes, of course," I say. "I'm sorry I let them get out of control. I'll do better next time." I hope my mask holds up. I don't want him figuring out I'm upset.

"At the start and close of every class, the instructor indicates what should be done with her actions, but it is the highest-ranking student who voices the commands."

I turn my chair to fully face him and take in whatever message he means to impart, but as I look in his eyes for a couple of seconds, I realize that may be all he says. He's not always cryptic, but he certainly can be. "Yes, Grandmaster."

He lets a few seconds pass before he puts his hand over mine. "I stepped in because it is distasteful for an instructor of your caliber to have to bark for your own benefit."

I smile and nod. "Thank you, Grandmaster."

"Now, do you want to talk about what happened in Atlantic City last night?"

I rub my hands down my face remembering it. "I never should have reacted to her like that. I gave her exactly what she wanted. I disgraced you and acted like a goon. I thought I was going to shut it down, but instead I pretty much guaranteed it'll happen."

"Are you worried you can't beat her?"

From anyone else I would probably be offended, but not Jin. "No, I'll beat her. I'm just mad at myself for walking into her plan."

"You were always my best student, Eden, because there was so much I didn't have to teach you. When you were late, you did push-ups on the side of class until I prompted you in. When your technique was poor, you stayed after until you figured it out. When you misbehaved, you stayed and cleaned the mats. You indulged your pride for a moment. If the price is that her plan works, you'll fight her, but disgracing me? No. I feel no shame when I look at you."

My throat knots up, and all I can manage is a nod.

"Take the rest of the day off. No classes, no martial arts, no UFC. Do something for your soul."

"Yes, sir."

I retreat to my room. My laptop is open, and the first thing I see from the doorway is a three-digit notification count on social media, so I shut it before temptation can get the better of me. Normally, I would resist taking the day off. I don't need days off. I love what I do. But today I feel like every time someone mentions this mess, they chip away a piece of my sanity. I switch my dobok for shorts and a tank top and glance around my room. It's the size of most dorm rooms, only big enough for a twin bed, a small bathroom and kitchen, and a loveseat that faces a dresser that also acts as my TV stand and desk.

It feels a bit like never moving out of your childhood bedroom in a way, but in another, it's not so different from how many New Yorkers live. I could afford something bigger and fancier at this point, sure, but for what? My quarters are separate from Jin's and allow for all the privacy of an apartment complex. The other three live-in student rooms on this side have been vacant for a long time now other than a night here and there for a kid in trouble.

I grab my phone to text Laila and see if she wants to get out for lunch, but she'll ruthlessly quiz me about Brooklyn Shaw. She'd probably be worse than the damn sports reporters. I slip my phone in my pocket and go out the back door, not sure where I'm headed. The cool spring air touches my skin like a kiss, still moist from morning rain.

The back door lets me out onto Merriam Ave. Living here used to intimidate me, but I'm so used to it now the area doesn't even occur to me often anymore. I attribute that largely to being grandfathered in. Jin earned his way into the good graces of the neighborhood because he was always willing to help out the kids, give them something to do and teach them something of value. He's always been so uncompromising with his training that the martial artists who attended his school were lethal and not good targets for robberies. Having a heart of gold but also being a walking weapon is a great combination for peace. It wasn't instant, but after spending enough time in the dojang, the immunity passed on to me. The second I became a contracted UFC martial artist I became the pride of the neighborhood.

I walk toward the bridge, actual High Bridge, and find a spot to look at the water and gather myself. I could catch a ride over to the Muay Thai or BJJ gyms I go to, but I can't ignore Jin's assignment even though he'd never know. I could find a spot in the grass and do some Tai Chi, but that's still off limits. Even meditating feels a little close for comfort.

Fuck. Is there not a single thing I enjoy that has nothing to do with martial arts? Not one friend outside this world? Surely, it's not my entire life. I search my phone for someone else to call, but they're really all acquaintances and semi-professional relationships. Forget a friend outside this world, I don't even have a real friend besides Laila. I feel a twinge of uneasiness at the realization Laila is my closest friend, and even we're not *that* close.

My phone buzzes. I'm relieved at the prospect the universe just sent me some long-lost friend right on cue, but when I look at the screen, it's my manager.

"Hey, Taylor," I say.

"Hi, Eden. I only have a minute, but I wanted to let you know the matchmakers really want to see this fight between you and Brooklyn Shaw happen. Anything you absolutely have to see in draft one of the contract?"

"Please be kidding." I rest my elbows on the railing of the bridge and look out over Harlem River.

He laughs. "Why?"

"What will that say? You can just stomp around the octagon saying you want a title shot and you'll get one? There are plenty of other women who have more years in, more wins, more—"

"You've already beaten them all, Eden."

"Brooklyn hasn't. It shouldn't work like that. You know the publicity and money she'll make from this fight. Other people have earned that. This is a stunt."

Taylor sighs. "Hey, I hear you, okay? I do, but the way they see it is she's not just any new fighter. She's a Shaw. She had a buzz long before she signed with the UFC, and she wins in spectacular fashion. They're convinced this is the right move. It's the fight people want to see."

I force myself to take a breath before I answer. They're right, really. I don't want to see bullying and disrespect rewarded, but I can't name another match that would make more sense. I'll have to put her in her place myself.

"If they want it so bad, I assume we're talking about a big ass check?"

"Yes, ma'am, I'm all over them about that," he says with a smile in his voice. That'll be good for the dojang at least. "You want to do it in New York?" he asks.

"Absolutely."

"You got it. That's home turf for her, too, in case you didn't know."

"Is it?"

"Yeah, she lives in Brooklyn."

"Of course, she does."

"But I've heard if it were up to her the fight would be in São Paulo, so you're still winning there."

"Brazil?"

"The roots go deep. They're die-hard fans."

"New York it is," I say.

"In four months?"

"Two."

He pauses. "Two?"

"That's eight weeks for fight camp, and as far as I know she didn't get hurt against Corelle. If she's so hungry she can skip her post fight vacation and come get some."

"I'm on it."

CHAPTER FOUR

My body feels heavy in my twin bed, like a force is pulling me deep into the mattress. After spending the whole afternoon bouncing a fight contract back and forth with the UFC, we finally reached an agreement. I could refuse entirely, but Brooklyn is twenty-two years old, which means if she wins this fight, she'll break my record for youngest champion. Maybe that's why she's making such a fuss. I suppose I can understand that.

With everything set in stone, I spent the evening on a ten-mile run. Sometimes it's the only way to wrestle my mind back into a quiet place. I'm not doing my inner peace any favors now by letting YouTube run a stream of suggested videos, but I try to digest them in a state of semi-meditation, letting them pass through my mind without granting them any emotional response.

Most of them are MMA "experts" talking over a video of Brooklyn's and my fight highlights, but there's a shortage of footage on Brooklyn. It validates my argument, but it also means I don't have much to study, and the little that does exist isn't very helpful. She's a Brazilian Jiu-Jitsu goddess, yet all of her wins have come through striking, so God knows what her takedowns or ground game look like. I scrounged up a few clips from the depths of the internet that are supposedly her early days in Brazil, but they're so low quality I can't even be sure it's really her.

My phone pings with a text message. Due to the crazy fast schedule of the fight, the match was announced immediately, and

I've been receiving a stream of people reaching out since. It's a nice surprise to see Laila's name instead of some unknown.

Did you see what Brooklyn just tweeted?

"Fuck." I sit up. "You try to be one with the universe."

I punch Twitter into the browser and go to Brooklyn's page. At the top, already garnering hundreds of likes after just fifteen minutes is the post Laila must've seen.

It's official. May 22 is the day I smash Eden Bauer and show you all what an overrated martial artist she is. No more weak champions. I'm coming for my belt.

I text Laila back. *I have now.*

Fuck her.

I laugh out loud at her response and scroll through more of Brooklyn's posts. This wasn't her first dig at me by a long shot. She's been calling me overrated for months, poking fun at everything about me from my fighting style to my interviews to my team and Emerald Tiger, calling us a band of ghetto karate kids. That sends a flash of anger through me, but Laila texts again and pulls me out of it.

Tweet back at her. Tell her you're going to break her dumbass face.

Break her dumbass face. *Sounds fun, but no.*

She texts back a second later. *You need to let a little of that Highbridge out on this one.*

In the octagon.

You're tense. Let's go get a beer.

I hover my thumb over the keyboard. Laila and I are friends, but I've always kept her at a certain distance because she's also a student and an employee. It feels out of bounds, but maybe that's silly. Jin didn't hold me at a professional arm's length forever. And when was the last time I was invited for a beer? I take too long to answer, and she texts again.

You're about to be in training for two months. It's your last chance.

Can't argue with her there. *You're on. The Lounge?*

Be there in fifteen.

I change clothes and walk the five minutes to the bar, weirdly nervous along the way. Taking her to the UFC event was different, damn near a work project, and we had something to watch. This is actual socializing, and I've never been much of a social person. When I connect with someone, they have a place in my heart forever, but it doesn't happen often.

When I walk up, Laila is waiting by the door in jeans and a skin-tight black tank top that shows off her toned shoulders and a bit of cleavage. Her short dark hair is styled and spikey.

"Hey," I say.

"Hey. So, is this where you usually hang out with friends?"

I laugh. "I don't go out much. Or have many friends. Or much of a life in general outside of the dojang, which is why we're at a place less than a mile from it."

"Sad, Eden. I'm getting you a shot."

"Have mercy."

"I'll go easy on you." She winks and disappears to the bar while I hunt us down a table. I find one in the back fit for two, and soon she's back handing me a shot and a beer.

"Thanks." The shot is sweet and easy to drink, whatever it is.

"So, you got a game plan for Brooklyn yet?" she asks.

"Not really. I have thoughts, but I haven't talked to Jin about it yet."

"Go on," she says. "Let's hear it."

"Pretty much what you'd think. Lots of takedown defense, keep her on her feet and exploit the striking difference. Get some extra survival Jiu-Jitsu training just in case. I'm not taking it as lightly as it sounds. I'm just a little exhausted with the subject."

"We don't have to talk about it." She props her elbows on the table. "What else is going on with you?"

I look away at the dimly lit bar speckled with people in the various stages of flirtation. I picture what it would look like to tell her something about my crazy childhood or my addict mom, but that's way too personal.

"Eden?"

"Huh? Sorry." I reach for a safe topic. "I'm worried about Mateo. He hasn't been back to class."

"It hasn't been long," Laila says. I can see she thinks I'm a little crazy to notice, but it doesn't come through her voice.

"I know, but he usually comes every day. He hates being at home. And if he couldn't pay dues, what else is he going without?"

"I'm sure he's fine. Maybe he's embarrassed. I can give him a call to make sure he knows he's still welcome if you want."

I nod. I've paid his dues before, so he should already know that, but it's better than nothing. "Thanks."

"Great, now you can stop thinking about the dojang and answer my question about what else is going on with you." She smiles a little mischievously, somewhere in that gray area between joking and flirting.

"There's nothing else going on with me," I say. "What about you?"

"You can tell me what's bothering you. I'm not going to run my mouth to the other students or anything. I hope you know that."

She has sincere eyes that pull me off guard, but I veer to the side of caution again and keep the conversation on the fight.

"Brooklyn's getting under my skin," I say. "I don't want to admit it, but it's true."

She reaches out and grabs my hand. "Eden, that stuff she said about you being overrated and weak is absolute garbage. Even *she* knows that. I promise."

"Thanks."

She leans back in her chair again, releasing my hand. "So, what're you going to do about her mouth?"

"What do you mean?"

"She obviously intends to talk shit every second of the day until the fight."

"How do you know?" I ask.

"She posted another one already just in the time it took me to get here."

"You're kidding."

"Nope." She pulls her phone out and opens Twitter. "And I quote, 'Eden Bauer, your time is up. Run away, little girl, before I break your little bird neck.'"

"Jesus." I shake my head. "What the fuck is her problem?"

"She's playing mind games. And you better start doing it back, none of this high road shit."

"You can't get in someone like that's head. She's too arrogant."

"Please, it's a front."

"You think?"

"Girl, she's just a brawler talkin' shit," Laila says. "It's nothing you haven't seen before."

"I don't know if that's what this is. She has real skills, and being from that family, I think she honestly can't fathom losing."

"At the very least you can piss her off, and aren't you always saying an angry fighter is the easiest to beat?"

I can't help but smile. "Hey, you actually listen to me."

"Of course, I listen to you. You're Eden fucking Bauer. Please quit acting like you've forgotten that."

The comment pierces me, and I instinctively grab it and put it in a cubby in my mind to look at later.

"You're good at this," I say.

"That's why I'm on your fight team." She beams a dazzling smile and takes a sip of her beer.

"Speaking of that, we start tomorrow morning. Game plan meeting with Jin to get the schedule together, then eight weeks of hell. I want this camp to be insane."

"Oh, I'll give you insane," Laila says. "Brooklyn Shaw is going to regret the day she forgot who the motherfucking champ is!"

"That's right!" I say. "Don't forget you can't cuss like that at the dojang, though." I smile and clink her glass with mine, then down the last beer I'll have until I've beaten Brooklyn Shaw.

CHAPTER FIVE

It's so liberating to be in the middle of a fight camp. There's no time or energy for my mind to get tangled in any kind of drama. I'm training twenty-four seven. Even my sleep is regimented for optimum recovery from the brutal exercises Jin puts me through. Having so many people volunteer for my camp soothes the fear that everyone wants to see Brooklyn crush me. It's just not true. Jin and Laila put their lives on hold to spend hour upon hour with me making sure I'm ready, studying Brooklyn's videos with me, holding pads, sparring, drilling, even running with me just to be there. There's just one face missing.

"Any word from Mateo?" I ask Laila for the hundredth time. He hasn't been back or reachable since the day his dues went unpaid. I had Laila invite him to my fight camp, a prospect that's so exciting to a kid I've never been turned down, but still no Mateo. Laila shakes her head. She manages a sad expression because she knows how worried I am, but she's still not taking it seriously. People quit all the time, and some of them find it hard to tell you they're quitting to your face. She thinks that's what this is, but I remember what it's like to have a scary home and just how much you look forward to class. I find it incredibly hard to believe he just quit, but I have no idea what I can do about it. I have nothing solid to take to the cops or social services.

The bell on the door rings, and Arlo Ruiz drops his gym bag just inside and holds his arms in the air with a huge smile across his face. Today is the first day of a four-week stint he's agreed to spend here in New York for the second half of my fight camp teaching me the finer points of Brazilian Jiu-Jitsu. I've already been in the dojang for an hour with Laila going through an insane workout Jin had the audacity to call a warmup.

"What's up, Sniper!" he yells with a beaming smile. "You ready to get up close and personal?"

I shake off my solemn thoughts of Mateo and smile back. "I am your humble student. I'm so sorry we didn't catch your fight in Jersey. I saw the replay. It was a beautiful win."

Arlo has gorgeous light brown skin and jet-black hair. Combined with his insane body, he looks like a movie star, something the fans haven't missed.

"Hey, that's okay. A troublemaker has to do what she has to do. I loved the power stance." He mimics the way I held my arms out to my sides at Brooklyn. Seeing him do it helps me see what everyone else did. I can only take myself so seriously, but it does look like a power move when he does it. "And the entourage around you when you bailed out. So cool. I hear the projections for sales on your pay-per-view are already through the roof. I'm taking notes, for sure."

"They're lessons from Brooklyn's book, but as long as it helps you."

"All right, killer, let's get it. Show me what you got."

Arlo follows me out onto the mats, and we start on the ground. We begin with him in my guard, a position in which I'm on my back, and he's on his knees with my legs wrapped around him. It looks like a disadvantaged position for me, but in the Jiu-Jitsu world, it's actually better, with many submissions available to me. In MMA, however, since strikes are allowed and he can punch from where he is, it's closer to even.

Arlo sets the tone early for a flowing practice in which we're constantly moving from position to position, attempting submissions but letting them go easily and early to move on to the next. Arlo moves fluidly, applying pressure, then backing off, then exploding the moment I relax. He easily has fifty pounds on me, which means my technique has to be perfect for anything to work, but if I get used to him, Brooklyn should feel much easier to deal with.

Though Jiu-Jitsu is designed to reward technique more than size, it still feels far from good when his hard shin digs deep into my thigh and drags across me with all his weight pressing down. He makes it to mount, a position that is exactly what it sounds like. He passed my legs and is straddling my stomach, creeping his way up toward my chest.

I try to sneak my elbows to the inside of his knees and inch my way back up, but he yanks my elbows up and slides his knees into my armpits. This would be the beginning of the end of a real fight. He's too high on me now for bridging my hips to be of any use. I could turn onto my stomach, but that would be worse. It's hard to breathe with his weight sinking down. I force myself to stop wasting energy on explosive movements that will never work and think, but before I come up with anything, he pats my side and jumps off.

"That's good, I get where you are," he says.

"Completely screwed?"

"I'm not going to lie to you, I can't make you as good as Brooklyn in four weeks. She's had a lifetime of training with the best of the best and it shows, but you're not as bad as people think."

"Thanks?"

"What are you in Jiu-Jitsu, a brown belt?"

"Purple."

"That works in your favor. They're underestimating you. You're not likely to tap her out, but I can teach you how to survive her for a round if she gets you down. And we'll work the shit out of takedown defense and getting back up to make sure you don't spend much time there."

"None if I can help it."

"I have some ideas. You ready to be sore in muscles you didn't know you had?"

"Please." I laugh. "If there's one thing I'm not worried about, it's conditioning."

"Believe me, I know all about your legendary cardio, but you strikers don't use the same muscles we do. It's going to get weird."

"Let's do it."

CHAPTER SIX

"Eden, you've been quiet in the leadup to this fight. Brooklyn has commented on your previous fights, your reign as champion, your Jiu-Jitsu, your team. Do you have any kind of response?"

It's not like me to zone out in the middle of a press conference, but the questions are just so predictable and mundane. It's like they're begging me to make a circus of this, and it strikes me as gross more than anything. The simple black table I'm sitting at houses my name tag and my belt. That says more than Brooklyn ever could. To my left is a podium where the UFC president, Dana White, is moderating. On the other side of him is another black table where Brooklyn is fielding questions. She's not getting as many as I am, which I'm sure is driving her nuts. I slowly pick up the microphone.

"Everyone gets ready for a fight in their own way. If she wants to concern herself with me and my team, that's her choice, but I'm not going to spend my time on Twitter. You'll see my response in the octagon."

"Jesus, what a boring answer," Brooklyn says on the mic, and a ripple of laughter makes its way through the crowd. "You're boring, Bauer. Your fighting is boring, and you're boring."

I just shake my head as the crowd oohs, annoyed they're buying into her grab for attention. When I don't answer, she cranes forward to see around Dana's podium.

"You're really going to let me talk about your people?" she asks. "What am I supposed to call that except weak? If you said half of what I've said about my brothers, I'd have knocked your fucking head off by now, but you know you can't, so you just shut up and sit down like a good little girl."

"My team is world class," I say. "They're not any more concerned over the opinion of a newbie who hasn't even earned this fight than I am."

"You're the only one crying about me being new. You're just scared."

"Make no mistake, Brooklyn. You didn't get this fight because of what you've done, you got it because of what *I've* done. I've crushed everyone else. That's the only reason you're here."

"Then why do they all think I'm going to win?"

"The odds are heavily in my favor last time I looked. They *don't* think you're going to win. You'd know that if you paid attention to anything other than your own delusional Twitter feed."

"All right, ladies, let's get to the next question," Dana says, and points to the next reporter.

"This one's for Brooklyn. Your family has achieved so much in Brazilian Jiu-Jitsu, but you're the first to have a chance at an MMA world title. Do you feel a lot of pressure to uphold the family name?"

"My family name carries itself. I'm not going to destroy Eden because of pressure, I'm going to destroy her because I'm a Shaw and that's what we do."

"Another for Brooklyn, your commitment to competing is clear. It's all we ever hear you talk about. Do you make time to have a personal life?"

"What the hell does that mean?" Brooklyn says.

"Like, do you have a boyfriend?"

"Jesus Christ, next question."

"Or maybe a girlfriend?"

I smile at the unexpected question, interested in this press conference for the first time. It's refreshing to see her off balance. I glance across at her to see how she'll answer.

"Next. Fucking. Question."

"Eden, I see you chuckling over there," the reporter says. "Same question?"

I laugh and pick up the mic. "Look, if you're poking around about whether we like girls or guys, I've been very clear and open that I'm gay. I'll agree with Brooklyn on one thing though, we're here to talk about the fight. You would never ask one of the guys if they're dating."

The room fills with applause, the first time I've felt them overwhelmingly on my side in a while. I'm usually a fan favorite, and though I've tried not to give it too much weight, it sucks that at least half of the fans seem to be team Brooklyn.

"All right, it looks like you're out of real questions," Dana says. "Let's wrap this up."

I'm all over his invitation to bail. I give a short thanks on the mic and am up from the table before someone can try to start a new series of questions. Brooklyn does the same, still looking significantly miffed, and I can't help but be tickled. She does have a soft spot.

Jin is waiting for me backstage and nods when we make eye contact. We unceremoniously head for the door. Some competitors love the lead up, the spotlight, the attention, but I hate being pulled away from training to prance around for the cameras. When we go out the front door, there's a fairly large crowd gathered, prevented from getting too close by a waist-height metal fence.

"Eden, we love you! Kick her ass!"

As much as I hate the pony show, I love the fans and never feel right blasting past them. I accept the first Sharpie that's offered to me to start signing. One person asks me to sign a Brooklyn shirt. I could write across her face. I've seen other martial artists do things like that, but I don't.

"If I sign this, you have to trade it in for one of mine when I beat her," I say.

The guy holding it out for me is a super thin kid in green shorts and a yellow shirt, probably Brazilian judging by his color choices. The Brazilians adore Brooklyn.

"You got it," he says. It's not like he'll follow through, but it doesn't matter. Fans like who they like, often with little to no reason why. I'm not exempt.

A wave of cheers flows through the gathering, which must mean Brooklyn just came out. I glance over my shoulder and confirm it. She's walking down the stairs in sunglasses and a leather coat, looking sharp and deadly. Samson Shaw, her father, is at her left, and her brother Théo is on the other side, each of them world renowned Jiu-Jitsu competitors.

Samson is still trim and toned, showing his age only in his refined air. Théo is a beautiful young man with a masculine, defined jaw and a glowing complexion. But Brooklyn still steals the show. She's a gorgeous creature with a smile that makes her instantly approachable, but she's also a well-tuned machine of an athlete to be feared. I reluctantly admit it's hard not to be a little starstruck by the martial arts royalty on parade.

"Brooklyn, take a picture with me?"

"Théo! Sign my chest!"

They show no signs of hearing the crowd.

"Brooklyn, marry me!" a woman yells from the front row. Samson stops on a dime and turns, picking out the woman who shouted it, deliberate and careful, then rips off his sunglasses. He steps closer to her, direct and intimidating, but not quite threatening. I still have the T-shirt I'm signing in my hands, but I'm locked on what's happening down the rail.

"Get this straight," Samson says, loud enough for everyone in the immediate area to hear, though he's only addressing the one woman. "My daughter is no fucking dyke. You got it?"

He turns and walks away, catching back up with Brooklyn and Théo, who show no signs of the horror I would hope to see on their faces. The crowd is silent, like they've all been collectively knocked off their feet.

"Fuck you!" someone finally yells, but they're already fifteen feet away and don't turn back.

It takes me a second to snap out of it. It's not totally shocking that he could have anti-gay sentiments, but they're so aggressive.

People yelling out at celebrities of all kinds to marry them is beyond common. That he would respond to something so lighthearted so viciously feels like a glimpse behind the Shaw veil. Is that how he acts with his children? Is that how he turned them into combat machines?

I finish scribbling on the shirt in my hands and give it back, then walk over to the young woman Samson yelled at. As I get closer, I realize she's younger than I thought, not yet twenty-one, maybe not even eighteen, and I'm hit with a new wave of disgust for Samson. Her expression is hard and angry, but her eyes have a watery look.

"Hey," I say. She looks over, on edge like I may yell at her too. "I know I'm not Brooklyn, but I'll take a picture with you if you want. Or sign something or whatever."

She looks down bashfully at the Shaw shirt in her hands.

"It's okay," I say. "I don't care if you like her."

"I don't anymore."

I wave her closer. "Come on, selfie it up." She leans in and snaps a few pictures of us in different poses smiling and pretending to fight. I sign the shirt and hand it back. "Chin up."

She nods and shows her friends her signed shirt, holding it tightly. I return to Jin and wave at the crowd one more time as we move toward the car. That reporter started unnecessary trouble, but she isn't the only one to misjudge Brooklyn. I certainly had her pegged as a lesbian. Apparently, Brooklyn's either homophobic or in the closet. Or both. Not inspiring options.

CHAPTER SEVEN

Arlo bends his knees and lunges his shoulder into my hips hard, knocking me back a couple of steps, a takedown maneuver called shooting. His hands wrap around my calves and he yanks up. I sink my weight, trying to sprawl my feet behind me, but his grip holds and prevents me from launching them backward. He shoves his head into my ribs and blasts forward until I lose my balance and slam to the mat. He scrambles to get on top of me while I struggle to put distance between us.

"Get. Up!" Jin's voice vibrates through the mats. He has a remarkable way of sounding like he's coming through a speaker, so loud yet never yelling. He's losing patience, a hard thing to make him do. I grab Arlo's ankle and pull it out from under him. He crashes to the mat on his side even as he tries to keep a hold of me. I pull back and toss his leg away, then spring to my feet as his heel whooshes past my head in an up-kick, narrowly missing. I couldn't blame him if it connected. With only two weeks to go, we're drilling hard.

"Good. Switch!" Jin yells. Arlo sprints off the mat and Laila jumps in. She comes at me with a lot of forward pressure, mimicking Brooklyn's style the best she can, then throws a bomb of a punch at me. I duck it and land a counterstrike combination. One punch connects extra hard. I feel a jolt of remorse, but Laila eats it like a champ and marches forward, leaving me no time to think on it any further before she shoots at my legs. I try again to sprawl out of it, but she switches the double leg hold to a single leg, picking my front foot off the mat and turning.

"Get out of there, Eden. You have to get this!" Arlo yells. Laila's still holding my front leg in the air with both arms, but she doesn't have the position to pull me down yet. "Move your foot to the outside of her leg, push the head away, and stomp."

I know the steps, and I'm trying like hell to do it, but she has my leg in a vice grip. I can't stomp down hard enough to break it. I focus on pushing her head down, trying to ruin her posture, but Laila slips her right foot behind the one foot I have on the ground and trips me, landing on top and going straight for a flurry of punches. I wrap my arms around her neck and pull her head down, then try to maneuver a hip out from under her so I can sweep her onto her back.

"Stop!" Jin says. We break apart. Laila offers me a hand, but I don't think I can stand. Four hours ago, I was nailing this exercise, but I have nothing left, and Laila and Arlo are switching out so they're always fresh.

"Get up," Jin says. He's said little else since we walked in this morning. Get up, get up, get up. I hesitate for less than a second, but he's on me like school of piranhas. "Stand up, jeja."

Jeez, it must be bad. He hasn't called me that for a long time. It means student, not a derogatory term, but a reminder of my position. I peel myself off the mat. My shirt is soaked with sweat. Everything aches and weighs a thousand pounds. I force myself to stand up straight even though doing so spots my vision with black. Hopefully, I don't pass out, but at this point I'd rather go ahead and do that than fail to stand before Jin. He comes close, looks into my eyes with an expression that seems to be anger, but then he gently puts his hands on either side of my face.

"This is the difference between victory and defeat."

"Yes, Kwan Jang Nim." Grandmaster. "Ahlge seoyo." I understand.

"You're sloppy," he says. "You know the movements, but you don't do them. Do you not respect Professor Ruiz?" Brazilian Jiu-Jitsu black belts are called professors. Jin knows I respect Arlo, but he also knows attacking me like this works.

"I'm sorry, Professor," I say to Arlo. This isn't his world, but all martial artists understand this kind of interaction.

"Then why don't you do what he says?" Jin asks, a bit of a trap. I know better than to say I can't or I'm trying. There is no can't. There is no trying.

"I'll do better, Kwan Jang Nim."

"You're tired," Jin says.

"Yes, Grandmaster."

"Are we to stop training once you're tired?"

"No, Grandmaster."

"You must defeat yourself first. Then your enemy."

"Yes, Grandmaster."

"Again."

He nods Laila back in. She faces me, pausing to meet my eyes. "Don't you dare go easy," I say.

She explodes down and forward, smashing into my hip with her shoulder and reaching deep around my calves. I pull reserves of energy I didn't realize I had and force my entire body into action to resist her, blasting through her grip so my feet are well behind my hips and out of reach, then shove her down face first as I escape backward. As she stands, I throw a spinning back kick, pulling it so it goes right over her head instead of connecting, but we all know it would have knocked her out cold if I wanted it to.

Arlo whistles. "There it is!"

Laila smiles and bows, an unofficial way of saying, "Thanks for not taking my head off."

Arlo puts his hand on my shoulder. "That was it. Once she realizes she's no match for you on her feet, she'll try to take you down. If you do exactly what you just did, you win."

"Yes, sir," I say, still in danger of passing out or puking. Fight camp is always such a blend of teammates bolstering your confidence and coaches putting the fear of God in you. Each is essential. It may be the exhaustion, but I'm teary with gratitude for each of these lunatics who are willing to spend hours breaking their bodies with me.

"That was sick," Laila says and hugs me. "You good?"

"Of course." I'm barely okay and too hot to be hugged, but I don't want her to know that. Jin has a way of finding my breaking point no matter how hard I try to wear a poker face.

"Take an ice bath." Jin's voice cuts through the chatter. "You run hills in the morning."

❖

The last week before weigh-ins, Jin starts to take it easy. My body needs to recover, it's too close to the fight to risk an injury, and I have to start cutting weight, which means I won't have much energy. As much as my team has been saying Brooklyn doesn't deserve this fight, they're behaving otherwise. All through camp I could feel it in the air, though they would never say it. They knew I could lose this. I don't feel that anymore.

"You see the latest?" Laila asks while holding the focus mitts in front of me, her left hand slightly forward to indicate my combo should start with a jab. I throw a simple jab, cross, hook, exhilarated by the hard thwap of each blow landing in the sweet spot before I pull it back.

"Nope."

"Brooklyn released a training video. She's just working the heavy bag, but at the end she faces the camera and says she's going to shock the world and beat you at your own game. She threw a head kick and said you're going to end up in the morgue if you don't respect her striking."

I slip the jab Laila throws and snap into a cross, uppercut, roundhouse. "Her punches look any better?"

"A little," Laila says. "Worth looking at if you want to call it a night."

I glance at the clock and realize it's already nine, much later than I thought, an excellent sign my cardio is where it needs to be. "Sure," I say. I slip out of my gloves while Laila pulls off the mitts and finds her phone in her gym bag. She slides down the wall and invites me to sit next to her. I join her and look over her shoulder at the video.

It's just like she said, Brooklyn working the bag. She does look better. That's to be expected. She'd be an idiot not to train striking just like I'd be an idiot not to train Jiu-Jitsu. I'm just not so attention hungry as to make the mistake of showing her. Brooklyn faces the camera and delivers her threat, then the video ends. I see a handful of comments, people encouraging her to kill me.

"Does no one even think about what they're saying?" I ask. "Don't they know you really could die doing this?" I regret saying it the moment it comes out of my mouth. I don't want Laila to think I'm afraid or being dramatic. No one has ever died fighting in the UFC, but it does happen in boxing every year, and that's a bit close for comfort. "I just mean—"

Laila puts her hand on my knee. "I know. She loves crossing lines."

"She's scared," I say. "She must be. To try this hard to get in my head, I must be in hers."

"She'd be insane not to be scared of you. You're the greatest woman in the game. Ever. And you've held the title for four years without breaking a sweat. She's either afraid of you or a complete idiot." She refreshes to the top of Brooklyn's Twitter page, and a brand-new tweet pops up.

Eden's team is a joke. Mr. Miyagi, a cashier, and a fighter with a 50-50 win/loss record. Hopefully they at least know how to throw in the towel when I'm smashing their girl. The Shaws are coming for you pussies. Iron sharpens iron.

"Oh, hell no. This bitch." Laila taps to comment back.

"Laila, don't."

"Fuck that, you can be miss Buddhist monk if you want, but she's talking about me now."

I put my hand on her wrist. "It's distasteful for someone of your caliber to bark on her own behalf."

Laila stares at me like I spoke another language.

"I'll take care of her," I say. "I promise."

"Why does it matter to you so much? You should be relieved someone else can clap back without you breaking your whole enlightened thing."

"I care because you're my student. You're an Emerald Tiger black belt, and we're better than that. You say more by saying nothing."

"I don't know about that. I say a lot saying something."

I laugh and shake my head. She looks at her phone again and bursts out laughing. "Oh my God, I love Arlo."

"What?" I lunge to look at the screen. "What'd he do?"

Arlo's tweet back at Brooklyn reads, *Iron didn't sharpen shit. Your brothers are on steroids, and you probably are too.*

"Holy shit, Arlo." I start hunting for my phone to text him.

"Oh, you leave him alone. Someone had to do it."

"What's the steroid comment about?"

"Jesus, Eden, you really should know more about the Shaws. You're a pro, for fuck's sake."

"Jiu-Jitsu is not my world, so shoot me. Just tell me."

"Her brother Leandro is one of those repeat steroid scandal guys. He won a world title, but they took it away when he tested hot for like the fifth time. It ruined his career."

"God, that's not fair game, come on."

"But what she said is?"

"No, it's not. None of this is. Why does competition have to be so nasty? Can't we just find out who's the best because we want to know?"

"Oh my God, how are you so pure?" Laila laughs.

"Shut up."

"I'm serious. It's a miracle. You make me want to be a better person and shit."

"Whatever, you're a good person. You just like to sound tough."

"Phf, I *am* tough," she says with a smile.

"All right, killer, you're tough. I need to get to bed. Please be good. And lock up the front on your way out, yeah?"

"You got it, boss."

I hear the bells and the front door latch just a few minutes later. I'm tempted to get on the computer and see how Brooklyn responded. I'm sure it was a fiery string of attacks, but I don't really want to know. I just want all this to be over.

CHAPTER EIGHT

Cutting weight is never fun, but I have it down to as much of a science as possible. I normally walk around at one hundred fifty-eight pounds, but I need to be down to one forty-five for weigh-ins. Thirteen pounds doesn't sound like a ton, but I don't have much to spare. I'm already lean at my normal weight, which leaves me with mostly water and muscle to lose. Extreme dehydration isn't a good feeling and freaks me out. It's a practice I wish combat sports would do away with. We're all cutting weight, which means we're competing with the same people we would at our natural weight anyway, rendering the whole thing unnecessary. It's just one of those old traditions we can't seem to shake.

I start two weeks out from the fight by drastically lowering my caloric intake, cutting carbs and salt and drinking tons of water. The idea is to lose as much body weight as humanly possible in this stage so I don't have to dehydrate myself as much in the water cut, but it usually only amounts to five or six pounds, leaving me with seven or eight pounds of water to lose. It's not unheard of or even drastic compared to what a lot of athletes do, but that's an absurd fact. It's not all that rare for someone to end up in the hospital trying to do a crazy cut. Even if they're successful, they often go on to lose the match because they haven't fully recovered.

I'm hours into the water cut now and just over an hour from weigh-ins. I haven't gotten on the scale in a while. It stresses me out to watch my weight creep down a tenth of a pound at a time.

I've been wearing a sauna suit for hours, a garment from hell made of non-breathable material that makes you sweat more than you've ever sweat in your life when you combine it with exercise. Running on the treadmill like that, unable to drink water, is a special kind of torture. I'm so close and so weak now I resort to sitting in the sauna.

The heat is insufferable. I can't even sit up straight and have to lie down across the bench. It's like my blood is boiling. The heat wants to rise off of me, but it's trapped in the sauna suit, which is squishing around on my skin. It's disgusting. Laila opens the sauna door and comes in. Even the tiny touch of cool air that sneaks through feels incredible.

"You want to see what you're at?"

I'm so drained I can barely even answer. I grunt.

"You have to be close," she says. "Let's check."

"If I leave and I'm not there, I don't know if I can get back in." A wave of nausea hits, and I wish I would just puke. That would probably do it.

"Five more minutes then," Laila says. "Then you need a break. You don't look good."

"Don't say that to me."

"Don't worry. You'll be fine."

Laila watches the time. It feels like five minutes has passed six times over, but it's too hard to ask her. Finally, she stands up.

"All right, come on."

Being this drained makes the brain fuzzy. I know this building, these halls, yet I can't quite make sense of the route we're taking. When we reach the scale, I peel off the sauna suit with Laila's help. It's damn near orgasmic having the cool air finally touch my lava skin. It's always a little strange letting Laila see me in nothing but underwear, but it's just part of the life, and I'm too exhausted to think too much on my appearance even though I must look emaciated and far from my best self.

"Ready?" she asks when it's off.

I nod and step up. She reads the scale from the other side, waiting until it's settled. She wordlessly holds her hand up for a high five.

"Really?"

"One forty-five, baby."

I've never failed to make weight, but it always sucks just enough to worry me. I shower and put on clean clothes. Once I've done that, I feel balanced again, energized by the fact that this is almost over. It feels like it takes forever waiting for the official weigh in, but it finally comes. It's ironic we do face-offs at weigh-ins, that we're all standing there trying to scare one another while we're about to fall over.

Once I'm to the stage and hear the crowd, I feel myself starting to smile. This is it. The fight is tomorrow. I'm about to walk out and see Brooklyn up close and personal, finally. As the challenger, she goes first, and she enters from the other side. They announce her over the speakers, and the crowd erupts in cheers. The floor is shaking with the vibration of their adoration. They love her. Unbelievable.

Brooklyn signals the crowd to get even louder and shouts something I can't make out. She has on a black baseball hat and a chain around her neck. She's shredded beyond belief with deeply defined delts, six-pack abs, and a chiseled back. She's still stronger than I am, even with my absolutely ruthless training, but I don't let it bother me. It's just a different body type, and it costs her other things. I'd keep my own body for fighting given the choice, but hers is awfully pretty.

She steps on the scale, and they announce her as one hundred forty-four pounds. She flexes for the photo. A pound under.

Laila appears behind me and drapes my championship belt over my shoulder as the announcer moves on to me, yapping about my hometown, style, and record before he finally screams my name. The crowd explodes, a nice surprise. It shouldn't be shocking, but the way they went off for Brooklyn, I thought I'd lost them.

I walk out swift and stoic with my belt draped over my shoulder. The weight of it reminds me who I am, what I've done. I'm the youngest UFC champion ever, and the longest reigning women's champion. I'm everything Brooklyn wants to be. I take off my shirt and sweats and step onto the scale, confident I'm every bit as intimidating, whether she wants to admit it or not. The announcer calls out my official weight, one forty-five on the nose. The crowd cheers, and I look to the back of the room, taking in the roar of all those people before I step off the scale to face off with Brooklyn.

We each walk to center stage, locking eyes. This ritual has always felt archaic and a little silly. This is the first time I've been remotely interested in what I may see in a fighter at this stage. I reach center first and stop, facing her in a fighting stance. She cracks the smallest smile and closes the distance so she's only inches from my face, her own arms raised.

Having her so close is surreal. It highlights her height disadvantage. I feel like I'm towering over her even though it's only three inches. Her features, both her body and her face, are hard and strong and beautiful all at once. Now that I'm closer I can see the chain around her neck is a cross. Her eyes are every bit as hypnotic as they looked in her pictures. Her thick lashes and full lips make her entire look snap into place for me. She projects such aggressive strength and toughness she manages to come across as masculine, but when you're right here looking at her, she's actually quite feminine.

"That's my belt on your shoulder," she says.

"You're going to have to take it."

"I will. Believe that."

"You're not ready, Brooklyn. You think you're good, but really, you're just strong. It won't be enough."

Brooklyn lunges at me. Dana White shoves himself between us with his back to me and two hands outstretched toward Brooklyn, but she's not trying to push past him. She just wanted to make me flinch. She winks at me and backs away.

"You're going to the hospital tomorrow, Bauer."

The crowd starts chanting, split between my name and hers. They're so loud we can't hear the people on the stage anymore, so I just smile and hold my arms out to my sides again. I'm here.

Chapter Nine

The day of the fight is gray and rainy. The sound of tires across the wet road is soothing. The limo driver's easy turns lull me into a kind of hypnosis, and I sit with my head leaned back and my eyes closed under sunglasses. Jin is to my left. Laila and Arlo are across from me, but I don't have anything to say to any of them right now. All I have room for is peace and focus. We're three hours out from my fight, depending how the other bouts go. A couple of first round knockouts could bump us up in a flash. I'd almost rather that happen.

"You good, Champ?" Laila asks. She's been calling me that for the better part of fight week, trying to creep some confidence into my subconscious.

"I'm gold."

"You sleep?"

"Not for shit." That's not a great thing, but it's not unusual, either. What's more important is that I successfully rehydrated after weigh-ins and feel well today. Some people experience cramps and weakness even after rehydrating if they overdid it, but this may be the best I've ever felt going into a fight. It's rare not to have some kind of injury or discomfort, but I have no complaints. That also means I have no excuses. It's my title, but I feel like I'm carrying my team's dreams, all their hard work. It's like being the last runner in a relay race.

"Circle again," I say to the driver. He takes another lap around the arena.

"You want to go through it again?" Laila asks.

"No," I say. "I just need quiet."

I know the plan so well it consumes all my waking thoughts. It even consumes most of my dreams. Being this prepared brings a level of acceptance for whatever happens. I'll win, but even if I don't, there's nothing else I could have possibly done. We go around a few more times before Jin touches my knee.

"It's time."

I sit up and nod at the driver, who's looking at me through the rearview for confirmation. He pulls up to the curb. I leave my sunglasses on and get out with my team at my sides, powering into the arena on a mission.

Jin wraps my hands, always the exact same pattern. I can do it myself, but there's something to this ritual. The calm in his movements transfers to me, and I feel still inside. When he's finished, I put my gloves on and warm up on the pads with Laila. There are televisions showing the current fight. I can't be distracted with watching it, but Arlo keeps an eye on them to update me on how long we have. When the fight before mine starts, I get a nasty jolt of adrenaline.

The audience has been getting louder with every passing fight. That's exactly how it's supposed to go, but it gives the impression of a rabid colosseum audience. I'm sure Brooklyn and I will be splitting the crowd roughly fifty-fifty again. That's a little crazy considering how long I've been around and how new she is. I want to believe it's because we're both New Yorkers, so we're bound to have to split the hometown. Really, the dynamic is deeper. It's the respectful versus the trash talker. The long versus the strong. The technical versus the brawler. The intellectual versus the intuitive. We check every dichotomy that's ever interested fans.

"They're not going to make it past the second round," Arlo announces from the other side of the locker room. "Get ready."

No sooner than he says it, there's a huge reaction from the crowd that must mean the fight is ending. I shake out my arms. This is the worst part, when all the adrenaline is raging and your skin feels full of chemicals and you're sick to your stomach. The reality sinks in that there's basically a trained killer about to try to hurt you. And someone like Brooklyn really *wants* to hurt you. Her comments flash through my mind. There have been so many over the last two months. She wants to take my belt, break my neck, put me in the hospital, send me to the morgue, but none of that matters. When you walk to the octagon, you walk ready to die. It's the best way to win.

"Eden," Laila says. "They're announcing Brooklyn."

I nod and move to the inner mouth of the walkout tunnel. Staff lines the sides, ready to walk with me. I'm glad I don't have to listen to Brooklyn's army of angels walkout music at full volume. A moment of quiet passes, and then my song plays over the stereo system, "Fuel" by Metallica, blaring much louder than Brooklyn's, small perks of being the champ. I start down the hallway at a steady, deliberate pace. The moment I pass through the opening, the crowd is domineeringly loud.

When I get to the side of the octagon, I strip down to my shorts and sports bra. My hair is braided now, the best way to deal with it. I hand Laila my clothes and give her a hug, followed by Arlo and Jin.

I face the athletic commission staff member who's waiting to prepare me for the octagon. He swipes along my arms, sides, and waist to make sure I don't have anything I shouldn't and that I'm not greased up, a cheater's trick of making yourself slippery so your opponent can't grab you. He checks inside my mouth, looks over my gloves, and puts a small amount of Vaseline along my eyebrows and cheeks to help prevent cuts, then waves for me to get in the octagon.

My world goes silent then, walking up those steps. I bow at the entrance and step inside the cage to thunderous applause. Bruce Buffer enters the octagon and makes his way through Brooklyn's introductions, the same as last time except now she's at three wins and zero losses. The very thing that made me so upset she got this fight is almost funny now. Three fights. It's such a disadvantage for her. Buffer moves on to my introduction.

"Fighting out of the Bronx, New York, standing five feet ten inches, one hundred forty-five pounds, holding a professional record of twenty-five wins and no losses, the defending featherweight champion of the world, Edeeeeen, the Sniper, Baaaaauer." I can't help but smile at Brooklyn when he says it. Her eyes are locked on me, her posture leaning forward like she wants to sprint at me the moment he says fight. The ref calls us both to the center of the octagon.

"All right, I want a clean fight. Obey my commands at all times. If you want to touch gloves, do it now." Neither of us move. "All right, to your corners." We each back up to our side of the octagon. He puts his hand between us in the middle of the octagon, then yanks it away and yells, "Fight!"

The crowd's energy is electric. Brooklyn rushes forward to claim the center of the octagon. That's not going to happen. I close in, staying just outside of her range, studying the way she moves. She bounces on the balls of her feet, dancing around in front of me, much more movement than the last time I saw her fight. They must have coached her to do that thinking it would be harder for me to catch her that way. Depends how fast she is. She's both more active and more reserved. Last time she would be throwing by now, but she waits.

"Good, Brooklyn, find your range," someone from her corner says.

I inch into her space to goad her into an attack without entering her range. She doesn't budge. Interesting. She might've figured out her striking distance. As we stretch toward twenty seconds without a strike, I feel the crowd getting anxious, something that doesn't bother me, but that I'm positive will drive her crazy. I can see in her eyes she's choosing an attack, so I snap a jab out to interrupt her, to let her know I can. It slips through and hits her gloves, and she throws a jab back. It's short. I don't even have to move to avoid it.

I step forward, and just like that, take the center of the octagon from her. She throws a jab cross to try to stop it, but I slip both and counter with a hook to the body that lands. It's like hitting a brick wall. She doesn't react other than to swing back big. I duck and feel her glove whoosh over my head. There she is. Those insane punches are the key to my advantage, but mess up and eat one, it'll be lights out.

I come up from my duck with an uppercut that clips her chin. She corrects her stance and tries to take the center back with a flurry of punches. I circle out, giving it to her momentarily, but once she's finished I slip a straight right hand between her guard, cracking her hard right in the nose. Her head snaps back, and the crowd reacts big. She comes forward again, throwing five shots in a row, desperate to get the clean shot back.

"Watch it, Eden!" Laila yells. I duck, pull back, slip left. She's catching air everywhere, and it floods me with energy. I chop her thigh with a nasty low kick that slaps loud enough for the cameras to pick up. Brooklyn gets back to her stance, dancing around on the balls of her feet again, this time circling the center that she's conceded to me. She thrusts into the pocket and throws another combo. I dodge two aimed at my head and counter with a jab that lands flush on her mouth and follow with a cross that gets through too. It lands so hard I expect it to wobble her, but she fires back with a right hook with a ton of heat on it. I get my hand up just in time to block, but the impact still sends a shock through my head.

She fires again to the other side of my head. I block that one with similar effect, then she follows with a hook to the body that slips past me and connects to my abdomen. A shock of nausea shoots through me on impact. I choke it down and try to keep a straight face, but I know she saw it. I've never felt that kind of power from another woman. It shouldn't be a surprise. That's what she's about, but even with all my expectations, it's more than I thought it would be. She definitely sees the pain because suddenly she's launching at me, throwing one after the other. I can feel her excitement as she rushes me, aware she only needs one of those to my jaw and intent on throwing until she gets it.

I forget about everything except my vision, watching her, studying her hips and shoulders for what's next and dodging each strike. Blocking isn't enough, I want her missing, and she is. Once I get the rhythm of her style, I hit her with a counter every time. I'm in my comfort zone now, picking her apart in a way she won't be able to ignore no matter how tough she is. She springs forward, and I back away with a quick shuffle.

She reaches, trying to catch up, stretched two feet past the front of her stance, exposing her body. I launch a front kick right down the middle and feel it land clean in her solar plexus. She finally reacts big, recoiling and stumbling backward with one arm crossed over her body and the other still poised to strike. The crowd screams, sensing an opportunity for me to finish, but Brooklyn's too dangerous to rush.

With her arm down, her head's open. I close in and throw a roundhouse. She gets her hands up, but my shin lands hard against her forearms, and I see a ripple of uncertainty pass through her. The collision sends a clang of pain through my shin, and if it hurt me, it certainly hurt her. I throw it again, positive she wants absolutely none of this. This time she blocks stronger, but I still see the impact shockwave through her body. She cuts away from me diagonally, trying to find a comfortable distance. I can get her with another minute, but the horn sounds to end the round.

Jin and Arlo spring into the octagon and slap a stool down for me to sit. Arlo squirts water in my mouth. "You're doing great," he says. "You hurt her bad. Watch for the takedown next round. She's had enough of your hands."

"Turning back kick," Jin says.

"What about it?"

"Look for it."

I nod and the break ends. The time between rounds feels comically short when you're in the match. Brooklyn and I each stand and face each other. There's something different in her eyes now. I'm sure there's something different in mine too. The ref checks with each of us, and upon a nod signals the start of round two out of a possible five. I expect Brooklyn to hang back and try to recover more, but I'm dead wrong. She sprints at me and jumps into a flying knee aimed at my head.

I lunge out of the way and fire back an aggressive cross. It lands to the eye, but she walks right through it like it didn't happen and shoots for the takedown. Arlo just finished telling me it's coming, yet I'm still caught off guard. Stupid. So stupid. This is Brooklyn Shaw. This crazy bull who's an absolute professional at blasting into people isn't going to stop from a punch. I sprawl hard, latching my hands behind her neck, digging my forearms into her collarbone, and shooting my legs behind me as hard as I can to break the grip she has around my calves. I get the back leg away, but she still has the front.

This is exactly what we trained for. I know what to do, and there is no can't, there is no try. I shove her head down and stomp my foot to the canvas as hard as I can. Even I'm a little shocked when her hand pops off. Free of her, I try to back away, but she's still hurling at my legs, so reckless. Everything in me wants to blast a knee at her low head, but I can't risk giving that leg back. I throw an elbow and connect with her face, splitting her open. With her dazed, I risk following it with a knee. It lands so clean I expect her to go down, but she doesn't. She's the fucking Terminator. She wraps her arms around my leg and slams me down so hard it rattles every bone in me, and we're on the ground, less than a minute into round two. It couldn't be worse.

She lands on top of me hard, her shoulder driving painfully into my chest. I throw up my legs and wrap her in my guard before she can pass to side control or mount and really ruin my life. She's bleeding badly from her brow, but she's collected and starts working to break my guard. Her posture alone puts a strain on my interlocked ankles, her rounded back applying way more pressure than I've ever felt from someone doing so little. I try to wrap my hand around her neck and pull her down where I can control her better, but she straightens out of my grip and rewards me with a punch to the face that makes the back of my head bounce off the canvas.

I punch her back, a desperate and ineffective move from the bottom. She throws another punch, but I expect it and swivel out of the way. The movement brings her close enough I manage to get my arms around her and cling to her like a koala bear. She somehow weighs a thousand pounds as she applies pressure chest to chest to interrupt my breathing and backs me into the cage.

"Stay calm, Eden. You're okay," Arlo says.

"You're not okay," Brooklyn says. "You're done. It's over." She presses into me so hard I literally can't breathe and lands short punches to my side. They don't hurt bad, but it doesn't feel good either. She slips her hand between our bodies and pushes away, creating enough space to drop an elbow at my face. It lands hard and draws blood, but I'd still rather she be preoccupied with strikes than submissions. Just as I'm thinking it, she makes a move to break my guard again.

"Twenty-three!" Arlo yells, a code we created so Brooklyn wouldn't know what I'm trying to do should this exact thing happen. I try to execute the move he's commanding, trying to get onto my hip and use the cage to press out, but she's all over me. Her pressure is overwhelming, smothering. She starts trying to sneak a grip on my arm for an armbar, so I move to protect it. She switches and tries for a Kimura, another arm attack, but I use the fence to help me roll out of it. She abandons the Kimura at the possibility of taking my back as I roll, but I manage to flip over just in time to lock her in guard again and eat a punch.

"Thirty seconds," Arlo yells. Brooklyn is giving me so much down pressure I want to try to throw a triangle, but Arlo told me any submissions I think I see on Brooklyn are probably traps to lure me to do something she plans to take advantage of. Brooklyn shoves down on my knee and makes an explosive movement into side control, moving quickly toward my chest and attempting a choke. She sinks her arm around the far side of my throat and starts to squeeze as she rotates to crank it.

"Give up, it's over," she says. "You can't handle me."

Fear shoots through me, but she doesn't have it locked in, not yet, and time is running out. Arlo taught me well. I can handle this. She's much better than me, yes, but I don't have to beat her here. I just have to survive her. She tightens the hold hard, squeezing with all she has. She knows she doesn't quite have the choke all the way in place to rely so much on muscle. I shove her elbow away and slip my head out of the back of the hold. She rears back in frustration to punch. The horn blares as she connects. Blinding pain erupts through the side of my face. She might've broken my jaw, but I'm not sure.

The ref leaps on her and pulls her off of me. The crowd is freaking out, boos and cheers combined. They must've thought it landed late, but if it did it was by so little I can't be mad. This time only Jin jumps into the octagon because the cut on my brow needs attention from the cutman, and only so many people can be in the octagon at once, but Arlo is right at the fence and can still talk to me anyway.

"Breathe," Jin says.

I don't tell them about my jaw. I don't want anyone to know, and I'm a little afraid to talk.

"You're one and one." Arlo references the scoring of the rounds, which is so obvious it's not helpful. "You've been a whole round with her on the ground now. You know you can get through it. She's going to want to do that again. Be ready for it."

Jin presses ice on my back between my shoulder blades to bring my temperature down. My lungs are on fire. The back of my head is thudding. The cutman has successfully held my bleeding brow at bay and slaps a big glob of Vaseline on it. The break ends, and round three starts.

Brooklyn launches at me, coming straight for another takedown. I see it a mile away and haul off a front kick as hard as I can. It misses her face but lands on her collarbone, almost certainly breaking it and sending her to the ground. She turns so her legs are between us to try to stop me from attacking with the ground and pound she assumes is coming, but like hell am I following her to the canvas, even if it is on top. I stand back. She waits, looking for an up-kick, but I back up another step and wave her to come on.

"Get up," I say. The ref motions for her to stand, and she labors up. She goes back to her bouncy stance, but it's lost most of its energy. Every time she gets close, I use kicks to back her up, going to the body again and again to disrupt her breathing and drain her energy. It's wearing on her. I know she's hurting, but so am I, and I'm not sure who's better off anymore.

She shoots for a takedown again. I sprawl and hook under her arms, then yank her back to a standing position. She tries to sink her weight, but I pull with everything I have. I won't survive another round on the ground. Finally, she has no choice but to straighten up, and we're locked in the clinch. I lock my hands behind her head, my forearms pressed into her chest and against her broken collarbone with my elbows tight. She tries to step out and leverage a throw, but I yank her head down and drive a knee into her gut. I feel her react and do it again, this time aiming for her head. She starts throwing wild hook punches, but I render those too weak to matter by keeping her off balance. The crowd is so loud neither of us can even hear our corners.

She drops low in the clinch and wraps her arms around my waist. I try to drop my weight and pull her off balance, but she squeezes, inching down so she's around my thighs now. She disregards the sweeps and takedowns she can't get and instead picks me up entirely. She holds me like I weigh nothing even as I slam my elbow into her head as hard as I can. She calmly regains a solid footing and starts to tip me. The canvas looks so much farther beneath me than seems possible. I have nothing to hold onto, no control whatsoever. As she angles me, I know it's going to be bad. Really bad. She slams me to the canvas headfirst, her full weight landing on top of me. It knocks the wind out of me and pain explodes through my head, neck, and back.

For the longest second of my life, I half expect she's killed me, that my head is gruesomely crushed or my neck is snapped in half. I can't move. I can't breathe. She's hitting me in the face, and it isn't even registering. I see the ref out of the corner of my eye about to intervene. I have to do something right now. I can't wait until I can breathe again. It'll be over by then.

I try to move my arm, and holy shit, it moves. I wrap her arm up and hold it tight against my body so she can't punch anymore, bridge my hips as hard as I can while pulling her trapped arm to the canvas, and it works. I sweep her off of me. I leap up and run to get my feet out of her reach as she swipes for my ankles. I finally manage to find a gulp of air, but something's horribly wrong. It's so wrong I need this fight to end, but Brooklyn is on her feet now and chasing me. I don't think I can even concede without taking another punch first, and I can't take another punch.

I face Brooklyn, still backing up as fast as I can as she launches after me. She knows how close she is to ending this. I stomp my back foot down hard to stop my backward momentum in one motion. I turn so I'm looking over my back shoulder, jump, and launch a back kick. Brooklyn is so sure I'm on the run she doesn't see it coming. The kick lands to her head, and she goes down, out cold.

Normally, we're supposed to continue until the ref tells us to stop, but I'm in shock. By the time I register she's down, it's clear she's unconscious, and I walk away as the ref waves off the fight. It's over. I won. Yet it feels so otherworldly. I'm not even sure I'm here. Slowly, the sound of the crowd screaming registers.

Arlo, Laila, and Jin flood the octagon. "Fuck yeah!" Arlo screams, so hyped. "Who's the motherfuckin' champ!" Laila grabs my hands and raises it. She moves to hug me, but I hold her at arm's length.

"No, don't."

Arlo tries to pick me up, but again, I motion for him not to touch me. "Don't."

I turn and walk toward Brooklyn. She's just barely coming to. The ref has one hand on her neck and one on her side so he can try to steady her as he explains what happened.

"Is she okay?"

"Get back," the ref says. As he says it, she sits up. She looks dazed and lost but seems to be catching up. Her brother is at her side saying something I can't hear, and soon she's nodding. I turn back to the others, who are all looking at me with confused, eager expressions, as if asking if it's okay to celebrate now, but something terrible is wrong with my neck, and I'm afraid to let them touch me. It's like something's been severed, and I have the strangest feeling I shouldn't be alive, like I'm going to drop dead any second. Like maybe I'm not even alive now. It's like the slam killed me and my miraculous win was some kind of death experience. Jin approaches and gently touches my back. Even that hurts.

"Keep breathing," he says. I mean to nod, but I don't want to move my neck. I almost speak, but I don't want to use my jaw.

I've sustained as many injuries as the next fighter, but they've never scared me like this.

"Hey, you need to announce this," Laila says to the ref. "She needs to see the doctor."

He looks from me to Brooklyn. Brooklyn could clearly use a few more seconds to recover, while I clearly need to get off my feet. He seems stuck in indecision, but Brooklyn gets up, so he waves her over. Buffer's announcement feels like it takes a year, and I don't care even a little what he's saying. Finally, I hear the words, "And still, the undisputed featherweight champion of the world, Eden, the Sniper, Bauer!"

Joe Rogan comes into the octagon to interview me. It's only ever a few questions, but I have no idea what I'm even saying. I'm pretty sure I don't manage any semblance of happiness. The moment the mic is out of my face, my team is guiding me through the hallways to the back, motioning for the doctor. When I tell him what my neck feels like, he immobilizes it with a brace and helps me lie down on the stretcher, and it all fades away.

CHAPTER TEN

I'm falling through the unconscious like I've been thrown into a lake with concrete boots. Time is peeling away in layers that don't make sense. I'm in the void, touching eternity, holding stillness, both weightless and restrained. Velvet against my ear, a voice I don't know, wrapping around me.

"Please don't die."

Is that where I am? In the mouth of death?

"You won't," the voice says. It's warm and calming and soft, somehow familiar but out of reach, too far to grasp at. "You're tough as nails. You'll be okay."

A hand wraps around my forearm and squeezes. I know that's what it is, but it isn't like any touch I've ever felt before. I feel it as faint pressure, but not as skin. I interpret it from a space above my head, not an occupant of my body, but I'm not an outsider either.

"I want you to be okay."

The pressure disappears and the presence in the room goes with it. I can't know that for sure, but it feels empty now. Everything is ever expanding, stretching me into nothing.

Consciousness seizes me in a violent embrace. I hear the room all around me, the sound of voices. It takes me several seconds to realize there's no meaning to the noises. I can't place the spaces between words or comprehend them. It takes a minute before it occurs to me to open my eyes. The room is too bright.

"Eden?"

I know her, but I can't make sense of her face. It's young and lively, with golden eyes and a fresh white smile. Her hair is dark, short, and spikey, her clothes tight to a fit body.

"It's Laila," she says. "I'm here, honey. You're in the hospital. You got hurt in the fight, but you're okay. Try not to move."

I must be on a lot of drugs because my mind is definitely not functioning well. I see her fingers interlaced with mine. She's holding my hand, but I can't feel it. A bolt of fear floods me, and I struggle to make my way back to movement or sound. I'm thrashing inside a lifeless body. It's like trying to wake up from a dream that won't release you. God, am I paralyzed? Terror. I internally shriek at my limbs to move, at my voice to speak. Finally, I hear myself squeak, a strangled, panicked sound.

"We need some help in here," Laila yells at the door. I gather all the energy in my being and launch it through my arm like a tidal wave, and finally it moves. My fingers flit, just tightening around Laila's. Something akin to a twitch tightens in my thigh. That's enough to calm me down from terror. Something is horribly wrong, but I'm not paralyzed.

A nurse jogs into the room and comes to my side, opposite Laila. "Eden, I want you to try to stay calm. You have a fractured vertebra in your neck. You're in a neck brace and on some pretty strong medications. We don't want you moving right now. It's very important we keep your neck stable. Try to relax for me, okay?"

I don't answer her. I'm not sure if I can. In fact, no, I can't. My jaw is wrapped. Guess that's fractured too. God knows what else is wrong with me. Certainly a concussion.

"I'm going to let the doctor know you're awake, and he'll come in and check on you. Is your pain bearable right now?"

Bearable. Not the most optimistic target, but I guess it is. I reflexively try to nod and am met with the restriction of the brace and a nasty flame of pain flaring in my neck. I close my eyes and wait for it to taper off. It takes longer than I expect, and just when I think it's not going to subside, it fades.

"Mhm." My voice sounds strangled.

"Okay, if you need anything, you just click this button." She slips the button into my hand. I'm not sure I have the strength to do that, but telling her so isn't worth the pain it would cause. The nurse disappears, and I meet Laila's eyes. I feel tears welling up. It's not the pain. Pain is part of this life. It's the helplessness.

Laila scoots closer to the bed and hugs my forearm. "You're okay, Eden. I promise. Don't be scared. They said there's a lot of swelling in your neck that can cause decreased feeling and muscle weakness in your arms and legs. The swelling will go down in a few days and you should be able to move better. And they didn't wire your jaw. It's just the wrap. Just hold tight."

Thank God for Laila. She has an innate sense for what I need to know. It sets me enough at ease that I close my eyes and let the dark pull me back in.

❖

My team is family in a way I've never known. They're always by me, holding me together. Waking up mentally is more challenging than it was physically. This is waking up to a new reality. It's having the doctor's words sit in my brain but being unable to compute them. You cannot fight. It will kill you.

He tones down the doom and gloom when Laila and Arlo jump all over him for details, clarifying that a full recovery is possible with time, but only if I take healing seriously. It's also possible I will never be the same, and he leans into that. It's true that fighters tend to rush recovery, but he doesn't need to scare me. What I felt when I was coming to was plenty scary.

He's a testy, unpleasant man who seems to take pleasure in delivering statements like, "She was a couple of millimeters from paralysis, and a few more from death," and, "I know it's not what you want, but this is a lucky outcome."

You can't look badass with a neck brace on, but I give it my best go as I leave at the fastest pace my battered body will allow. Walking reminds me my neck isn't the only thing wrong with me. My legs feel chopped to bits, my left ankle isn't too keen on bearing my weight, my back is so sore it hurts to breathe, being in the light feels like standing right next to the speakers at a concert, and my jaw is screaming, but most of those are familiar feelings. Laila and Arlo help me into the back of the SUV before Arlo gets in the driver's seat and starts us back toward Emerald Tiger. Jin sits next to me in the back, ever stoic.

The beginning of the ride is silent as I stare at the back of the leather seat, pissed I can't turn my head to look out the window. I don't know what I could possibly say. The doctor is right, of course. I'm lucky. The fighter in me can't prove him wrong fast enough, but the part that knows what it felt like to be paralyzed, even though it was only for a minute, even though I was wrong, that part would never let me risk it.

"You'll be back in there in no time, Champ. Don't even worry about it," Arlo says.

Just picturing myself in the octagon again makes me queasy. I can't stop replaying the fight, a full body recoil hitting each time I have the overpowering, visceral memory of my neck bending too far, hearing the pops, the shock of pain and numbness. I don't know how I got to my feet. It feels like it was someone else. But it snaps back into excruciating detail when my heel connected with Brooklyn's head, the scary solidity of the blow, the way she slammed lifelessly to the mat.

I've always thought martial arts were beautiful, that competition was honorable. It's a shared moment with your opponent where you each find out exactly what you're capable of. I've never been oblivious to the risks, but coming that close to paying the ultimate price puts a new tint on the art that has been the love of my life, and I can't pretend it didn't shake my foundation. I don't think I even want to get back into the octagon. Inflicting or enduring that type of violence suddenly seems crazy. Worse than crazy, wasteful.

"You think I could make it as a coach?" I ask. Speaking sends pain shooting through my jaw and up the side of my face. They each look at me, examining me like they're trying to decipher what I said.

"Of course, you can," Laila says.

"Don't let that doctor get in your head," Arlo says. "You'll make a full recovery. You're young and super healthy. You don't have to coach."

I sigh as I let the thought settle in my mind. I crave the incense and stillness of the dojang, the ceremony and respect. Just the thought of returning to teaching Taekwondo full time soothes my soul. It's still combat, but there are so many more rules, so much less risk, and the atmosphere is as much about character as it is about fighting.

I don't know how to look them in the eye and tell them I don't want to go back to the UFC. A fighter's fighter doesn't quit because they got hurt. Champions don't get scared when their body breaks. Black belts don't cower in the face of danger. Warriors must be ready to die. And yet, do I not have a responsibility to honor and care for my body? Can I still disconnect from inflicting harm?

"I'm not going back." I try not to say it like a scared little lamb, but it still comes out quiet. There's a long beat of silence, and Arlo spins and looks back from the driver's seat.

"You're not talking about retiring, are you?"

"Yeah. I think I am."

"I know you got rocked, girl, but you'll never forgive yourself if you don't go back. You can't go out like that."

"Like what? On top?" Laila asks, shocking me.

"No," Arlo says slowly. "Because of a scare."

He craftily avoids saying because I'm scared, but it's the same thing.

"She achieved her dream," Laila says. I was prepared for her to side with Arlo. It's surprising and heartwarming when she rushes to my defense instead, but it makes me wonder how badly I must've freaked her out to make her feel this way. "She's the greatest female to ever do it. Youngest champion, most title defenses, and she'd be retiring undefeated. Why fuck with that and risk everything when she probably wouldn't be the same fighter she was anyway? Don't start with the macho shit. There's no reason to risk her health."

"Whoa," Arlo says. "Easy. I just think she'll regret it, that's all. And you don't know she won't be the same fighter. Don't shortchange her. Eden's a savage."

"Yes, she is, no matter what she does. She doesn't have to come back to prove to you she's a savage. If she wants to coach, she should coach."

"Still here, guys," I say.

"Sorry," they both mumble.

Laila turns back. "You know I think it's a good idea. I always have. Have you two talked yet?" She points from me to Jin, and I cringe. She thinks I'm planning to do what she's been suggesting for years and turn the dojang into an MMA gym. I've considered the financial state of the dojang, but I'm far from sold that's the only way to save it, and I've definitely not talked to Jin. I can't turn to look at him, but I feel his eyes on me.

"About what?" he asks.

"Nothing," I say. "There's no need."

"Eden, it's time," Laila says.

"Laila," I warn her sharply.

"It may be a good time to consider converting the dojang into an MMA gym," she says quickly, spitting the words out before I can stop her.

"God damn it, Laila," I say. "She's speaking out of turn," I say to Jin, but to my horror, she goes on anyway.

"The dojang has been losing money for years. Eden's been putting her winnings into keeping it going, but she can't do it forever, especially now."

"Laila!" Pain shoots through my jaw, but I can't stop my anger from coming out in a snap of venom. There was a time she'd never ignore my authority this way. Have I lost her respect so soon? She just keeps talking.

"If we convert it to an MMA gym it will make so much money. You would never have to think about it again. MMA is what everyone wants now. And Eden could coach."

"That's enough," Jin says. I have no doubt it's for my benefit more than his own. I wish I was in the proper condition to strangle Laila.

The silence drags for what feels like a decade. I understand Laila's intentions, but she's never ignored my will before. I could stomach her politely mentioning the idea, but to tell Jin the dojang is failing is too far. Acting like I'm on the brink of collapse when I actually have more money than I have ever had is enraging. Jin puts his hand on my knee.

"Is that what you want?"

"No." I wish I could look at him when I say it so I could stand a chance of making him believe me.

"How much money have you spent on the dojang?" The stillness in the car is excruciating. I'm fairly certain none of us are breathing except Jin.

"I would never keep track of that. It hasn't hurt me. It's been one of my greatest joys. It's my responsibility to give others what you gave me."

"It won't make it as it is," Laila says.

"Silence," Jin says sternly. "Your instructor has already informed you you've forgotten your place." Laila looks like a beat puppy, but I'm too furious with her to care. Jin addresses me again. "If it's your wish to convert the dojang, you needed only to ask."

"Jin, please don't," I say, grasping for his hand, not sure where it is. He reaches back out and holds it.

"You can't ask, can you?" he says. "I should have known that. The dojang was always meant to be yours. It doesn't grieve me for you to make it your own."

A tear spills down my cheek imagining losing the dojang, but even more so imagining Jin losing it. "It is my own."

"Make yourself whole, Eden. However you need to."

I've had an idea in the back of my head since Laila brought this up to me the first time. Not my first choice, but a contingency for this exact situation. It's still difficult to mention, but it's better than Laila running her mouth.

"What if we do both? We could convert the south side student housing into an MMA space. I have more than enough money to do that. I'll coach MMA during the day, and the dojang will operate as usual." I tense waiting for a response. This is the best way to save the dojang with the smallest amount of change, but it's still a change. It still means the dojang can't survive. I hate the thought of Jin feeling that.

"It's a good idea," he says. "I want your future secure."

There's a beat of silence before Arlo tentatively speaks up. "I think it's brilliant. I pay my gym ten percent of my winnings, and I don't want to brag, but that alone is a pretty penny. A few decent pros or one absolute stud, you're already bringing in quite a lot, especially if that's on top of what you're already doing."

"Yes," I say, excited he sees my vision. "I don't want a lot of clients. I still want the dojang to be the focus. Do you think they'll come if I don't have many training partners to offer them?"

He tilts his head side to side considering it. "You're a specialized coach, and they get all your attention. That's what you're selling. You'll bring in partners when you need them."

"Does my name carry enough weight for that? You think they'd want to learn from me?"

"All right, I already went down your list of accomplishments," Laila says. "You're just fishing now."

"I got my ass handed to me in that fight," I say.

"What the fuck are you talking about?" Arlo asks. "You did *not*. You won. You were winning anyway, and then you knocked her out. There's no dispute."

"Yeah, I knocked her out, but it's not going to be a secret who almost died and will never fight again. And it wasn't just the slam either. She was rockin' me."

"You need to watch the fight," Laila says. "Nobody saw her rocking you. Not like you were rocking her. She was hell-bent on beating you on your feet, didn't work, then she took you down and that didn't work either. You were owning her and she panic slammed you. The story is that you had a freak landing, not that she should have won."

It feels like a lifetime ago. Normally, I would have re-watched it a dozen times by now, but I haven't had the chance in the hospital. I probably could have gotten someone to show it to me on their phone, but truth be told, I'm afraid to see it. It's already playing on a loop in my mind. Maybe seeing it would take some of the bite out of my seared memory.

I slowly turn my whole body so I can look Jin in the eye. "I need you to know I love the dojang. I would never do anything to hurt it. If this is wrong, I can find another way."

He squeezes my hand. "I know you love the dojang. That's why it's yours."

"Tell me what you need," Laila says. "I'll work on it while you heal. When you're ready to come back, I'll have the gym and your first client ready."

CHAPTER ELEVEN

Twelve weeks in a halo-vest is hell on earth. It's a contraption you wear on your chest that circles your head and holds it still with rods that are screwed into your skin. They explained it before they put it on, but I didn't fully comprehend the apparatus or just how cumbersome it would be. I thought going home was going to be a sweet relief, that I was going to take it easy for a few weeks, watch a lot of stupid videos on the internet, and then more or less get back to life, even if it was going to be Diet Life.

Instead, I found out that for all freaking twelve weeks I was going to need help with basic things like getting up, and I had to be monitored like a fucking baby by Laila and Jin. They took turns staying in the student room across the hall to be close. A week of it is humbling. Four is humiliating. After that it was soul crushing. Getting back to eating solid food helped, but independence is the very thing I've built my life around since I was a kid at the mercy of my train wreck of a mother's whims, and now it's gone. A week ago, I went to my own doctor back home to finally have the halo-vest removed, only for him to slap a collar on instead because I was too weak to hold my head properly.

The collar was obnoxious, but don't get me wrong, being rid of the halo-vest is euphoric. Today, I'm finally rid of the collar, too. I can completely take care of myself again, but I still feel something close to panic about my physical condition. I haven't been able to exercise for fourteen weeks, and I feel it everywhere. I'm weak. I'm vulnerable, and it's horrifying. It's not like someone is going to run up and attack me. That's not my life anymore, but not being able to stop them if they do is still the worst feeling I've ever carried.

My head weighs a thousand pounds, and sometimes it feels like it's getting away from me like I'm a baby. My neck is stiff and tight all the time. It feels like it's been permanently immobilized, and it still hurts more or less all the time, but it's a dull pain that's become a familiar companion. I consider it a reminder of how bad things could've gone.

Seeing the fight brought that home. I've been watching it obsessively, almost on constant replay. I lean forward and click to the place in the video that I've memorized to be the start of the third round. Brooklyn came out in the third so aggressively, so sure she had me. I pause the video on her first attempt that round to take me down and look into her eyes. Her arms are so wide trying to wrap me up. Her brow is cut, her legs and body splotched with red where she's taken hit after hit. And still she's coming in with no regard for protecting herself. She wanted it so bad. I hit play and watch the rest.

Laila was right. There's no question I was winning the third round, which means I was winning two out of the three we fought, in addition to getting the finish. And she did have her chance on the ground and couldn't end it. There's no question, but I still can't help but look at her and wonder if she was in half the pain I was, if she took half the damage I took. I've watched the slam so many times now, but it still sends a shudder through me. When she lifted me, because she managed to sneak down past my hips to my legs, it was a top-heavy configuration, which made it possible for her to dump me on my head the way she did.

Sometimes the worst injuries come from maneuvers that look like nothing on video. This isn't like that. You can see that it was brutal. You can feel the crowd hold its breath. But as quickly as they do, I'm moving to defend myself, and they come back to life tenfold. I thought I was lying there lifeless for a century, but watching it now, I barely paused. I stop the video again and look at my own face, searching for signs of the terror I felt at that moment. Nothing.

A tap at the door breaks my concentration, and Laila sticks her head into the room. "Don't tell me you're watching it again."

"I'm not insane."

"I think you may be."

I sigh and shut my laptop, then wave her in. "What's up?"

She sits on the end of my twin bed. "I need to talk to you."

"Okay." I pull my knees to my chest to give her more room. "Go ahead."

"I promised I'd have the gym ready and your first client lined up by the time you were well enough to come back," she says. She looks down and scratches the back of her neck, falling into silence.

"It's okay if things are behind," I say. "I'm still trying to figure out how to hold my own head up anyway. Probably not the most inspiring thing for a client to witness." I try for humor, but she doesn't laugh.

"It's not that. The gym is close to ready. We separated off a space for you. It's lined by a fence that you can use to mimic the octagon. We have all the equipment you could ever want. You should come see it."

I haven't been able to walk back into the dojang. I'm afraid to see it changed, afraid I'll realize this was a huge mistake, or that it'll remind me of too many things I've lost. I still feel good about retiring, but Arlo, Laila, the UFC, even Jin, have all asked me to wait before I announce it, insisting I have time to sit on it and should use it, convinced I'm going to come out of this and want to fight again. It's not unheard of for a champion to wait a year between title defenses, especially when there's an injury involved, so there's no pressure.

I've never been an indecisive person, but their unanimity on it makes me nervous. Part of me is afraid seeing the finished MMA space will wake that dormant thing they all insist is waiting under the surface. I don't want it awakened. No one fights forever, and most fighters wait too long to get out, waiting to be pushed out by age, injury, and losses. Even if I go now, it won't exactly be in one piece.

"What's wrong then?" I ask. "No clients?"

"Not the interest I hoped for. We only have one pro offer. Everyone has good things to say, Eden. It's mostly that they can't move to New York or they're locked in contracts with current trainers or they just think you should have a bit more time to heal. In a year or two you'll have plenty of options. Or you could work with amateurs. There are plenty of those. You'd just need more of them because they can't pay much."

"Wait, there's one pro offer, though? I only need one right now. Who is it? Do I know them?"

"Yeah, you know them."

"What's wrong?" I ask, but she can't seem to spit it out. "Jesus, is it Arlo or something? You tell him to take his ass back to Canada. I don't want pity clients."

"It's Brooklyn Shaw."

I feel my face scrunching up, my brows pinching together even though I don't mean to do it.

"What are you feeling?" she asks.

"Huh? Feeling? I don't... Huh?"

Laila nods. "I know. I wanted to just tell them to go fuck themselves, but Jin told me I had to at least run it by you. Just say the word, and I'll tell them to drop dead."

"Brooklyn Shaw wants me to coach her? *The* Brooklyn Shaw? 'Eden Bauer is an overrated, weak champion' Brooklyn Shaw?"

"Yes."

"Called Jin Mr. Miyagi, called you a cashier, Brooklyn Shaw?"

"That's the one."

"Why the fuck would she want to train with me?" I'm not even as mad as I sound. I'm too confused to be mad. "Is this some kind of joke? Is she mocking me?"

Laila pauses for a long time before she speaks. "I hate the woman, but no, I don't think she's mocking you. I didn't speak to her directly. It was her father who called."

"You talked to Samson Shaw?"

"Yeah, I did. Man, he's a smooth talker. He says everything leading up to the fight was just business to get big pay-per-view numbers and she never meant for you to take any of it personally."

"Hah."

"He said you're the champ, and you're the only one to ever beat Brooklyn, so there's no one better for her to train with. He thinks she can learn a lot from you. She just accepted a fight offer with Julia Mendez. They want you right away."

"I see." I still feel like I'm waiting for the punchline.

"I'm not saying you should do it, but if it matters to you, he did sound sincere. And he offered a truckload of money."

"How much is a truckload?"

"It pays for the renovation and then some."

"Whoa." I sit forward a little despite myself.

"And that's just to get you to let her through the door. Then you get ten percent of any of her winnings too."

"That's crazy. Why would he do that?"

Laila dips her head to the side. "I think he knew it was going to be a tough sell, and he didn't want you to be able to say no. They have that Shaw money, so they can. They want her to go down as the greatest of all time, and they think you can take her there."

"Jesus." I can't picture Brooklyn Shaw in Emerald Tiger. It's an absurd image. Trying to conjure it just lands me with a vision of her standing an inch from my face telling me what a fraud I am. I can't buy that it was all a show, but why not? People do it all the time. It *does* raise PPV numbers. We did both get paid way more because of it. She was so over-the-top the whole time it did occur to me it was fake, but does that even matter? Can I let someone who disrespected me and my family into my gym?

"What do you think?" I ask.

Laila raises her eyebrow and shakes her head. "That's not my call, Eden."

"I'm asking."

"I don't think she deserves you. But I do think you deserve this."

Is it some kind of poetic gift from the universe? Brooklyn Shaw breaks my neck and steals my career, then hands me another? The bond between a coach and a martial artist is a sacred one. I'd be testing every limit she has and guiding her not just in how to win, but to protect herself. I'd be intertwined in her mental state, emotions, dreams, and health. The trust requirement is too great a canyon to leap and the stakes too high.

"I can't do it."

Laila stares at me for a long moment. I half expect her to ask if it's my final answer, but she finally nods.

"I'll tell him."

"Thank you."

"I'll just tell Samson Shaw no."

I laugh. "Do you need me to do it?"

"No, no." She shoves her palm toward me on a straight arm. "I've got this. Watch." She clears her throat. "No, Samson Shaw, we won't be bought. Wow, what a power move. I like it."

"It's not a power move. It's just the right call." I hope it is anyway.

CHAPTER TWELVE

Being rid of all the contraptions on my head and neck feels like a thousand pounds off my shoulders, but being able to move through the world freely again feels like a thousand pounds off my soul. My doctor isn't a jerk like the ER doctor I saw, but he does keep telling me to take it easy even though everything in me is screaming to exercise around the clock and figure out what normal is going to be now. He allows me to start working my way back into teaching, and a little exercise as long as I don't try to be a hero about it.

Still, getting back in shape has to start somewhere, so I pop my headphones in and head for the back door. As soon as my shoes hit pavement, I start a slow jog. Running in this area isn't the best idea in general. People have been scolding me about driving to a real path rather than running the streets, but the Hudson River Path is close enough I can't be bothered to drive to it even when I do use it. I thought my lack of fear of these streets was because I'm close to the community and don't expect them to hurt me, but now that I can't defend myself, it's clear it was never that. I'm on edge in a way I haven't been in years, scanning all around me.

I shake myself for being a coward. Doing this during the day is already a concession. I usually prefer to run at night. There's something about hearing your own breath in the quiet dark, feeling the coolness of evening air against your skin. I used to run ten miles a few times each week. Now it only takes a quarter mile for my limbs to feel heavy and clunky. By a half mile, my lungs and throat burn, and my heart rate is easily over one fifty. Jesus, it's even worse than I expected.

The thing about running is that if you can convince your body you're not listening to it, that your mind is stronger, it will eventually cooperate. I enjoy that battle, but I've never had to fight it so soon. I'm only a mile from the gym when my neck's protest to activity escalates from tightness to pain and spasm. I cuss under my breath and slow to a walk. Everything in my nature wants to shove it into a corner, but my instructions are to let the body win right now. I can't imagine even touching what I used to be capable of from this place.

I stretch my neck as I walk, soaking in the familiarity of the businesses, friends laughing in front of their busted houses, and the sound of tires peeling across the street. A mile and a half in, my heart rate has been down for a while, but my neck shows no signs of improvement, so I start heading back on the next street over.

I'm cruising down the road just a few blocks from the gym when I hear thumps and hollow clangs. I try to spot the source and notice a dumpster on the side of an old sign shop with someone standing by it. My head is stuck in an involuntary sprinkler motion that sends pain crackling out as I do a quadruple take. The person by the dumpster has an arm raised, offering a hand to someone who's inside. And of all bizarre things, the person is Brooklyn Shaw. I squint, still not convinced this could be what it looks like, but there she is, in all her muscled glory. As I stare at the strange interaction, I slowly realize Brooklyn isn't the only face I recognize. The hand she's holding belongs to Mateo. Relief and confusion battle for control.

How does she know Mateo? *Does* she know him? And what in all hell is he doing in a dumpster?

"Hey!" I say. They must not hear me because neither looks. I jog the half block to them. I'm almost there when Mateo jumps out of the dumpster with her assistance. I catch up in time to hear them laughing. They're laughing? I stop next to them and plant my feet firmly in an awkward social paralysis. Brooklyn looks every bit as flabbergasted to see me as I am to see her. I force myself to speak.

"What the hell is going on?" I look from one to the other, undecided on who I'm even asking. "Where the hell have you been?" to Mateo. "And what are you doing here?" to Brooklyn. "And what are you doing in the dumpster?" back to Mateo.

Brooklyn holds up a hand. "Whoa, easy. You know each other?"

"What are you doing here?" I ask again, surprising myself a little with my aggressive tone.

"I was on my way to see you." She sounds testy too now, the smile she shared with Mateo gone. I can't compute why she would be on the way to see me as if it were a normal thing.

"What? Why?"

"To talk you into training me." There's no edge now. It's just matter-of-fact, with surprising confidence. "I heard you said no."

"I did."

"And why's that?"

"Because it's an insane idea," I say.

"You still mad I said you were overrated? You obviously proved me wrong. I'm the one who has to swallow my pride. What do you care?"

"You're disrespectful. I don't want it around my kids. They see enough of that."

She scoffs. "Oh, what a load of crap."

Mateo's eyes have turned to saucers soaking this in. I don't have time for this conversation, and he doesn't need to see it. I ignore her retort and turn to Mateo.

"What happened?" I ask. "I've been worried about you."

He looks at his feet and shrugs. "I got fired. I can't afford my dues."

"You don't have to, Mateo. I want you in class. You know you can always come to the dojang."

He shrugs again, unable to look at me. I can feel the shame weighing down his head, and it breaks my heart. I brace both of his arms. "You are more important than any dues, Mateo. I could never afford mine either."

"You couldn't?"

"No. Now what the hell were you doing inside that dumpster? Did someone put you there?"

He shakes his head.

"Hiding?"

"No."

"What then?"

"I was hungry."

"Oh, kid." I want to crush him in a hug, but it'll embarrass him. I take in Brooklyn at my side all over again. She's in a simple white T-shirt and jeans, but it must be one of those two-hundred-dollar shirts that only appear to be plain, because she looks incredible.

"And you saw him in the dumpster and just decided to help?"

"Shocking, I know," Brooklyn says. "Look, I promised your dude here a burger. You want to come?"

My emotions are cascading and churning like the bottom of a waterfall. Just seeing Brooklyn sets off a twinge of distaste and anger, but that doesn't mix well with the involuntary affection I feel toward her for pulling my sweet Mateo out of the trash and offering him friendship, no questions asked. Regardless of my inability to make sense of her, I'm not ready to lose track of him again.

"Sure."

"Perfect." She looks a little surprised, but she leads the way to the burger joint across the street. We get a table and order a truckload of food. Brooklyn and I ask for appetizers and shakes in addition to burgers for everyone. I can't tell if she genuinely eats a ton or if she's in sync with my plan to order more than enough food to ensure Mateo gets his fill without worrying about the cost.

When the food comes, he shovels fries into his mouth at a staggering pace. Brooklyn and I sit quietly, exchanging loaded glances until he slows down enough to have a conversation.

"You been going to school?" I ask.

"Sometimes."

I can't bring myself to scold him. I know how stupid school feels when your world is falling apart. I want to know how he got fired, but I can't quite ask him. I feel like it'll imply he did something wrong when really it makes me crazy he's even working and that a boss would fire a kid who's clearly in such a desperate situation. But then, a lot of the kids around here are like Mateo.

Brooklyn seems to notice I'm stuck and jumps in. "How old are you, Mateo?"

"Twelve."

"How long you been training with Eden?"

He shrugs. "Two years maybe."

"That's good," she says. "You stick with that. And stick with school. Going sometimes isn't going to get you out of here."

"Nothing's going to get me out of here." He's not a cynical kid. Whatever's transpired in the past weeks has left a mark.

"Hey." She grabs his hand with an urgency that makes him jump a little. "Whatever you tell yourself is true, becomes true. Don't say that shit unless you want to be here forever."

He nods reluctantly.

"You like martial arts?" she asks. He nods again. "You want to be a fighter?"

"I'm not good enough."

"What did I just say?"

"But I'm not strong," he says. "And I can't even buy my own food."

"I see," Brooklyn says in a near whisper. Her deep brown eyes fill with such warmth and sadness she looks like an entirely different human. "But Eden just told you she couldn't pay her dues when she was your age. And you know what? I couldn't buy my own food when I was a kid. Didn't stop us. It doesn't have to stop you."

"Whatever, you're lying. You're a Shaw."

"Look it up, Wikipedia. Hand on the bible."

"But why?"

"What do you mean why? Because we were poor, dude. We lived in Brazil then. What do you know about Brazil?"

"They're really good at Brazilian Jiu-Jitsu."

She smiles and fist bumps him. He laughs as he returns the gesture. The sound is magic. "We *are* really good at Brazilian Jiu-Jitsu, but we also have some of the most dangerous cities in the world, and my family lived in one of them. When my dad opened up his Jiu-Jitsu school, he put every penny he'd ever won in competition into it. For the first few years before it started to take off, we couldn't afford anything. Not even food. My oldest brother, Nicolau, got tired of being broke, so you know what he did?"

Mateo shakes his head. I know she's not even talking to me, but I'm inexplicably honored she'd let me know anything personal about her. She's so unexpectedly sweet with him. Brooklyn, sweet?

"He started robbing businesses," she says. "Know where he is now?"

"Jail?"

"That's right. Now, he had money for a minute. He brought us all presents and food. He was the man. But look at him now. And look at us now. He could've done what I do. He could've been the best of us, but he didn't believe there was a way out. He started hanging around the wrong people and stopped training with us. By the time he gets out of jail it'll be too late for him to compete. You understand what I'm saying to you?"

He nods. "Yeah, I think so."

"You have to surround yourself with the right kind of people. Don't disappear on the ones who're trying to help you. I'm not saying your life isn't rough, but you hit the jackpot in one way. You have one of the best fighters in the world just down the street trying to look out for you, trying to train you for free. You know you'd be crazy not to show up for that, right?"

He breaks into a smile and looks over at me. His shoulders finally relax. "Yeah, I know."

"All right, then."

"Hey, Brooklyn?" he asks.

"Yeah?"

"You think maybe you could show me some stuff too? Like a Kimura?"

"You like Kimuras, huh?" She smiles at him, then glances at me. "Well, I don't know. What do you think, Eden? Should I come by the gym?"

Mateo spins to me with excited, innocent eyes, and Brooklyn smiles out of the corner of her mouth, looking pleased with herself. Jesus, that's checkmate, and she knows it.

I roll my eyes. "Yes, you can come by the gym and show him some stuff."

"And us?" She points from herself to me a couple of times.

"Come by tomorrow morning, and we'll *talk* about it. No promises."

She smiles a sneaky smile, like I'm not supposed to see it. "Fair enough."

CHAPTER THIRTEEN

That the Shaws show up in style should not be a surprise to any of us, but I can't help but laugh at the black Escalade that rolls up to the Emerald Tiger parking lot booming hip-hop. Théo Shaw emerges from the passenger seat looking slick in all black clothing to match the all black SUV. His hair is cropped almost all the way down with a series of three lines shaved along the side of his head for stylistic value. He has a showstopping smile, deep brown eyes, the body of a god, like the rest of his family, and carries the confidence of a champion.

Then, the puzzling Brooklyn Shaw emerges. She wears her hair natural with its beautiful thick curls a few inches long and shaved sides with some stenciling a bit more elaborate than Théo's without getting over-the-top. She's wearing a white sleeveless shirt and jeans. Her eyes are hidden by black sunglasses, but I feel them on me through the glass panel entryway just the same. She laughs at something Théo says to her, and her face lights up.

I can't help but examine her as she approaches the door, her body, her posture, her walk. She moves with relaxed power, casual purpose, like a tiger. My stomach twists as she gets closer. The bell on the door jingles as she and Théo walk in. Laila, closer than I am, greets them first.

"Hello," she says. "Glad you could make it out. I'm Laila."

Théo and Brooklyn each nod and shake her hand, awkwardly spitting out their names as if they haven't had to introduce themselves in a long time. They probably haven't. I knew Théo's name was pronounced without the h, but the way he says it still sounds a little different, richer, than when most people say it. Théo turns to me wearing a smile, but I feel the heat of resentment radiating off of him. Funny, I never took time to consider that he may be mad at me. Between all of Brooklyn's trash talk and how badly she hurt me, I never bothered guessing how the legendary Théo Shaw feels about the way I knocked out his baby sister.

"Eden." I hold out my hand for him to shake. Théo doesn't break his smooth demeanor for a second. He slips his hand into mine and squeezes my upper arm with the other hand in an unexpected gesture that warms me to him instantly.

"The one and only," he says. "It's nice to officially meet you, Eden."

"You as well." I try to form some kind of compliment, anything to indicate that I realize and appreciate who I'm talking to, but everything that runs through my head is asinine, and soon the moment is gone.

Brooklyn steps closer and finally takes her sunglasses off. Her striking brown eyes grab me. I'm impressed with the confidence with which she can hold my gaze. I expected uncertainty or guilt or at least a little self-consciousness, but I see none of that.

"You look good," she says, throwing me off balance right away. Is that intended to remind me she mutilated me and it's a miracle I've recovered? Or a bona fide compliment? I don't have time to decipher it, so I just hurl it back at her, whatever it is.

"So do you."

"What's on the agenda for this meeting?" Théo intervenes right away like an overbearing manager. Maybe that's exactly what he is, something I'll need to know moving forward. I nudge my head toward the gym a bit to indicate they should follow me and guide them toward the new MMA area.

"I was surprised to hear you wanted to train here," I say. "Given our history."

"Look, Ms. Bauer, it was a fight," Théo says from behind me. His impatience is already thick. I have a flare of doubt we'll survive this conversation. "Pre-fight is part of the fight in our camp. We believe in attacking the mind as well as the body. It was never anything personal. I thought our father explained that on the phone."

"He did." I stop just inside the MMA space. It's set back from the rest of the gym inside what used to be the other four live-in student quarters. It's a shame to lose those, but only in a nostalgic sort of way. We haven't had more than one or two live-in students for years, and they never stay long. The three extra rooms on my side of the gym will be enough, and I could easily move out to provide one more if it ever comes to that.

The new area is larger than I imagined it would be, about twice the size of the octagon and rectangular. It looks amazing. There are three heavy bags set up on the right wall that can be detached to offer more mat space if needed, with additional clips if we ever want to put up more.

The design is sharp, all black mats, bamboo walls except one accent wall at the back, which is black with an explosively eye-catching emerald tiger head. The left wall displays all the medals and awards the students of the dojang have received, a common MMA and boxing gym practice that wasn't appropriate in the dojang. It's an impressive display, filled with mostly Taekwondo tournament medals and prominently featuring my UFC championship belt. Brooklyn's eyes catch on it, but I don't see any of the negative emotions I may expect.

"Laila did tell me what your father said," I say. "But if we're going to do this, we're going to spend a lot of time together. I need to know how you really feel about it."

Théo opens his mouth, but Brooklyn beats him to it. "I did think I was going to smash you."

"Brooklyn." Théo glares at her.

"Go on," I say.

"I told the whole fucking world I was going to smash you, and then I lost. I thought I was better. Still do, if you must know, but don't think that means I don't realize you're a legend. That's the whole reason I wanted to fight you. I never hated you. You're actually one of my idols." Her eyes are full of emotion, anger, maybe even rage, but also despair. "That fight fucked everything up. I hated you after it more than I ever did before it. My dad was ready to kill me for losing. When he heard you were starting to coach, he told me I better get my ass over here so you can show me how you beat me. I don't know if he's trying to punish me or what, but I told him it was the stupidest idea I ever heard."

"Brooklyn," Théo attempts to chastise her again, but I can appreciate this kind of honesty. I shake my head at him to indicate it's okay. I'm almost tickled more than anything she just told me she still thinks she's better than I am. I'm weirdly happy her spirit isn't broken. She'll need that. Still, I can't see her respecting me as her coach if she thinks her loss was a fluke.

"So, you don't want to be here," I say. "This was just a show meeting you can take back to your dad to say you tried."

"I turned twenty-three last month. You were two months older than I am now when you won the title. I can't break your record," she says. "I'm just four fights in and already lost the undefeated thing. That means I need to do something incredible to leave the mark I'm trying to leave. I can't lose ever again."

She breaks eye contact to slip out of her shoes and circle the mat, examining the room. She gets to the heavy bag and throws a light jab. "You know how people don't like to watch grappling? Always bitching it's just people holding each other down?"

I nod, walking farther onto the mat, watching as she throws a cross with a little more sting on it.

"I always felt the opposite," she says. "Jiu-Jitsu is complex, so many steps and submissions and counters and counters to the counters. Striking, though? Punch, kick. I figured I could master that in a weekend." She throws a hard body kick that moves the bag and rattles the chain. "When I started knocking people out, I figured I was right." She turns and faces me. "But then I got in there with you."

I expect more, but she stops. "You want me to show you the complexity in striking?"

"Théo has been my coach for years, and it's been working. I trust him with my life. You…" She looks me up and down. "Yes,

I want to be able to strike like you, but I'm not sure I can believe you would ever really help me. I'm the reason you're a coach right now."

"I've always been an instructor and a corner," I say. "Coaching is not some half-assed grab at a new career. I love it."

"Yeah, but you were a champion. You were the one, the baddest bitch ever. I'm supposed to believe you're going to help me overshadow your own legacy?"

"Then what are we doing here?"

"My dad is not a guy you ignore," Brooklyn says.

"That's not a good enough reason."

"I do believe you can make me better. I just don't trust you. What about your belt?"

"What about it?"

"One person tells me you're retiring. The next says if you were, you would have done it. We fight in the same division. I need to know which it is. I'm not going to train with someone who's planning to fight me."

"I'm not coming back."

"Then what are you waiting for? Are you just milking your reign until they strip you?"

"No. I've been asked from everyone in my life to wait. My coach, my friends, the UFC. They all think it's just a reaction to getting hurt. No one believes I mean it, but I do."

"If they don't believe you, why should I?"

"It doesn't serve me to work with you either if I'm planning to come back."

"Serves you much better than me," she says.

"How do you figure that? I'll be making you better at striking, but you won't be making me better at Jiu-Jitsu."

"If you really teach me."

Jesus, does she think I'm hatching some plot to fake coach her just to make her a weaker fighter so I can come back and beat her? After I've already beaten her in earnest?

"Brooklyn, I don't have that kind of time to waste. My competition days are over. I don't want it anymore. It'll be final soon enough."

She studies me for a long time before she speaks again. "I want Théo involved in all our training."

"As what?"

"My coach."

"Your Jiu-Jitsu coach?"

"My head coach."

"How do you suggest I be your coach if you already have one?" I ask.

"You'll be my striking coach. He oversees everything. He does conditioning. He does strategy."

"No."

"No?" She says it with a smirk and twinkle of amusement in her eyes. "And why not? It's less work for you. We're offering you a small fortune. What's the problem?"

"I'm not a kickboxing class, I'm a coach. I can't change your results with a quarter of your attention. I'm not attaching my name to someone who's barely listening to me and bound to lose to the next elite striker she faces."

"Hey now," Théo intervenes. "You've been coaching MMA for five seconds. I've been doing it for years. You should count yourself lucky to have a first client like Brooklyn."

"She's not a client at all if you're her coach, Théo. Now, you don't have to do this." I meet Brooklyn's eyes again. "You have your family thing going on. You made it to a title fight by twenty-two. No one's saying you aren't a great team, but if you want change, you have to make a change. There are serious holes in your striking. I won't be the only one to see them."

Brooklyn looks away, her jaw clenched.

"He can be in the room," I say. "He can speak his mind, but I'm your head coach, or we don't do this." I'm a little shocked I'm even officially offering to do it. She's arrogant, stubborn, and doesn't trust me. She's also special, though, and if she can be honest, maybe we can get there.

"You have a lot to learn, and you're *not* better than me." I power through before she can lash out. "Right now. But you can be. If you do this, I can put that belt in your hands and take you on to break my record for title defenses and beyond. The sport is young, Brooklyn, especially for women. My record isn't going to hold up forever regardless of what you do. I don't care about that, and if I did, I'd just turn you away. I wouldn't jerk you around and ruin my name as a coach. If you're my martial artist, your fights are my fights. I will take you there."

Brooklyn holds my gaze for a long time. Her hunger for glory is palpable, filling the room with energy. She looks at Théo, but he's stone-faced. She looks back.

"All right. Let's get it."

CHAPTER FOURTEEN

Just some light drill work, okay?" I say to Laila. I don't like having to put her in with Brooklyn at all. I wish I could do it myself, but my neck isn't there yet. I've been cleared to do most everything, but I'm still not supposed to take hits to the head. It seems like the kind of thing no doctor is ever going to green light. I may have to take some liberties at some point, but the last thing I want to do right now is hurt myself again.

"You're the boss." Laila slips into her gloves. I bump her side in thanks and jog over to where Théo is finishing wrapping Brooklyn's hands.

"Ready?"

"Yep." She yanks on her black and gold gloves and slaps them together. "Whatcha got, Obi Wan?"

"We're just going to start with a simple one-two. Then Laila will counter. I want you to slip it, then a counter of your choice. Very light. I'm looking for touches only. Focus on movement."

Brooklyn stares at me dead faced.

"What?" I ask.

"One-two, slip, counter?"

"Yes." One-two is universal striking language for a jab and a cross, straight punches with your lead and back hand. Three is a lead hook, four a rear hook, five a lead uppercut, six a rear uppercut. One-two is the most basic combination that exists, which I'm sure is why she's looking at me like I'm an alien right now.

"Come on, just let me see it."

She steps up to Laila. Brooklyn is in a tank top that shows off her buff shoulders and arms. She probably has fifteen pounds of muscle on Laila. It shouldn't matter in this context, but I can see Brooklyn sizing up the mismatch.

"Ready?" Brooklyn asks and winks at her.

"Light," I snap before either of them moves.

Brooklyn throws the jab cross, nice and light, to my relief. Laila uses her gloves to absorb the punches like they're pads, then throws a cross that Brooklyn dodges. Brooklyn returns with a hook to the body that Laila shields with her elbow. The form is terrible on all counts, but I don't say anything. I let them work through a few reps. They've been going for around three minutes when Brooklyn starts glancing over at me. She doesn't say anything, but she's obviously anxious to move on.

"Move your feet," I say. "Find an angle."

Brooklyn takes a quick step in and fires off the one-two.

"Good, now get out." She doesn't move quickly enough, and Laila's counter lands to Brooklyn's cheek, light as a feather but clean. Brooklyn pivots on her front foot and returns a strong punch to Laila's ribs that catches mostly elbow again. It's harder than I want, but not ghastly.

"Again," I say when Brooklyn drags her feet to reset. She throws the combination, this time dodging Laila's counter with a swoop down and to her right, then coming back with an uppercut.

"Way too big of a slip. You're out of position," I say. They reset and go again. The minutes are ticking away as Brooklyn cycles through the same handful of mistakes. For every one that looks good, ten are a mess, and I'm starting to doubt if she's had any formal stand-up training at all or if she just brawled with her brothers in the garage. I call out guidance every few reps, trying to slowly key her into the different pieces of her body and how they need to move. Laila's getting sharper as she figures Brooklyn out. Brooklyn is getting sloppier, moving like a teenager who's been told to clean their room. She leans back and drops her arms, then snaps the jab forward, a highly relaxed and stylized approach, so overconfident.

"Put your hands up, Brooklyn. Quit messing around," I say.

"Oh my God, give us a new combination already. Enough of this baby shit," Brooklyn says.

"You don't need a new combination. You haven't figured this one out yet."

"Haven't figured it out?" Brooklyn spins on me.

"You're risking too much doing too little. You reach when you should move your feet. You'd rather take a punch on the way in than be patient enough to find an opening. These are basics that absolutely have to be mastered."

"Get out of here, I know the fucking basics," Brooklyn snaps.

"Okay, well, it doesn't look like it."

"You're awful cocky for someone who barely beat me. Don't let this coaching shit go to your head."

I laugh. "You think I'm the one with an arrogance problem here?"

Laila steps away from Brooklyn like it's dangerous to be close to her. Brooklyn steps toward me.

"I think you're trying to flex on me or something. Don't act like I don't have any idea what I'm doing over here. Don't forget if we'd been in a real fight, I would have won."

"How do you figure that? You were unconscious."

"You were saved by the bell, Bauer. In real life you would have never gotten back to your feet after the second round. I would have choked you to death with another minute or two."

"Please, if you want to talk about a street fight, you would have been done in round one if I hadn't had gloves on."

"All right, all right," Théo says. "Let's just cool it."

"I can throw a fucking one-two," Brooklyn says, quieter but every bit as angry.

"Maybe you can, but you haven't been giving it an honest effort since you got here. You think you're too good for drills? And I'm supposed to pat that weak effort on the back? You want to move on, do it right."

We stare at each other for a long time. How the hell did she pull me into this? What *is* it about her that makes me so much more reactive than I've ever been? Am I intimidated? Is it that simple? God, I hope not. And how the fuck is her face so gorgeous even while she's trying to burn me into a pile of ash with her eyes? Working with her is like trying to tame a tiger, trying to move a gorgeous killer that's never had to move for anyone. Every time I face her I can feel her checking me for weakness.

"Change it up at least," Théo says. The interruption breaks the tension. "Give her a little something new to work with."

"Fine, but I want to see it sharp," I say. "No attitude. No playing around. You keep your hands up, control your distance, stay on balance. Cross, uppercut, duck a right hook, counter."

Brooklyn nods and goes to work. She's throws the cross and uppercut hard, pushing Laila back. I see the reaction on Laila's face, but she recovers and throws the hook for Brooklyn to duck. Brooklyn swoops under it and launches a left hook to the body.

"Better," I say. "Sharp, not hard. Still just touching. Go."

She runs the combination again, faster than before, still landing too hard. I study Laila to make sure she's okay. She's still brushing it off.

"Smaller duck," I say. "Just enough to make her miss. No extra movement."

She goes again, pushing forward and really cracking Laila this time.

"Touches," I snap.

Brooklyn resets and goes again without pause. Laila blocks the cross and uppercut, throws the hook. Brooklyn bobs under it well this time and returns with a mean right hand that slips through Laila's guard and hits her in the nose. Laila stumbles backward and cups her face. Brooklyn resets, but I step in between them. I put my hand on Brooklyn's chest and back her up a step. She's like a brick wall but moves back with her hands up.

"What do you not understand about touches?"

"I'm fine," Laila says.

"She's fine," Brooklyn repeats, but I look at Laila, and she's wiping blood from her nose. When I turn back to Brooklyn, she's staring at me with playful curiosity, like she can't wait to see what

I'll say. When another second of silence passes, she drops her hands in exasperation.

"What the hell do you want from me? You said to step it up. I stepped it up. Don't put little twigs who can't handle my hands in here if you don't want anyone to get rocked. Put a big ass dude in. He'll take it."

"Is that how you're used to working?" I ask. "You fight giant guys so you don't have to control yourself?"

"I *usually* fight real fighters."

"She is a real fighter," I snap. "And like it or not, she's been beating you on the counter. She could have done that to you too, but she didn't. She respected you and me and this space."

"Oh, cry me a river. We're fighters. It's not training until someone bleeds."

"You train like that you won't have a body left by the time you're twenty-six. We're here to hold the title for a decade. Is that what you want or not?"

"You're not taking me there with this garbage. You're just a control freak trying to suck all the life out of my style."

"You think this is garbage?"

She steps closer. "Yeah. It's fucking garbage."

"Laila, get me my gloves."

"Eden."

"Do it."

Brooklyn raises an eyebrow and smiles. "You sure you want to do that, Coach?"

"Oh, I'm sure."

Laila shows up with my gloves, and I slip them on without bothering to wrap my hands first. It won't be long. Brooklyn smirks watching me do it.

"I feel like you should have to sign a waiver to fight me," she says.

"Your ego is what needs to come with a waiver," I say. "It's going to get you hurt."

I shouldn't take this risk. The fracture in my neck is healed. It won't kill me to take a knock, but it could put me back on the couch for a few weeks fairly easily. It would destroy this arrangement for sure, but it's already hanging in the balance if I can't make her listen to me, and drilling with her isn't as crazy as it may sound. We were closely matched in the octagon because I had to worry about things like takedowns and submissions, but in straight up striking, she's no match for me, and she needs to understand that.

"Go on," I say. "Either combo."

She flies forward, throwing a hard jab-cross. I slip the jab and move back a couple of inches from the cross, then pivot hard into a hook that hits her in the body. She curls over the punch, seeming to forget she's meant to counter at first, then throwing a sloppy left hook I duck easily. I'm circling into position again before she can recover. She straightens up and throws the second combination, a cross and uppercut. She knows the right hook is coming, but she's so out of position from overcommitting to her cross she can't dodge it. She abandons the duck and tries to block instead, but she's late and has to absorb most of the impact. Then I'm gone, leaving her swiping at the air in her attempted counter.

She's slow to move into the next combination. I can see her selecting which she'll attempt with care, examining my stance and guard for openings. I suspect she'll choose the second combo again because in that one, she knows exactly what punch I'll have to throw, and that's exactly what she does. I slap her cross away, slip the uppercut to the right, then rack her again with a hard hook to the face that sends her to the ground.

Théo moves to her side, but she holds her hand up angrily to signal him not to. She touches her face and looks at her glove to check for blood. There isn't any, and she pulls away from eye contact like she's embarrassed to have checked. She makes a slow motion to get up.

"Just sit." She looks surprised when I sit across from her. "Breathe."

"I'm fine."

"I know you are." I pull off my gloves. She slowly does the same and unravels her wraps. She looks at the floor for a long time before she meets my eyes. There's a blend of anger and vulnerability in them that makes me uncertain what she could possibly be thinking.

"Look," I say. "I'm not trying to torture you. I know you don't want to hear it, especially from me, but you don't have this down. You're an incredible martial artist. You still have to be realistic about your weaknesses if you want to get better. Go home and think it over. Decide if you really want to do this. Come back tomorrow if you do."

Her gaze is so intense I'm sure she's about to cuss me out, but she doesn't. It's like she's trying to pull my soul out and examine it. Given she has such a tight-knit family, I can't fathom what's made her so suspicious, but I recognize the lack of trust. I feel the familiarity of it panging around my chest.

I stand, then offer her my hand. She hesitates before she grabs my forearm. I return the grip and pull her to her feet. The warmth of her palm seeps through my entire body, and I find myself reluctant to let go. There's something safe and dangerous mixing in her touch. I don't want to notice, but there's no denying she lingers too.

Théo breaks the spell when he walks up and slaps my upper arm before leading the way out of the gym. Laila and I follow them out and watch them leave in the Escalade.

"You okay?" I ask.

"I'm good."

"Think she'll be back?"

Laila tilts her head and stares at me like it's a dumb question. "Uh, yeah. I do."

CHAPTER FIFTEEN

The sound of rain smacking metal fire escapes has always been comforting to me. I'm never upset to get stuck in bad weather, but it's only a little surprising when a black SUV pulls up to rescue me. There are any number of people it could be, but I slowly realize it's the Shaw Escalade. The windows have such a dark tint I can't see Brooklyn until she rolls the window down.

"Don't tell me you don't have a car," she says with a wide, amused grin.

"I don't break it out for little trips around the neighborhood."

"Can I give you a lift?"

The introvert in me wants to turn her down, but after our argument last night it wouldn't be good messaging. I crane my neck a little and see Théo isn't with her like I expected, and damn does she look beautiful smiling down at me. How can she be so friendly and inviting one second and so ruthless the next?

"Sure." I circle the car and step up into the passenger seat with my grocery bag. Brooklyn looks over and smiles before she pulls off. She's in a tank top again, prepared for training even though she's early. The bizarre urge to trace the lines of her arm startles me, like I'm afraid my fingers are going to act on their own.

"Really not sure why you insist on walking alone in this kind of area all the time," she says. "Most girls as pretty as you know better."

It feels like the words reach out and shake me they're so unexpected. Did Brooklyn Shaw just call me *pretty*? And wrap it up in a reprimand? A dozen responses jump into my mind, but none of them come out of my mouth before she speaks again.

"I guess they must leave you alone, huh? Perks of being the Sniper?"

"Ugh." I groan at the nickname. I haven't been able to shake it since an announcer coined it when I won two fights in a row with one punch. "If you could never call me that, it would be great. And yeah, it helps, but I've been walking these streets since I was a kid."

"You grew up here?" Her look of genuine surprise humanizes her, and it's strangely endearing.

"Just up the road. I used to pass the dojang to and from school every day. One day I was huddled up in the alcove trying not to get jumped, and Jin pulled me inside. Never really left."

"No shit? I didn't have you pegged for a Bronx kid."

"Why's that?" I ask, repressing a laugh.

"I don't know. You're just so…" She waves her hand around searching for the word. I have a feeling whatever it is it'll be mildly insulting.

"Ugh, what? Soft? Naive?" I ask. She keeps waving at the air for the word. "White?"

She throws her head back and laughs. The sound is so pleasing to my ears, free and full and easygoing. "Nice. You're so nice. When I was talking trash before the fight and saw you getting all worked up about it I thought no one ever talked to you like that before, but they must have if you grew up here."

"Yes, they definitely have. I just didn't expect street talk from a world class martial artist."

"You have some very romantic ideas about martial arts, don't you?" The sun catches her deep brown eyes and lights them up in a flame of gold as she looks at me.

"Yeah, I guess I do."

"Not very Bronx of you."

"No, it's Korean."

"They should have called you the Shaolin Monk, not the Sniper."

"That would be Chinese."

"Whatever, it's Asian. And it suits you."

"Beats the Sniper." I smile.

"You really don't like it, huh?"

"Do you like yours?"

"Brutal Brooklyn?" She shrugs. "The whole name thing is kind of cheesy, I guess, but I don't hate it."

"How'd you get it?" Probably a stupid question. It's definitely fitting.

"It's been around since I was a kid. I always mostly trained with my brothers, but when people, especially girls, came through the gym and wanted to train with me, that was kind of a warning label my brothers used. '*Okay*, but she's brutal.'"

I laugh as I picture a tiny, cute, kid Brooklyn shocking people with her savagery. "Sounds about right."

"Humor me with what you hate about the Sniper?" she says. "You stay back where you're safe and dial it in, then put them down with one precise shot. Definitely not the worst name I've heard."

"Snipers kill people who don't know they're fighting."

"Ah," she says. "It's an honor thing. I should have known."

"Yes. And I engage plenty. You talk like I'm a runner." Her smirk is so subtle I don't see it until I dare to look right at her. "What? You think I am?"

"No, I didn't say that," she says. "You definitely try not to get hit, though."

"Well, yeah. That's kind of what the sport is. Hit them as much as possible while getting hit as little as possible."

She shrugs. "I guess. It's sure fun to watch two people just go for it, though. You could do that too. You're tough as nails. I didn't know that about you, but you can sure take a shot."

"Thanks, but I can take a shot when I have to because I haven't been knocked out a million times. It's all connected."

"Mm."

We settle into a silence, and I realize there's an MMA podcast playing through her speakers, one I listen to all the time. I know the voices so well they almost feel like friends, but it takes me a second to realize they're talking about me.

"Look, I wouldn't count Eden Bauer out yet, Matt. We've seen people come back from devastating injuries before."

"I hope you're right, Bill. She's still young and had a lot more to show us. I certainly wasn't done watching her, especially after what she did to Brooklyn Shaw. Just incredible. I mean, she survives this absolutely brutal slam by Shaw. I thought it was over. I think we all thought it was over, but then she not only gets up, she throws this insane jumping back kick *while she's backing up*! I mean come on!"

"Hey, easy, you're spitting on me," Bill says.

"I'm sorry. I got excited. Look, the way Eden Bauer always finds a way to win is just unprecedented. That was one of the nastiest knockouts I've ever seen. She just flatlined Shaw, and she did it with a broken neck. About took Shaw's head off."

"Oh Jesus, turn that shit off," I say.

Brooklyn smiles and cranks the wheel to make a left. "I'm fine."

The hosts go on. I want to turn the volume down, but it's her car, and it feels rude. "I guess one thing we can look forward to is a much more competitive featherweight division. Whether Bauer retires or not, she's out for a while, and I think we're in for a hell of a battle between the other contenders. Who do you think is the one to watch? Do you give the nod to Brooklyn Shaw for giving Eden her best challenge?"

"I'm not so sure," Bill replies, and I cringe. "Shaw has a fight coming up with Julia Mendez, and I think she may be a real problem for Brooklyn. Julia is experienced, well-rounded, and we know now just how vulnerable Shaw is on her feet. Look, Brooklyn took a hard knockout. She should have taken a longer break to heal and gone back to the drawing board to figure out her striking. She's not a true mixed martial artist yet. I think there's a good chance we'll see a rerun of what Eden did to her."

"Yeah, that's enough." I reach out and swipe the volume down, relieved when I can't hear their crap anymore.

Brooklyn laughs. "It's just talk, Eden. I'm fine, heard it a million times. My dad will never let me live it down anyway."

"What do you mean?"

She glances over, more alert now, like she's realizing she shouldn't have said anything. "Shaws aren't supposed to lose," she finally answers. "And they're definitely not supposed to be on someone else's highlight reel."

"Surely he was more concerned about *you* than that?"

She shrugs. "He loves me, if that's what you're asking, but he's no stranger to seeing his kids get hurt. I'm the baby of the family. He's been watching my brothers rip up their joints and get choked unconscious since I was learning to walk. A little knockout won't freak him out. His takeaway was that another one of his kids failed."

"Failed?" The word bursts out of my mouth. "You're at the highest level the sport has to offer competing for the title at twenty-two years old."

"That's what we're supposed to do, Eden. We're Shaws."

"You know that's not fair, right? What you've done is amazing."

She shakes her head. "If I had beaten you it would've been amazing. Youngest champion by way of defeating the greatest of all time in her prime? Undefeated with plenty of years to build a legacy? *That* would've made him happy. But no matter what I do from here it'll never be the same. My legacy will always be scarred with your name. The best except for you is the most I can ever be, and even that's far away. Right now, I'm just a new contender with a record of three and one. That's not amazing, that's average."

She doesn't say it with self-pity, but it sinks deep into my chest, and before I know it I reach out and grab her hand.

"Brooklyn, you are *not* average."

She squeezes my hand lightly before pulling away to steer into a parking space in the back of Emerald Tiger. I glance at the clock on her dash and realize we're still well before our training start time.

"Were you in the middle of something else?" I ask.

"No, I was coming to talk to you."

"Oh. Well, come on in."

I hop out and walk to the back door, searching for my keys.

"What's in the bag?" Brooklyn asks.

I'd nearly forgotten the grocery bag I'm carrying and feel weirdly self-conscious about it now. "Uh, toothpaste and soap."

Brooklyn beams. "Interesting gym supplies. You have some students with hygiene issues?"

I let us into the narrow dark hallway, then flip on a light to paint the brick passage in warm yellow. "They're mine, actually."

"Oh, right. To take home later."

"To take home now." I stop at the door to my room and unlock it, glancing back at Brooklyn. She looks like a mystical creature in the dim light of the brick hallway, like an impossibly sexy vampire, but what the fuck am I doing thinking of her like that?

"You live here?"

It comes into vivid reality that I'm about to let Brooklyn Shaw into my place. Had I thought about it sooner I might've avoided it by taking her in the front, but it's too late now.

"Come on." I nod and walk inside. It's clean at least, simple and decorated in the elegant Asian décor consistent with the rest of the dojang, but seeing it as Brooklyn must is a reminder it's little more than a glorified closet. Brooklyn steps in and looks around.

"You live here," she says, disbelief on her face. "Full time?"

"I don't need much."

"You're a millionaire," she says. "I mean, aren't you? You have to be. Do you have a gambling problem or something?"

"I like it here." I set the bag down on the bed. When I turn, Brooklyn is holding a picture of my mom. It's been on my dresser so long I barely ever even register it, not like I have to now with the image in Brooklyn's inquisitive hand.

"Who's this?" she asks. I walk over and slowly take it from her. It's a picture I pulled from the security camera last year of Jennifer wielding a crowbar as she jumped to smash my window. It's not the highest quality image, and Brooklyn probably can't make out the details, but I can, and I keep it around to remind myself what she's like before I let her talk her way back into my life. A bit heavy to share, but I don't want to lie.

"It's my mom."

She looks stunned and cranes her neck to try to look at the picture in my hand again.

"What did you want to talk to me about?"

She lets a second pass before she answers. "It feels kind of stupid now, but I wanted to tell you I'm going to try to be more cooperative. I do want to learn from you."

"That's good to hear."

"I'm sorry for yesterday. I shouldn't have gotten rough with your girlfriend."

"My girlfriend?" It catches me so off guard I break into a smile. "Who, Laila?"

"Isn't that what she is?"

"No." I laugh. "No, of course not. She's a student."

"Oh, come on."

"I'm serious."

"Well, she sure looks at you like one."

"Oh, whatever. She does not." I roll my eyes and put the picture in my dresser drawer.

"And you looked ready to take my head off for poppin' her," Brooklyn says with a teasing grin. "You sure you're not feeling a little something?"

The notion that Brooklyn is talking to me about dating a woman so casually is unexpected after she came across so horrified at the idea herself in the press conference, not to mention her father, but I decide it's better not to ruin it by calling it out.

"I've known her since she was fifteen," I say. "I don't see her like that. And if I did have a girlfriend, I wouldn't put her in there with you."

"So, you're single?"

That's so forward I have to pause. I can't read her expression. It's so matter-of-fact. What does she really want to know? "You're asking me about my dating life?"

"I'm just trying to imagine you bringing ladies home to this place with your little twin bed, there."

She's teasing me. That's new and kind of nice. "Don't worry about my bed," I say. "I do fine."

"I'm sure you do." She smiles. "I'm just curious what your game is. You a hotel girl? I can't see you staying with them. Or maybe you're not the bed type?"

"That's a lot of information to give someone who wants to pretend she doesn't like women." I wish I hadn't said it as it comes out, but thank God, she smiles.

"Oh shit." She laughs. "Damn, you don't have to come at me like that. You don't know."

"I forgot you can't take your own medicine."

"It's true. I'm sensitive."

"Yeah, you're a real flower."

Brooklyn punches my arm playfully. "Points for bravery, Bauer, but go back to being the nice girl, jeez."

I shake my head and throw my soap and toothpaste into the bathroom. When I come back, I prop myself in the doorframe. This isn't some weird alternate universe that doesn't count. This is reality, and Brooklyn is in my home. I would've bet any amount you gave me this would never happen, but there she is, looking completely enticing and I swear to God, flirting, all under the banner of straightness.

"You know you can tell me, right?" I say.

"There's nothing I need to tell you, Eden."

"Anything you say to me will be between us."

I can't imagine why Brooklyn would be hell-bent on being in the closet. It doesn't seem to match her hell raising style. And how deep does it run? Does her family know? Do they help her cover it up? Is she in denial herself? Or is this all a grossly arrogant assumption?

"There's only time for one thing in my life right now," she says. "The belt. I promised to win it and put it in my father's hands, and I have to deliver. That's all there is to know."

"All right, then. Let's get you ready for Mendez." I lead the way out of my room.

"Now?"

"You have somewhere to be?"

"No, but Théo and Laila won't be here for at least an hour."

"I know. I'll go with you. Just don't break my little bird neck again." I turn back and smile to make sure she knows I'm messing around, but she doesn't look amused. She reaches out and pulls me to a stop.

"Eden, you know I didn't want that, right? I never thought that would really happen."

Her expression catches me off guard, more than sincere, almost distraught.

"Okay," I say. "Don't sweat it. We all know the risks, right?" I slap her arm and guide her through the empty dojang to the MMA mat, pull both our wraps and gloves from the closet, and toss hers at her.

When we're geared up, I step toward the center of the mat facing her. I don't let myself think too much about her lethal hands or my neck or what we've taken from each other. It's just me and my fighter on the mat, in my home, practicing my truest love.

"You wanted to do something more advanced," I say. She nods. "Watch me. Stay with me." I step toward her in a fighting stance, initiating a dance she picks up effortlessly, stepping back as much as I stepped forward, maintaining the distance. I move in and out, circling and cutting, slow for a long time. I watch her eyes for boredom, but her pupils are large and focused. Her steps are measured and precise. Soon she isn't reacting and mirroring me. We're moving as one.

"Yes," I say. "Now…" I reach out with a jab while moving to my left. I throw the punch like I'm under water, at quarter speed but with good form, letting it touch her chest, just touch. "Always smooth," I say. I move and put my right against her cheek, then circle out. She returns a cross, touching my chin and moving backward.

As she sinks into it, we move a little faster, but never give up the flow, never break the connection. She comes in. I back away. I circle left. She circles too. We trade techniques, never reaching, never competitive. It's such a delicate ballet, when she's off she knows it. I never say a word out loud. I just watch her soak it in, giving her a lead to follow. Soon she's always in step and centered. We're deep in the rhythm of the same breath. Time falls away. I don't notice the activity in the dojang stirring up until Laila and Théo walk in together with curious expressions on their faces.

Brooklyn and I straighten up, holding eye contact a moment longer. It's like coming out of a dream, breaking a serene trance.

CHAPTER SIXTEEN

Laila looks overwhelmed behind the front desk despite the early weekend class already being mostly cleared out, so I help the stragglers into their coats and shoes while they jabber at me.

"Miss Bauer, I'm testing for my yellow belt soon."

"I know you are, Jordan. Have you been practicing?"

He nods and tries to wiggle into his shoes. His mom smiles at me as she guides him out the door. Once they're gone, I go over to Laila.

"You okay?"

"Yeah," she says. "Just busy. Brooklyn is already back there warming up. We have an extra Shaw tonight."

"What do you mean?"

"Her brother Leandro is back there too with Théo."

"Did they say why?"

Laila shrugs. "Her fight is real soon. I figured he was here to support her. Jesus, he's a big motherfucker. Is he serious with that 'I'm all-natural' stuff?"

"Shh!" I slap her arm and chuckle. "You coming back? I could use you for a few rounds. Fight week. All hands on deck."

"Sure, boss."

"Hey." I grab her hand. "You haven't asked for one-on-one mat time in a while. You know you still can, right?"

She waves her hand. "It's okay. You're busy with the prodigy."

"You think I can only handle one prodigy?" I wink at her, ignoring her sour mood.

"Oh, don't be a suck-up." She laughs.

"When have I ever not had time for you?"

She shrugs. "Okay, okay, I get it."

"I'm sure Brooklyn will roll with you too if you ever want to practice some Jiu-Jitsu here instead of driving across town."

"You've really changed your mind about her, haven't you?" She looks a little sad even though she seems to have warmed up to Brooklyn too.

"I guess," I say. "She's driven and loyal. She'll help you if you want, I'm sure."

"Jeez, picture that."

"She would."

When Laila and I get to the back, Brooklyn is already geared up and roughhousing with her brothers. Leandro's giant hands are pinning Brooklyn's wrists crisscrossed over her chest from behind while Théo punches her in the stomach.

"Jesus, it all makes so much sense now," I say. They make mock guilty faces and disentangle.

"Don't worry, we didn't hurt her," Leandro says as he shakes my hand.

"You better not have," I tease him. "We ready to rock? We're down to a week. This'll be our last blowout. I want it looking tight."

"Give me your worst," Brooklyn says.

"We're sparring all night. Laila and Théo will alternate."

"Hey, let me at her," Leandro says. He's only ever been in Jiu-Jitsu matches as far as I know, but I nod.

"Sure, you can rotate in after Théo. I want her exhausted, but not hurt, guys. No injuries. Hard but safe. Don't forget she needs to be able to get in the octagon in a week. Laila." Laila steps in with Brooklyn. I start the first three-minute round and off they go.

Brooklyn looks like a different person out there, relaxed and loose instead of pure barreling aggression. Laila is missing more than she's landing, a new and welcome dynamic. Brooklyn used to be willing to leap off a cliff if she thought she could clip you on the way down.

"Good, Brooklyn," I say as the timer buzzes. Laila jumps out and Théo takes her place. His style is a lot like Brooklyn's old one, aggression at all costs.

"What're you waiting for?" he taunts her.

"Watch him, don't chase him," I say.

Théo springs forward and comes after Brooklyn hard. He pops her in the gloves once, then shoots, lifts her legs, and slams her down onto her back. Watching two Shaws grapple, the best two, is a piece of art. I don't even notice I've crouched down for a better look until I'm inching forward to see every grip, every movement.

Théo gets her in a position called knee on belly, which is exactly what it sounds like and a disadvantaged, not to mention hellacious, place to be. She works on curling her body out from under him, shoving his knee away. He hooks under her shoulder and swoops his foot in an arc around her head, yanking her arm straight as he leans back into an attempted armbar, but she gets her leg free of his other hand in time to back roll over her own shoulder and alleviate the lock. He scrambles for her back. She turns and wraps her arm around his neck, but he grabs her ankle and pulls, pushing his weight forward to flatten her again. She puts her shin across him and floats him right over the top of her and ends up in mount.

They're so much more mobile than other Jiu-Jitsu grapplers I've watched. So often, you see people spending many seconds to minutes working their way through a single position, but Théo and Brooklyn make it look so easy and flow from one position to the next. The second one of them looks screwed, somehow it flips.

The round ends and Leandro leaps in to replace Théo before they've even completely separated. He doesn't have the finesse of Théo or the timing of Brooklyn, but he has a confidence in his approach, a methodical, precise pressure. I wish I could see the last Shaw sibling, Nicolau. The timer goes off, and Laila cycles back in. Brooklyn stands back up, clearly tired. She's on her fourth round, which is draining against someone who's doing it with you, but a nightmare against fresh opponents.

"Quit panting, you're fine," Théo says. "Go get her."

He's right about half of it. Breathing through your mouth is dangerous and leaves the jaw vulnerable, a good way to get knocked out. "Close your mouth," I say. "Stick to the plan."

The plan is to save her power for good openings she creates with movement, angles, and setups, not to charge into fists like she has her entire life. If you want to land a giant cross, you hit them with your jab first. Once you land a good one, it won't be long until they throw one back, subconsciously trying to even the score. When you know it's coming is when you can find that big shot. Brooklyn's so dangerous she's never had to think like that, but she'll be a nightmare if she does. The other part of the plan is to get to the ground where her expertise is, not to risk everything to make some kind of point.

"Go! Go!" Leandro says, and Brooklyn lunges at Laila swinging. Laila eats one, but dodges the next and cracks Brooklyn with a solid right.

"Counter!" Théo yells. "Cross!"

Brooklyn tries, but Laila moves and hits her with a jab.

"Kick!" Théo yells.

Laila hits Brooklyn with a three-punch combo, landing all of them.

"Back her up!" Théo is losing patience.

"No, get out of there, Brooklyn," I yell. "Reset."

Brooklyn bounces in and out of the pocket, undecided.

"Suck it up and go get her," Théo says.

"Théo," I snap.

"She's getting muscled."

"She knows what she's doing."

"Doesn't look like it."

"Stop," I say. Brooklyn is getting sloppier and sloppier, but everyone does as they tire. Théo isn't helping, but I can't tell how much is him and how much is Brooklyn's own instincts re-emerging. When you're fatigued and feel like you're in danger, you go back to what you know best, even if it's wrong.

The timer buzzes and Théo leaps in with a vengeance, hitting her hard. "Come on, kid," he says. "How bad do you want it?"

"Théo, back off," I say. "That's not how Mendez fights."

He ignores me and pops Brooklyn in the nose. Brooklyn retaliates with a vicious windmill of a punch.

"Don't lose your cool, Brooklyn. You set the pace, not him."

"Come on," he says. "Let's see it."

He responds to her blocks by trying to hit through them with more power. Body, head, body, head. A glove gets through and impacts hard enough Brooklyn's head snaps back.

"That's enough," I say. Théo tags her again and anger shoots up my spine. I storm up behind him, wrap my arms around his chest and pull him away. "I said that's enough. What do you think you're doing?"

"I think I'm coaching my sister."

"We're supposed to be polishing this plan, and we're getting further and further off track."

"Tell me about it," Théo says. "Why do you think I'm going after her? She's not ready. I'm not letting her out there like that."

"I know you want to help, but you're making it worse."

"You think she's going to be able to ask Mendez nicely to back off in there?"

"Of course not, but she needs to handle this with technique, not fear. I need you to stop trying to force her to brawl."

"She can get me off her any way she wants, bottom line is she isn't doing it, and I'm not easing up until she does."

"Théo, I think it's best if Brooklyn and I finish this session alone."

He breaks into a smile like he thinks I'm kidding. "Are you crazy?" he lashes out. "You can't even fight."

"I can fight enough. I don't know why you think going full contact and trying to hurt her is necessary, but it isn't."

"I'm not trying to hurt her. I'm trying to protect her before another chick kicks her skull in." His eyes are full of anger, burning into me. I let a long pause pass before I speak again.

"I understand what you're doing, but you two have fought so many years you have patterns we need to break."

"You're throwing me out of my sister's last training session?"

"I'm nicely asking *all* of you to leave so I can work with my martial artist one-on-one."

The way Théo's gaze is burning into me makes his face look even more predatory than usual. "Is that what you want, Brooklyn?"

"It's not up to her," I say before Brooklyn can answer him. Of course, it's up to her, but I don't want to put her in that position. I don't particularly want to be the bitch that threw her brother out, either, but if those are the only options. "I need you to go."

"If you're wrong, and she loses, this is over." He jerks his head to motion Leandro to follow him out. "Get your shit together, Brooklyn!" he yells back, and the front door slams. The silence feels heavy. I avoid Brooklyn's eyes and turn to Laila.

"Right." Laila springs back to life, moving for the door. "Call if you need anything." She touches my arm before she goes. I turn to Brooklyn and try to read her face.

"You didn't have to throw him out," she says.

"I did have to, but I'm sorry. I know you two are close."

"We're closer than close, and he was right. I'm not doing well."

"He was right that you're off, but bleeding isn't going to fix it. He wasn't helping. Put it out of your mind, Brooklyn. He's mad at me, not you. You'll talk to him about what an ass I am tomorrow and have a good laugh. Right now, we have work to do."

"And you're going to be the one?" she asks. "You're going to risk that? You're crazy. He was right about that too."

I wrap my hands in a kind of meditation, around the wrist, around the knuckles, between the fingers, wrist, hand, until the wrap runs out and I slip my gloves over them. We usually spar with sixteen-ounce boxing gloves because they're bigger and less dangerous. The extra surface area means it's easier to block and the impact disperses more when you do connect, but this close to the fight, we need to mimic the real deal, so I put on the four-ounce, fingerless MMA gloves.

"You need to learn control," I say. "Fighting someone you could break may be the best thing for you."

"Fuck, Eden, I don't want that responsibility."

"Look at me." She rolls her eyes before she does. "I trust you."

She shakes her head and sighs. "Everything's open?" she asks, referring to takedowns and grappling.

"Everything's open. Execute the plan start to finish."

She moves at a more rational pace from the jump. We trade shots, much harder than we usually do, but still short of what Théo was doing. She lands a cross to my eye that sends a jolt into my neck and a tingle of fear through me, but as I circle out and check in with my body, it's fine. The fracture is healed. I have to stop acting like I'm hanging by a string. I'm strong.

As we get deeper into the round, her technique fades again. She's swinging hard but wild. It's a little disconcerting she's not concerning herself more with my safety, but she shouldn't have to. That's my responsibility.

"Don't force it," I say. "You have plenty of power. You don't have to sacrifice your balance. Move your feet. Don't lean to reach me, use your length. Full extension."

She ignores me and continues, which would be fine if she improved, but she gets wilder, taking bigger swings. I escape and land some stern counters. She lunges for a takedown she isn't in position for that I easily sprawl out of. I shove her back to her feet and jab her, leaving a hook open if she wants it, but she doesn't react in time. She gets annoyed and rushes forward again, following her entry attack with three more. I absorb them with arms and gloves, deflecting all the damage.

She should cover up before I make her pay, but she pushes me backward instead, insisting on a takedown now. Being on the receiving end of all her power is always a little shocking and nerve-racking. It's hard to believe we're in the same weight class.

She pushes me into the fence that lines the wall, and I wrap her up in a clinch with both my hands around the back of her head and neck in a double collar tie, a hold that breaks her posture and gives me control of her balance. She fights for underhooks, a smart move for her since she's shorter and wants to set up a takedown. She tries to slide her arms under my elbows, but I keep them locked against me and yank her off balance to stop her. Only now with her so close do I realize how exhausted she is. She's slick with sweat, heaving for breath, and using bursts of power because she can't sustain more.

Her skin is hot, her body solid and flexed. She's let me break her posture to the point her forehead is on my chest. The feeling of her struggling in my grip but being unable to control me the way she wants is surreal.

"Calm down," I say quietly, as if I can bring her down with my voice. She explodes with power, trying to tear me to the ground, but her hips aren't under her, so I weather it. She tries again, but I raise my knee in what would be a devastating strike if I followed through.

"You're not in position," I say. "Calm down and think. Break my hold." She ignores my advice, intent on keeping her underhooks rather than addressing the vice grip I have around her neck. Her arms tighten around me. Weirdly and suddenly, I'm aware of just how much contact we're sharing. We're glued to each other, something that's happened in sparring more days of my life than not, so why am I thinking about it now?

She pauses, then pulls me away from the fence. Her arms strain as she tries to topple me. I pull the clinch tight, step right, and yank her so she has to slam her foot down to catch herself, forcing her to abandon her own maneuver or fall.

"You can't muscle your way out of this."

"Shut up."

"Use your head. Break my hold."

She finally listens, putting her palm to my chin and straightening her arm, twisting my face away from her while pushing and loosening my hold enough she can back away. The second she's free she throws a right hand. I duck just in time and hear it rattle the fence behind me.

"Good," I say, but as soon as I can compliment her, she's throwing wild looping punches, leaving absolutely everything open. I could light her up if I wanted, but I circle under and out.

"You're brawling again."

"Yeah." She raises her hands to her side for an instant, then swings again. "I'm a brawler. That's what I do."

Her anger is intriguing more than anything. I send a few straight down the middle to slow her down. "You can be more."

"I'm not a calculated fighter, Bauer. I'm not brainy like you. I'm just guts and muscle. You said it yourself."

She swings, and I feel the wind of it against my cheek. "You're a Jiu-Jitsu specialist. Of course, you're calculated. You don't just go for a submission, you get in position, control, and exhaust them first. You time it. This is the same. You have to set me up. You can't just swing."

She feints a jab, but shoots for a takedown just before the end of my sentence is out. I sprawl, but she powers forward despite all my weight pressing her toward the mat. Her shoulder finds my hip and slams me into the fence. I try to flatten her down, but she has her legs under her now. She pauses with all her weight crushing me against the fence, bear hugs, and lifts me off the mat in such a powerful motion there's not a thing I can do about it. I'm hanging in that moment of zero gravity between raising up and falling, and all my instincts switch from the fight to my neck. It's a different motion, but the familiarity of it as her arms constrict around me and her shoulder drives down makes my very blood tense in anticipation. I orient myself for the best fall, attempting to square with the mat.

Then her hand is behind my neck, holding it, and the momentum of my fall slows by half. She switches from hurling me down to lowering me there, then moves into side control as if nothing happened.

She wraps an arm around the back of my neck and holds the back of my shoulder, then pushes her head to the mat so we're chest to chest and my own bicep is pinned against my ear. Her weight crushes down as she hops her legs over my body, using me as if I were the ground. She's in position now and starts cinching up an arm triangle, a technique that will choke me with my own shoulder and her bicep. She applies it so slowly and precisely it feels safe, but I can't stop her. When she tightens it up, I tap her back and she releases the choke. She leans back a little and holds my neck again.

"You okay?"

I nod, soaking in the ecstasy of this feeling, of my shirt soaked with sweat resting heavy on my chest, of muscles relaxed in a way they only can after drained of all they possess, of animosity morphing effortlessly to friendship to competition to survival to love.

Brooklyn slowly smiles. "Good. Crazy girl." She starts to sit up, but I reach out and grab her shirt before she does.

"Hey."

She freezes and looks at me.

"Forget what I said about you only being strong. I didn't even know you then. What you just did was smart and precise and controlled and aggressive and powerful. You can be all of it, Brooklyn. Don't let anyone call you just a brawler. You're an elite martial artist."

She leans down and kisses me so smoothly I don't know it's happening until her warm lips are fitted perfectly to mine and all the air is sucked from my lungs in a shock of exhilaration. My entire body responds and lifts up into the weight of her before I even know what I'm doing. The kiss is slow and comes in gentle surges, an unstoppable force, both soothing and dizzying.

I wrap my arms around her, running my hands up her back, feeling the shape of her, blindsided by the sensuality under the tough exterior. Her palm molds to me as she slowly moves up my side to my chest. Her tongue slips into my mouth. When our tongues meet, I feel her tense with desire in my arms, and she pushes her thigh between my legs, pressing against me in a motion that shatters all sense of reality. Her fingers thread into my hair at the base of my neck and close. Every piece of me dissolves into her, and I pull her deeper into the kiss, my palm on fire against the back of her soft neck.

She moves against me again, pressing firmly with her thigh and pulling a quiet moan I can't stop from my throat. She breaks the kiss to move down, breathing over the sensitive skin of my neck and kissing my collarbone. Her fingers trace the exposed skin showing across my stomach, and her hand gently moves under my loose shirt, pushing it slowly up while she kisses. I bring my left glove to my mouth, grab the Velcro strap with my teeth, and rip it to free my hands. The sound of it tearing apart seems to energize her, and she moves to pull my shirt over my head.

The cool mat is a pleasant shock against my screaming skin. I pull her shirt off too, and she crashes back against me. She kisses me hard and groans in a deep, visceral sound. I move my hand up her stomach while she rips off her gloves, feeling her ragged breathing on top of me, until I brush over her nipple and feel her strength buckle. She tugs on my earlobe with her teeth, setting off every path of pleasure in my body.

"Yo, Brooklyn! You ready or what?"

She leaps off me so fast I feel like my soul's been waxed. She yanks her shirt back on so haphazardly it's a wonder everything makes it through the right holes, and she's on her feet. I get up too and just kick my shirt and gloves against the wall where they look more appropriately abandoned as a normal end of session routine. Fighting in a sports bra is par for the course, so I'd rather Leandro sees that than me frantically trying to get dressed.

He rounds the corner and fills the doorframe. "What the hell are you two doing in the dark?"

"Training. Duh," Brooklyn manages. He flips on the lights while looking at her like she's an idiot.

"Didn't notice the sun go down," I say.

"What're you doing here?" Brooklyn asks.

"Théo took the Escalade," he says. "Figured you'd need a ride."

"I could've called a driver. You didn't have to do that."

"Okay, well, I'm here, so we going or what? Looks like you two were wrapping up."

"Yeah," she says, a little too fast. "Sure, that's fine. See ya, Eden."

I know it's an act, but the way her eyes pass right over me like I'm nothing is more convincing than I was prepared for.

"Later," I say as coolly as I can manage. She doesn't look back as she walks off with Leandro. In the long, empty minutes after I hear the front door close, I just sit in stunned silence. I figure a text will come any second, but it doesn't happen. What the hell do I expect her to say? Maybe it's coming to her now the way it is to me that we're out of our fucking minds. I can't *hook up* with Brooklyn. What kind of stroke did I just have?

CHAPTER SEVENTEEN

Finding a second alone with Brooklyn proves impossible. The Shaws seem to travel at least two at a time wherever they go. We even drive to the airport as a group to fly off to New Mexico for the event, then share a cab to the hotel. I spring to bring Laila along as part of the team just to not feel so outnumbered by them. Interviews, meals, weigh-ins, the face-off, morning jogs, always at least one Shaw brother. Now that it's fight night, there's certainly no room to talk. Don't get me wrong, the Shaw boys are lovely. They're focused but funny, fierce but friendly, opinionated but curious. They just happen to be making it impossible for me to gauge where Brooklyn is on the kiss.

I've snuck around with girls before, a friend in high school who didn't want her boyfriend to find out we were making out on the side, a coworker who didn't want the boss to know about us and separate our shifts, but those experiences don't touch this. Those situations were kept secret with a heavy dose of playfulness. We were still flirtatious, taking chances and daring anyone to say something. Brooklyn doesn't play around like that. There's no wink with her standoffishness.

Sometimes I think she intends to never talk about it. Maybe I should let that happen. The more time that passes, the stranger it seems to bring it up. If she was picturing a continuation, she could have made an effort to see me alone, or at least call, but she hasn't.

I zip up my Shaw hoodie, a UFC jacket with her last name up the left side of the back. It's the first time I've worn one with someone else's name on it. I grab my room key and head two doors down to Brooklyn's room. She answers all dressed and ready. Théo is sitting in a chair in the corner.

"Ready?"

She nods, and they follow me into the hall. We collect Leandro and Laila and head out. The prelims are half over by the time we make it to the locker room. Brooklyn is the second fight of the main card, so we have time, but not an excess amount of it.

I kneel in front of her and start wrapping her hands, much more deliberately than I ever am with myself. I don't say a word, just let her know I'm here with passing eye contact. The moments before a fight are intense and the way people navigate them so varied.

"I like the way you do that," she says, watching the pattern I'm using to wrap her hands.

I smile. "Good."

Théo, Leandro, and Laila are watching the fights on the TV around the corner, shouting at the screen as things happen.

"Eden, about the other night."

My eyes snap up to hers. "Really?" I ask. "Now?"

She laughs lightly. "In case she wipes my memory with a head kick or something."

I want to tell her that'll never happen, but she doesn't seem to be after reassurance. "Okay."

"We can't do it again," she says. Doesn't seem like the kind of thing I absolutely need to know in case she can't tell me later, but I nod, reacting as little as I can. "I meant to come talk to you about it," she says. "But I didn't trust myself not to do it again, and I can't."

"Okay." I focus on wrapping her right hand. "Got it." I have no idea if I manage the casual tone I'm going for. I figured if it didn't happen already, it wasn't going to. I was burning alive in my skin that night, and I'm pretty sure she was too. If she didn't come back, she had reasons, and they were probably good ones. She's my client. She's hyper focused on her career and needs to be. Whatever's going on with her family around the issue is obviously a problem.

And after a long, shaky road, we're finally getting along, may even be friends. Why jeopardize all that for a kiss? Earth-shaking or not.

"It was incredible, though," she says, catching me off guard. When I look up, she has a completely alluring, mischievous smile. God damn it.

I smile back and keep it simple. "Yes, it was."

"I just have to keep my mind on training. You understand. You've been there."

I've never actually cited my career as a reason to shut someone down before. I've never had to. Keeping people at a distance has always come so naturally it's never required a real conversation, but I'm sure I would have.

"Yeah," I say. "I understand."

"Are we cool?"

"Of course, we are."

"Yo, they're talking about you two," Théo yells from the next room over.

"Let's warm up," I say. I grab the pads and go to the area with the TV so we can listen while she throws some punches.

The announcers speak in their typical smooth rhythm. "Brooklyn Shaw is coming back to the octagon off a brutal loss to Eden Bauer five months ago and facing what a lot of people believe to be another tough matchup in the former kickboxing champion Julia Mendez." He looks to his cohost, who comes back in the same flow.

"That's right. Julia Mendez is on a tear right now, a five-fight win streak, her latest victory against the number six ranked Sara Tomil. She's coming in with a lot of confidence, and there's even talk that Mendez is on her way to being the new Bauer. Bauer beat her in just one round when they met in the octagon two years ago, but it's pretty clear Mendez is not the same martial artist she was back then. What adjustments does Shaw need to make to see a better result than she had against Bauer?"

I stay glued to Brooklyn's eyes as she thwaps solid hits into the mitts, ready to move her out of the room if she starts reacting to the announcers, but she shows no signs she's even listening.

"She's made a crucial one, and that's her team. The Shaws have been slow to confirm this, but it's official, Brooklyn Shaw has made what I believe to be a brilliant decision in bringing none other than Eden Bauer herself on as her new head coach. If anyone can get her ready for Mendez, it's Bauer. I mean, what a move. I never thought they would be able to patch things up enough to do that, but I'm so glad they did because that's the dream team."

"I get what you're saying, but I'm not so sure. It's such an important relationship. Switching coaches is a tricky thing even under the best circumstances, and here you have a ton of baggage, only a couple of months together, and listen, champion or not, Bauer is a brand-new coach. Mendez has had an ironclad training team for a long time now. She's a veteran of the sport. She knows what works for her. I think she goes into this fight with a giant advantage."

"We're about to find out! But first let's talk about our next match."

They switch to talking about the martial artists who are up next, and Leandro spins around.

"That was great," he says. "They love talking about you, Brooklyn. You've got star power."

"They talk about everyone," she says.

"Not like you. Not all excited and shit."

"He's right," I say. She looks surprised and smiles.

The crowd erupts. I look to Théo, who's staring at the screen. "That's it," he says. "One-minute KO. You're up, B."

I grab her gloves and look her in the eye. "She comes out hot, but fades. Control the pace. Work the legs and body. Get the takedown and tap her out, but don't rush it," I say. "She expects it from you. She's going to try to knock you out on your way in."

"Let's go!" someone shouts down the tunnel. Brooklyn makes nervous eye contact.

"You're ready," I say. "I'll be right there in your corner."

She nods and pulls up her hood. She starts her walk down the aisle with me, Théo, Leandro, and Laila right behind her. If she's still nervous, all signs of it are gone. She looks like a wrecking ball, powering forward. She kisses me and her brothers on the cheek before kneeling in prayer at the stairs to the octagon. Julia Mendez's intro is second, but Brooklyn has more fans. After the ref checks with each of them, he issues the start of the fight to roaring applause.

Brooklyn steps toward the middle but has to back away as Mendez comes flying in with a strong right. Brooklyn circles out calmly.

Mendez marches Brooklyn down, applying measured pressure. Brooklyn's hands are up, her eyes focused as she watches for Mendez to expose her next attack.

"Leg kick," I yell, and Brooklyn throws a banger of one that slaps Mendez's leg so hard her heel comes off the canvas. Mendez bobs and twists her shoulders, feinting three times in a row, trying to draw Brooklyn into a punching match.

"Hit the leg again," I yell. Brooklyn is halfway through the kick before I'm even done saying it. She responds instantly, the best I've ever seen at it.

"Inside!" I yell, and she does it, chewing up the inner side of Mendez's lead leg. Mendez moves in with a beautiful straight jab and cross that slips right past Brooklyn's guard. Brooklyn eats it without blinking and digs a left hook into Mendez's body, tight and vicious the way we practiced. Brooklyn hits the leg again without me calling for it. It slaps hard. Viewers are used to seeing people take leg kick after leg kick without much, if any, reaction, but it's a complete misconception that they aren't a big deal. When one really lands it hurts so bad you can't believe your leg is still attached. After too many of them your leg doesn't work right anymore, and you can't move well. All of Mendez's fancy striking will be compromised if Brooklyn can keep doing this.

Mendez knows that too, and this is when a martial artist is the most dangerous, when they're hurt enough to know they're in peril but not so much they've lost their weapons. Mendez comes at Brooklyn, throwing a snappy combo, ducking the counter, and going straight into the next combo. She cracks Brooklyn in the face and backs her into the fence. Brooklyn covers up, and the crowd roars as drops of blood trickle to the mat.

I'm not prepared to be so affected by seeing her rocked. It's so different when you're in there dealing with it than when you're watching helplessly as someone you care about gets hurt.

"Clinch up!" Théo yells. Brooklyn pulls the back of Mendez's head down and holds her there while she recovers, but Mendez slides her arms between Brooklyn's and takes control of the clinch, then launches knees. They're not hitting anything vital, but if they do it'll be a game changer.

"Control!" I yell. It probably sounds like useless advice to people around us, but Brooklyn and I drilled the clinch enough she knows what I mean. She adjusts her grip, pushes Mendez back, and thrusts a knee into her gut. Mendez wrenches free and goes into a flurry of punches. Brooklyn dodges two but eats a third. The crowd reacts big as Mendez starts firing off one after the other.

"Come on, watch her," I mutter. "She's open."

Brooklyn hauls off a single, powerful cross, and Mendez's knees buckle. The crowd leaps to their feet, and Brooklyn flies over to Mendez for the kill. She lands one more bomb, but the horn screams, and the ref throws himself between them.

Brooklyn sprints to the corner, and I jump in. She sits, breathing hard but looking excited. The cutman goes to work on Brooklyn's busted eyebrow. I kneel in front of her. She's already staring at me with striking focus for input, and in that moment, I can see and feel she trusts me completely.

"That was the worst of it," I say. "She's tired and hurt. She's going to start leaving her punches hanging. Look for the takedown."

"She ain't shit next to you, Coach." Brooklyn smiles and smacks my shoulder, and I can't help but beam back at her.

"Bring it home. This is your round."

The break ends, and Brooklyn stands back up. The ref signals them to resume and Brooklyn goes on the prowl. Mendez throws a long punch and Brooklyn goes straight for the takedown, wrapping up her legs and slamming her to the canvas, moving straight into mount as if it were the easiest thing in the world. Mendez twists and bucks for freedom, trying to roll away, but even the half of her back she's exposed is enough for Brooklyn to slide and take control of her from that position. Her arms and legs constrict around Mendez's body and flatten her out while Brooklyn starts inching her forearm under Mendez's neck.

"It's over." Théo grips my shoulder. "That's it. She's got her."

Mendez's struggle is like watching a fly in a web. She's not getting out, and her effort may even be making it worse as Brooklyn inches closer to the rear naked choke.

"She's done!" Théo yells.

Mendez makes her inevitable last mistake, lifting her chin as she tries to break free, and Brooklyn's arm slides into place. Mendez can only tolerate the choke for a couple of seconds before she taps. The ref pries Brooklyn's arms apart to end the fight.

Brooklyn leaps to her feet to celebrate, pounding her own chest with her fist as she circles the octagon. She stops in the middle and points at me, like the first time I saw her win, but this time with a huge smile and so much affection in her eyes. Joe Rogan comes in and pulls her in with his arm around her shoulder.

"Brooklyn, what a fantastic victory! Did the fight go how you planned?"

"Exactly like we planned. I'm so hyped to be here with you, New Mexico!" The crowd roars in answer to her, and she blows them a kiss.

"Brooklyn, your corner is looking a little different. We're dying to hear how you patched things up with Eden Bauer and what it's like working with her. Was the rivalry all a show? Are you really friends?"

The crowd roars so loud at the question Brooklyn has to wait before she can answer, a second she uses to flash a disarming smile at me.

"You just can't not respect Eden Bauer, man. She's a bad motherfucker. She carried that belt for four years, and when she's done with it, you can pass it straight to me, 'cause it stays in New York right at Emerald Tiger, baby. I don't care who I have to smash. Karinov, Brown, Silverton. I'll walk through any of them."

It's strange how much easier it is to contextualize her trash talk now that I know her. I'm sure everyone she named feels the way I did when we were about to fight, but now I also understand how her brothers felt, looking on with fondness as she shouts out my name and my gym. The receiving end stings, but, man, is it cozy over here where her loyalties lie.

We file out of the octagon and back down the walkout tunnel. Her brothers are all over her. Brooklyn absorbs it, returning their hugs.

Then she turns and hugs me. I squeeze her back, surprised by the gesture and unable to miss how nicely our bodies fit together but trying like hell not to fixate on it.

She squeezes again before she lets go. "Time to rage. On me." The guys and Laila whoop, and Brooklyn winks at me. "You too, Bauer. Don't even think about sneaking off to your room."

Chapter Eighteen

None of us know the first thing about New Mexico, but it doesn't slow us down. After a quick change of clothes, we're in the lobby of the hotel copying the location of a Brazilian club the concierge tells us about into our phones and waiting for the valet to pull the cars around. With five of us traveling together, we opted for two, a sensible Ford Escape and a flashy two-seater Brooklyn picked out, a red Maserati convertible.

They pull that around first and hand Brooklyn the keys. She makes eye contact just long enough I think she's going to ask me to ride with her, but Théo joins her without any indication another option even occurred to him.

"See you over there," she says.

The Ford pulls up and Leandro, Laila, and I jump in. We follow Brooklyn for a block before she smokes us. She must floor it all the way there because by the time we arrive, she and Théo are already in a VIP booth drinking something with lime on the rim. The music is thumping but not overwhelming. The dance floor is set back from the bar and VIP booths so that we have a view of it but are in our own world. Théo holds up his arms and beams when he sees us. He's still in sunglasses and leather despite it being in the eighties and dark.

Brooklyn is in the back corner of the wraparound booth with her arms propped on the back. She's in a red tank top and loose white shorts to her knees. Even in the dim light, I can make out tender patches on her arms and legs where she took punishment, areas that will be purple by tomorrow. Her split eyebrow is sewn shut with four stitches the back-stage doctor did just after the match on site.

Leandro slides in on the other side of Brooklyn, followed by Laila, then me. I'm so glad Laila is here. This would be so much harder without her. I pick up the drink menu, but Brooklyn practically lunges over the table to flatten it out of my hands.

"Don't even look, Bauer. We're all having caipirinhas."

"Cai whats?"

"They're Brazilian. Here, taste." She hands her glass to me. "That goes for you too," she says to Laila. I nod at the bright taste of the drink. "I can do that." No sooner than I say it, the servers are setting glasses in front of Laila and me anyway.

Laila holds up her glass. "To your win. And many more to come."

Brooklyn raises her glass back. "To the best team on Earth. Saúde."

"Saúde." We repeat the word with questionable success. The Shaws all smile.

"I'll get you there." Brooklyn winks.

"And to Eden," Théo says, holding his glass up again. "I know I gave you a hard time, but you're the real deal. Welcome to the family."

His sincerity is touching. "Thank you, Théo."

"Saúde."

The music seems to get louder as time passes, but so do we as the drinks start to flow. It's hard to talk to Brooklyn across the table in all the chaos. That shouldn't bother me. I don't know why I keep looking at her like something is still hanging. We've said all that needs to be said. She's right to focus on her career. It makes sense that she's over there with Théo and Leandro.

"Whoa! Eden Bauer!" A gorgeous blonde in a backwards baseball cap about does a backbend as she passes. She tries to come over, but the VIP area is roped off and guarded, and they're already ushering her on. Laila whistles as she walks off.

"You should go after that one." Laila elbows me, and the whole group laughs. I don't embarrass easily, but I may be blushing now. I'm not sure which of the Shaw reactions scares me most, but I'd rather not look at any of them, so I just swat the comment away.

"If she's not your type I don't know who is," Théo says as he slides another drink across the table, shocking me. I assumed his attitude would reside somewhere in the vicinity of his father's. God, wouldn't it be nice if I were wrong?

"Eden's never gone for fans," Laila says.

"Shut up," I say.

"Or students," she adds, and I'm pretty sure she winks at them.

"You make it sound like it happens all the time."

"Uh, yeah."

"Eden Bauer, heartbreaker," Brooklyn says. "I can see it." She smiles with her eyes and takes a sip of her drink.

Laila relieves me of the need to respond when her hand lands on my arm. "Well, you're officially on vacation. Have a little fun and dance with me." I snap over to meet her eyes, taken totally off guard. She's leaning forward with intense eyes, but her tone is airy and casual.

"I should probably stay behind the ropes here."

"Why?"

The directness of it leaves me with nothing. After a second of silence, she pushes me to let her out of the booth, and I let her drag me toward the dance floor. I catch Brooklyn looking on like she's amused. Yes, definitely amused, though I don't know what that means. I follow Laila, and soon we're mixed into the heat of moving bodies, the thumping bass vibrating up my legs. Laila faces me and puts a hand on my waist as she starts dancing.

"Relax, Eden. It's just a dance." I feel stupid admitting it even to myself, but it feels wrong dancing with Laila in front of Brooklyn. How ludicrous.

"Yeah, okay. You're right."

The caipirinhas are finally going to my head even though they aren't strong. As the heat crawls over my skin, it starts to feel good to dance, and I lose track of all my obnoxious racing thoughts, who's trying to take a picture, what the Shaw boys are thinking, what Brooklyn is thinking, if she's watching, if she cares.

Soon there are so many bodies on the floor we can hardly move without bumping into the people around us, and the music is so loud it's like becoming aware of a new dimension. Laila and I are at once dancing with each other, by ourselves, and with everyone around us. At first, I think it's just a random person who's run out of room and inched into my space, but when her arm comes into view for a second and I see the black cross on her forearm, I realize it's Brooklyn, and she's shaped to my back, dancing in the same rhythm, very close but not actually touching me.

I turn to face her, unable to help my smile. The red and yellow lights circling the room glide over her, drawing my eye to all the sexy exposed skin, and I see her now, in the club, a little differently than I ever have before. I've never witnessed her removed from the martial arts world, and it's striking. You still can't miss her lethality, but she's soft and sensual too. Her face is structured with the hard lines of an ancient warrior, but her eyes and lips are thoughtful and mischievous. Everything about her is a duality between sex and war, the shine of moisture on her lips and the stitched cut on her brow, her soft brown skin and the deep purple bruises, her strong arms and the delicate hollow at the base of her throat.

"Sorry," she says.

"Sorry?"

She nods discreetly at Laila, who's in her own world now, then leans in and speaks low in my ear. "If I'm interrupting something."

My heart skips in my chest, and I'm pretty sure I'm doing nothing to hide what her proximity does to me. "You're not."

"I'm glad."

She says it like it's nothing, and it probably is nothing, but I feel a little out of breath. Does she not know how much I want to touch her? She smiles slowly like she's reading my mind and grabs my hand, pulling me farther into the crowd, closer to the speakers and away from Laila and her brothers, who are all dancing in a group now. And then she starts dancing with me.

The second she sinks into a rhythm it's like my brain shuts off and the only way I can hope to operate is by instinct. She's an incredible dancer, fun and free and sexy. But then, that's who Brooklyn is all the time, whether she's trying to slam you into the next dimension or kiss you so passionately you forget your name. She moves closer and touches me, her hand fitting to my hip. A surge of arousal and a jolt of fear flood me as I both want to reach out for her and can't believe she's daring to touch me this way in public, but then, she's from a dance culture. This is normal and platonic. She wouldn't do it if it wasn't. This smothering attraction is just the result of Brooklyn being Brooklyn, not an invitation.

Keeping that in mind while the drinks and music are swirling takes all my focus. I move with her, smile at her like none of this is difficult to navigate, like I'm not thinking about it at all, but I can't stay inside her space without losing myself in her warm scent and bare neckline, and she's doing nothing to help me stay out of it. She's inches away, radiating burning energy, just brushing across my skin in a whisper.

One moment, I'm deep in a hypnotic state, the next, reality floods back. Théo and Leandro are each within thirty feet of us dancing with Laila, all smiles and fun, nothing romantic or sexual to speak of. That's what this is supposed to look like, and I'm positive it's not. I'm positive I'm wearing my desire on my sleeve no matter how I try to hide it, and I don't want Brooklyn seeing it any more than I want her family to.

"I'm burning up," I say. Well, it's true. "I'm going to go to the bathroom and take a breather."

Brooklyn nods, and I squish through the crowd. The moment I'm free I cool down on the spot as cool air touches my sweaty skin.

To call this place high end is an understatement. The entry to the bathroom is grand, white marble and spacious with a sitting room before you enter what I suppose you'd call the actual bathroom, which is bright and elegant and split into stalls made of the same white marble that goes floor to ceiling and closes with dark wood doors. The stalls, if you can even call them that, each have sinks and mirrors so there's no communal area.

Being inside is almost as private and comforting as getting in your car at the end of a long workday, and I need it. Jesus, I'm wound tight. Luckily, I don't look like half the train wreck I expect to, but I take a second to finger comb my hair. The New Mexico heat and dancing are making it a little wavy, but that's the most it ever does. I splash water on my face and wake my skin up.

I check the time on my phone. One a.m. Seems like an acceptable effort. Maybe they won't fuss too much if I go now. I need to get away from Brooklyn. I can't be this buzzed around her and behave, least of all with her an inch away moving the way she does on the dance floor. Does she think I'm superhuman? I need to quit before I do something dumb. I'll take a Lyft if I have to. Yes, that's good. Run. I open the stall door and almost walk right into Brooklyn.

I stop just in time, straightening up in a jolt. One of her hands moves to my waist, the other to my face, and somehow, she's both pulling me closer and pushing me back into the stall. Her lips meet mine full and hot. She closes and locks the door, then pushes me into the wall and kisses me with a passion I've never felt before. I'm swallowed in a tidal wave of desire, confused and jumbled and so turned on. I can't begin to fight it. I hold her against me and slip my tongue into her mouth. She opens to me and leans into me hard so our breasts, stomachs, and thighs are pressed together. My skin is charged and sensitive. Her hand traces down to the waist of my pants, and she hooks a finger in them and runs it between my hips, low enough my knees go weak.

"Brooklyn, we shouldn't." I pull back long enough to whisper it, but as if they weren't words at all, I crash back into the kiss, licking her lower lip and meeting her tongue with another surge of thirst. Her hands are everywhere, running up my sides in an assertive touch, around the back of my neck, cupping my breasts as our kiss gets wild.

"You don't want me?" she finally whispers back.

"You know I do."

She pushes her thigh between my legs and pleasure rockets through my stomach and spine.

"Fuck," I say into her neck as she crushes me against the wall and I let her pin me there, enjoying the pressure of her, the tension in her muscles. I bite her exposed neck that's pressed close and feel her shudder. Her pleasure sends me to the edge of sanity. I just want to rip her clothes off, but that voice is still chirping in my ear. She said she didn't want to do this, and we've had a lot to drink. Is she going to hate me tomorrow if we let ourselves get caught up?

"Brooklyn, wait," I whisper. She pulls back enough to look me in the eye, our arms still tangled. She stares at me through deep brown eyes full of desire, confusion, apprehension. I touch her face, so fully under her spell. "You told me less than twelve hours ago you don't want this."

"I'm ridiculous. I've never wanted someone so much in my life." Brooklyn smiles, but I cling to seriousness, knowing I'll never recover it once I let it go. One of us has to look at this outside of this cloud of lust. Being Brooklyn's coach has gone from something I thought would never work to the centerpiece of my life in what feels like a heartbeat, and as much as I want her, if we're going to have to part ways because of it, I don't want to.

"I don't want to be a mistake," I say. She rests her hands on my chest and kisses me, light and soft.

"Eden, you would never be a mistake. I just didn't trust myself to stay focused."

"Are you still worried about that?"

"Yes, but staying away from you isn't going to help. You're already all I can think about."

"Fuck, I'm sorry."

"It's okay." She laughs. "It's nice." She kisses my neck. "If I'm honest, it's been that way for a while. Since before we kissed. Even before I liked you I couldn't keep my eyes off you."

The confession surprises me. I would have never thought so, but I guess her kiss didn't just fall out of the sky.

"I think of you too," I say.

"Yeah?"

"All the time."

"What do you think?" she asks.

"It's like time with you is all that counts, and the rest is just waiting to be with you again. And ever since you kissed me…"

She looks into my eyes, leaning into me. "Yeah?"

"I can't stop thinking of the way you touched me."

Her hand moves to my lower back and holds me close while her other hand moves up my neck, her fingers in my hair, and she balls her hand into a fist at the base of my head.

"Like this?" she whispers.

"Yes."

"What else?"

"How you make me feel like I'm going to come without even taking my clothes off."

She moans softly in my ear as she moves against me like we're fucking slow, the way that makes your whole body weak.

"Tell me more, baby," she whispers.

"I want to feel you inside me. And I want to fuck you until you can't move. I want to hear you come over and over again until the sun comes up."

"Fuck, Eden," she whispers, breathless in my ear.

"Let's get out of here."

She looks into my eyes hard before she finally nods and kisses me, then opens the door and leads the way back into the roaring main room. Théo spots us immediately and fills me with dread. I'm definitely flushed, but I trust he'll assume it's the alcohol. I just don't want to get tangled up with him and the others and lose the night. Brooklyn flashes a peace sign at him to indicate we're leaving, but he jogs over.

"What happened to you two?" he asks, but there's no suspicion. He's smiling ear to ear.

"Getting air. Bathroom. Bar."

I try not to laugh as she names off everything she can think of rather than choose something.

"Don't tell me you're leaving."

"Got to, brother," Brooklyn says. "Fight is catching up to me. I guess she did hit me once or twice after all."

"Ah, shit. Okay, sis. You'll take care of her, Coach?" He looks to me and takes me totally off guard.

"Of course," I say. He pulls me into a tight hug. I've never been ashamed to be gay, but something about this gives me a small twinge of guilt. As soon as he lets go, we bolt for the car before someone else can spot us. The valet brings the Maserati around and we hop inside.

"You okay to drive?" I ask.

"Yeah, I danced it all out. I wasn't that drunk to begin with." That means she did all this sober. I try not to give that more power than I should. She zips out of the bay. Once we're on the main road she opens it up, pushing seventy in seconds. The warm night air rushes through my hair and pushes against me like a hug from the beyond.

We drop the car off in front of the hotel and head upstairs. When we're walking down our hall I notice she keeps checking over her shoulder, but I just smile to myself.

"Whose room?" I ask.

"Shh."

"They're at the club, Brooklyn. No one's here." I laugh.

"There's always someone listening."

I take out my room key and wave it at her with a question on my face. She nods and walks a bit farther down the hall like she's not with me while I open the door. Once I'm inside, I wave her over with fake exasperation. She looks down the hall again before she comes over. I teasingly stand in her way to delay her, but she just bear hugs me around my waist, picks me up, and carries me inside.

"Fuckin' rebel, huh?"

"You do know it wouldn't be that weird to be caught in your coach's room after a fight, right? If only you had an ounce of cool in you," I say, still in the air in her arms.

"No amount of cool is going to explain the sounds I'm about to pull out of you, troublemaker."

"I see." I lean down and kiss her softly, feeling her strong arms holding me effortlessly. Being alone in a real room slows us down from the hunger of the club or the gym. Maybe because we know this can really happen now, that it's not just a stolen moment. She carries me farther into the room until she can set me on the bed, following me down as she lowers me to my back. I pull her tank top over her head and toss it on the floor, desperate for the feel of her hot skin. She lowers onto me, pulling my shirt off too and pushing her hips between my legs. She moves in a fluid rhythm, grinding into me in a motion that's already edging me toward orgasm. No one has ever made me feel so much so fast. She's all-encompassing, somehow touching me everywhere at once.

I kiss her neck as she grinds and move my hands up her smooth back. A simple gold cross hangs from her neck. I take in the overpoweringly sexy image of Brooklyn on top of me in a black lace bra. I reach down her stomach and unbutton her shorts, then slip my hand inside. She takes a sharp inhale as my fingers trail down, tracing lightly over her underwear. I slip my hand under the fabric and slowly move down, shuddering from the rush of feeling how wet she is. I slowly stroke her opening, waiting to fuck her even though she's ready now. She's holding herself up on her forearms on either side of my face, close enough I can feel them tremble when I touch her, close enough I gently bite and pull the flesh of her shoulder.

She kisses me hard and desperate, slipping her hand under my bra and squeezing my nipple. The shot of pleasure sends me arching off the bed into her hard body over me. She squeezes again, and I hook my free arm around the back of her neck, holding her close as I press harder against her opening with the pads of my fingers without actually fucking her just yet. Her strength dissolves on top of me.

"Fuck, Eden."

She sits up to straddle me. I sit up too, chasing her intoxicating kiss. Her hips roll against me, the hottest thing I've ever seen. I unclasp her bra with my free hand, and she tosses it aside. Her breasts are fairly small but full and firm and completely breathtaking. She leans down to my ear.

"I want to see you," she whispers. I smile and reluctantly remove my hand so she can take off my bra and throw it on the floor. My mouth goes dry and my heart beats like a cannon as I watch her look at me, her eyes swimming with want. "God, you're so beautiful." She cups my breasts, squeezing both of my nipples as she kisses me, pulling a moan from deep in my chest.

"Get rid of these too," I whisper as I pull at her shorts, and she moves so I can yank them off, taking her underwear with them. She straddles me again, this time naked, and I might have forgotten how to breathe the way it keeps coming in ragged gasps.

I can feel her wetness as she rolls her hips against me, and my thoughts are all a haze of heat. I grab her hip with my left hand, soaking in the rhythm of how she wants to be fucked, and slide my fingers into her in a slow but firm motion that breaks her cadence as her eyes close and she exposes her neck to look skyward. I pull my fingers almost all the way out, then plunge deeper, and she moans loud and bites her lip as she moves her hips to meet the thrust.

She holds me tight against her chest, her fingers in my hair as she rides me. I match her rhythm, going deeper as she rides harder. I take her nipple carefully in my mouth, sucking and teasing it with my tongue. She lets her head fall back as her body rolls and bucks against me, arching and pulling and scratching. She grabs a fistful of my hair and thrusts her hips into me.

"Eden," she moans, clinging on to me for release. I crush her against me with my free arm and fuck her in hard, deep thrusts as she comes undone in my arms until her entire body tenses and she rolls against me in big, slow motions as she cries out in orgasm. She grips me hard, her fist in my hair yanking my head back and her fingers grasping my shoulder until, finally, the tension releases, and she melts.

I roll her onto her back and kiss down her stomach, enveloping her pulsing clit in a hot kiss. She gasps, but her hips rise into me and she gathers my hair, pulling me against her. She asks for a lot of pressure, fucking my face slow at first but quickly building until another orgasm rips through her, loud and hard and long.

I'm prepared to keep going, but she pulls me up next to her. She looks almost confused or lost as she looks deep into my eyes. She kisses me slow, clinging on to me like I may disappear.

Then her hands trail down and pull off the rest of my clothes slowly with a striking hunger in her intense gaze. We're finally both naked, and just soak each other in. She's perfectly proportioned, her waist long and trim but strong, a crevice between her ribs where her abs transform if she flexes, but right now she's relaxed and soft. Her thighs are thick and powerful. She rolls me onto my side and shapes to my back.

She gently pushes her hips into my ass, and I return the pressure. Her arm threads under mine to reach my breasts as she runs her teeth over my neck. She teases me until my body is on fire and I need to be touched so bad I'm about to roll back over and attack her, but just as I'm about to she rolls me the other way instead so I'm facedown. She kisses down my back between my shoulder blades and runs her fingers over the inside of my thighs.

"Oh God," I moan into the mattress. "Fuck me, Brooklyn." I can feel her smiling behind me as she teases me. And finally, her fingers slip inside, pushing deep in a confident, careful thrust that fills me and shuts down my brain. It's like the world disappears to be replaced with a new universe inside. Her hand weaves into my hair. Everything she's doing feels so incredible I'd trust her to do anything she felt like.

She thrusts deep and slow, hard and fast, light and teasing, and somehow no matter what she does it feels even better.

"You know how long I've wanted you?" she whispers into my ear. "I'm going to fuck you until you scream my name."

"Hold me down."

She pins my wrist to the mattress and crushes her weight into my back so I can't move and thrusts in a consistent, maddening rhythm that pushes me close to the edge with each motion.

"Fuck, Brooklyn. Yes." My fingers curl around hers. She clasps my hand while still crushing me down. My orgasm starts to build. I'm on the edge of coming for what feels like an hour, and then it crashes over me, ripping through me in blinding ecstasy.

"Oh my God, Brooklyn." My body tenses as it floods into every corner of me, taking over. When it finally subsides, it takes every speck of energy with it, and I wilt beneath her. She gently kisses the small of my back, tracing her fingers over my skin. I slowly roll over as she settles beside me. I breathe in the heat of her and touch the soft skin of her stomach, resting my head on her chest. I can't fucking believe I'm in bed with her, but I should've known it would be earth-shattering.

"Brooklyn."

She looks down, but I don't even know what I wanted to say. All I know is I've never felt this, and it's a little scary but incredible and I have no idea what to do with any of it. She cups my face and looks into my eyes.

"I know. Me too."

CHAPTER NINETEEN

The feel of Brooklyn disentangling from me stirs me to a hazy awareness, but it isn't until I hear her getting dressed that I snap back to full consciousness. I look around the dark, unfamiliar room, disoriented, and spot her silhouette as she puts on her jacket.

"What time is it?" I mutter in a cloud of exhaustion.

"Four thirty," she says and comes to my side. She sits on the edge of the bed and kisses my head.

"Why the hell are you awake?" It's barely been an hour since we dozed off.

"I should get back to my room before my brothers notice I'm not there," she whispers. "They're going to come to my room when they're up."

I rub my eyes and force them to focus on her face. "None of your family knows you're gay, do they?"

"Of course not."

"Not even Théo?"

"No, God no." She sounds horrified.

"They've never questioned you about it? Hinted? Nothing?"

Brooklyn smirks. "No, they would be shocked. I know you find that hard to believe."

"I really do. Are they living under a rock?"

"What're you trying to say?" She pretends to be offended. "You think I look like a dude?"

"God no." I run my hands up her sides and lean up to kiss her. "You just have *all* the vibes."

"They think I'm like that because I grew up with three brothers. And the fighting. My dad never treated me any different than the rest of them. As long as I can remember, the only thing that's mattered has been winning and bringing glory to the family name. It just got more and more intense as my brothers let him down. I was never expected to date. It was never weird to them I didn't bring dudes home or that I was rowdy like the guys."

"You *are* a rowdy bunch, aren't you?" I drape my arm over her legs. My eyes have finally adjusted, and she looks like a goddess.

"A little bit." She pinches the air.

"So, you're born to be a rebel. What do they expect?"

"Not that much of one. I'm my dad's last hope."

"What do you mean?"

"Nicolau is in prison. Leandro will never be respected no matter what he wins with all the steroid shit. Théo got hurt in his world title match and has never been the same. People act like we're royalty, but the way my dad sees it, his children are letting the legacy fall apart. I'm it."

"That's a lot to carry."

She nods but doesn't look burdened. "It's okay. I'll come through. I'm going to win the belt and put it in his hands."

She came across so arrogant when I first saw her, but she doesn't boast or conquer for herself, she does it to honor her family. Not so different from what got me started, honoring Jin.

"But if people found out I'm a dyke…" She cringes. "Then none of it counts. Everything my dad has ever worked for is over. He'd never talk to me again."

"Oh, Brooklyn." It cracks my heart in two that she has to walk through life with that over her head, that she's so devoted to him but can't trust him to feel the same. "Are you sure it would be that bad? Maybe they'd surprise you." Her entire body tenses just at the mention of it. I rub my thumb over her taut forearm.

"Yes," she says. "Believe me, I'm sure, Eden. I've seen it."

"What do you mean?"

"I told him I had a crush once. On a girl named Olivia. I think I was eleven." She looks down, unwilling to meet my eyes, but I sit up a little, scooting closer with intense interest.

"What did he do?"

"He told me to take it back or he'd beat me bloody and never look at me again. I took it back. The next day he acted like nothing happened, except I wasn't allowed to see or talk about Olivia ever again. Théo brought her up once years later. Dad didn't remember her. Or he acted like he didn't remember her. I don't even know."

"Jesus." I squeeze her leg. "I'm sorry."

"You don't have to be sorry. I'm fine. I just need you to understand I know what I'm talking about with them. I don't do shit like this because I can't risk it. I shouldn't even be here right now." She starts talking faster, almost in a panic. "You can't think you know better than me on this. If you did something, if you told, you could destroy me. You could blow my whole life up. You could ruin—"

"Whoa, hey." I sit up and pull her into a tight embrace, holding her against my chest hard. "Brooklyn, I would never do that to you. No matter what. Not if I thought it would help you. Not if you broke my heart. Not even if I wanted to hurt you. I will never out you against your will. I swear."

She slowly relaxes. "Thank you." She squeezes my hand. "So, we're okay?"

Jesus, what a loaded question. I've never lived in the closet. Not giving a shit what your train wreck of a mom thinks gave me that one perk. I'm not thrilled with the images I'm getting of what closet life looks like, but I can do it for now. I don't expect her to come out right this second. But then, is that even what she's asking? Or is she asking me to pretend this never happened and go back to the way we were once we get back to New York? To store this away as a sacred secret for the rest of my life? "I don't really know what that means," I say. "I'm not mad if that's what you're asking."

"But…"

"I want to see you again, and I'm getting a little worried you're saying that's not possible."

"Believe me, I want to see you again too," she says, hunger flooding her eyes.

"Yeah?"

"God, how can you not know?" She leans over and kisses me.

"Then we're okay," I say as I kiss her back. The weight of even that much of a commitment already feels complicated. This isn't sneaking around at a job you can afford to lose anyway. This is the big leagues, sneaking around with the public eye probing into our lives looking for exactly this type of story with Brooklyn's family on the line. It doesn't mean glancing over your shoulder now and then; it means constant vigilance, fear, and restriction. It means even Laila and Jin can't know. It's not the kind of thing I ever thought I'd subject myself to. Having my hands tied. Being a dirty secret. Being with someone who's ashamed to be with me. That doesn't feel like a fair way to put it with Brooklyn, but I'm afraid I'm spinning it for her, afraid I'm just another girl who knows exactly what she deserves until someone makes her knees weak.

Then again, she's only twenty-three, a fact that has been in the back of my mind despite not quite registering as a problem. We're four years apart, which doesn't mean much to me on most levels, but I can't imagine Brooklyn won't be living her life very differently in four years with or without me. Maybe there really is a valid exception to be made here.

She kisses me again, soft and tender and hot. My head swirls, and God, who am I kidding? I'm not going anywhere. When we part, she smiles as she backs toward the door.

"Good night, beautiful."

She opens the door carefully, cracking it open just enough to peek out, then disappears into the hall. An empty bed isn't a rare thing for me, but stretching out on the king-size hotel mattress alone is a little hollow. The drapes are thick, but I can make out the glow of sunrise at the part between them. Our flight home isn't until evening. I'll be spending every second until then sinking into the dull ache in my body and dreaming of Brooklyn.

CHAPTER TWENTY

It's been three weeks since we flew back in from New Mexico. The onslaught of media attention has been overwhelming. Every time I step outside there's someone trying to run me down and ask about my training techniques, how I'm handling the transition to coaching, and what it's like working with the infamous Shaws.

New clients pour in, eager for a taste of whatever turned Brooklyn's striking around so fast. I tell them Brooklyn is an exceptional athlete, and that has a lot to do with it. It's not the best sales pitch, but I'm not sure I want Emerald Tiger flooded so soon. The Shaws pay big money for Brooklyn to have the kind of hyper focused training she's had, and let's face it, I like spending all my time alone with her.

Théo still comes to most of her sessions, but at least once per week, he can't, and at least once more he leaves early enough we can reasonably pretend we want to put in more work and spend a couple of hours goofing around or sneaking off to my room.

It seems the night she was with me in the hotel and left at dawn is about as close as she's ever going to get to spending the night. She has an endless supply of ways she thinks we'll be discovered that she's always compensating for. If someone sees her car here in the middle of the night, busted, but if she gets a ride and someone sees her here without her car, they'll know she's sneaking around.

Her apartment is an incredible modern loft in a high-rise in Brooklyn, but her family drops in on her so often we spend even less time there. She never relaxes when we're at her place. At least at the gym we have a built-in excuse to be together. If Théo did show up and we had to come out of my room, we'd be able to say we went back to watch video or get training tape or something. As it stands, the mind-blowing sex is always followed shortly by speed dressing and bolting.

It's constant waiting. Waiting for her to call, to text, to come over, waiting for Théo to leave, waiting for her phone calls to end so I can make noise again. But God, does she make it worth it when she finally does show. We talk for hours, laugh until we can't breathe, train until every demon we've ever carried is sweated out, and make love until we can't move.

The weeks after her fight are so free. She hasn't committed to a new fight yet, which means she's relaxed and loose. It's not all a fight to the death. It's just the love of the sport, and she teaches me as much as I teach her. We do Jiu-Jitsu for hours, and it's clicking into place in a way it never has. It's making me stronger. Being curled up on my back defending all the time has given me a core of steel, but it's also strengthened my neck. You wouldn't think it, but just holding my head off the mat all the time is a low intensity workout that's changed the game, and not being in constant pain is like a shadow lifting.

Mateo is in Taekwondo today. Having him around regularly is a relief, but I'm under no illusion his life has magically become wonderful. Brooklyn does a private lesson with him every other Thursday, more when she can. I sneak hundreds into his gym bag every so often, wishing I could just buy the kid a new life.

Laila closes class, and I bow them out. It's difficult not to run straight to check my phone, but I worked hard for my independence, and I don't want to abandon that completely, no matter how crazy I am about Brooklyn. When I do check it, I can't deny my heart leaps like it always does when I do, in fact, have a message from her.

Morning, sexy. Want to come to a BBQ with me tonight?

She never invites me on social calls, nothing that could in any world look like a date. I accept the invitation and ask for details.

"What're you smiling about over there?" Laila asks, looking amused. "Someone's smitten."

"Just a funny meme," I lie and put my phone away.

"So, not smitten?"

"Just with cute puppies."

Laila finishes shoving her dobok in her bag, then straightens up and comes over. It feels like an eternity of eye contact, but whatever she was going to say, she doesn't. She just pulls me into a hug.

"'Kay. See you tomorrow."

I check my phone again, and Brooklyn sent over an address with a header of "Shaw House."

Shaw House? I send back.

Family BBQ. And friends. People from the neighborhood. Casual.

My heart pounds as I try to picture it. I usually think Brooklyn is overcautious, but this feels risky. Then she texts again, and it falls into place.

Dad wants to meet you.

My stomach rolls. Samson Shaw wants to meet me? According to Brooklyn, he was the one who sent her to train with me, but my only experience with him in person was watching him tell an excited fan his daughter isn't a dyke. That's a dichotomy I haven't made sense of. She must feel my apprehension even though not much time passes.

It'll be fun. I promise. If not, I'll get you out early.

It's weird being asked to meet the parents when they won't know who you are to their daughter. It's weirder still when you know they'd hate you if they did. Play nice with someone who's doing the same. A futile exercise, but I text her back that I'll be there.

I'm tempted to dress up. It feels weird not to, but then, a barbecue does scream casual, so I just go with jeans and a nice button-down. I break out the Acura and make the drive to Brooklyn. When I pull up, a jolt of nerves makes me want to bolt and make up some reason I can't come, but that's a chickenshit move.

I hear a riot of fun inside, so much so I'm not sure they'll hear the door, but seconds after I knock, it swings open and a beautiful woman with deep brown eyes, long silky black hair, and a gorgeous smile answers in a rose red dress. I thought Brooklyn looked a lot like her father, but seeing her mother completes her. She's a blend of the best of them, Samson's athletic, strong body, his angled cheekbones that make him look like an eagle, his assertive, confident demeanor, and her mother's endlessly warm brown eyes, wide set and entrancing, her smile that hits you like a hug, her magnetism. What a genetic jackpot. People say that about athletes all the time, but being the product of a literal crack whore and a random myself, I lost faith in the idea.

"Eden," she says with a bright smile. "I'm so glad you're here. Come in. I'm Zaira, Brooklyn's mom."

It's not a mystery all the ways she could recognize me, but it still surprises me. "It's so good to meet you," I say. I step inside and take in the home. It's sleek but homey with grand open space, sharp furniture, lots of lush green plants, and music. It sounds like there are a lot more people here than there are. It looks like just fifteen or so, but they're a lively bunch.

Brooklyn and I spot each other at the same time. She's standing in the open area in the kitchen holding what I assume is a mixed drink, smiling that brilliant smile as she talks to Théo without taking her eyes off of me. She breaks away from him and comes over, pulling me into a hug.

"I'm so glad you're here," she says into my ear.

"Me too."

She guides me farther inside, introducing me to everyone as we go. She's so warm and comfortable. The persona she pulls out for the media is completely gone and she's the sweet, fun, much adored young woman of the family.

She takes me to relative after relative, Uncle Silas, Cousin Luan, Grandfather Ernesto. It's an overwhelmingly male family, but Brooklyn and her mother are shining elegant stars among them. It's also an overwhelmingly Latin family, clearly Brooklyn's mother's side even though Brooklyn has indicated most of them are still in

Brazil. Samson is a black man who grew up right here in Brooklyn. I expected the guest list to be much more heavily comprised of his side of the family. I wonder if he doesn't have any. It's not an uncommon theme among fighters.

Théo appears at my side and slips a drink into my hand with a wink as Ernesto talks about his first apartment in an accent that's completely charming but requires all of my attention. When he pauses, Brooklyn says something back to him in Portuguese. I could listen to that all day, but she must excuse us, because soon she's leading me out to the backyard. There's a grill smoking at the far edge of the patio. Samson is wielding the spatula with a glass of amber liquor in his hand.

"Théo." Brooklyn indicates for him to come too. Samson looks surprised when he sees me, but his handsome face lights up.

"Eden Bauer, good to finally meet you, Champ."

"You too, Mr. Shaw. It's an honor."

He waves it away, but it's clearly a comment he's used to hearing. "Let me get these burgers handed off and we'll go have a talk."

"Sure," I say. I'm lucky it comes out casual. Inside I'm scrambling for why we'd need to do that. What does he want to talk about?

"Why do I feel like I'm in trouble?" I whisper to Brooklyn as we walk off and Leandro drifts over to join us.

She laughs. "He has that effect, but there's no one my dad respects like a champion. Don't worry."

Brooklyn, Théo, Leandro, and I settle into a table in the back corner of the yard next to the fire pit. I get the urge to touch Brooklyn's leg under the table but don't. That's the exact kind of shit I wouldn't have thought twice about with the girls before her that is not a cute game with her.

"Your mom is lovely," I say, and all three of the Shaw siblings light up with affection.

"Yes, she is," Brooklyn says.

"Takes a tamer to deal with our dad," Théo says.

"Make no mistake, little brother, she'll fuck somebody up if she has to," Leandro says.

I can't help but laugh. I don't doubt it, but it's hard to picture. "She's an expert too?"

"Oh yeah." They all echo.

Brooklyn turns to face me. "My grandfather you just met, Ernesto, he's the Jiu-Jitsu genius. Without him, none of us would be anything. My dad moved from Brooklyn to Brazil to learn from him. That's how he met my mom."

"The Shaw legacy is really the Ramalho legacy," Leandro says.

"You're about to get your ass beat if you don't quiet down," Théo says and smiles as he looks over his shoulder.

"Why do you think none of us have been able to make it happen even though we're the best?" Leandro says. "We're cursed because Dad brought us back to the U.S. and started acting like it was all him."

"Yeah, had nothing to do with you taking enough steroids to kill a horse," Théo says.

Leandro punches him in the shoulder loud enough to make a resonant thwap, but the much smaller Théo seems unaffected and flashes his bright family smile.

"At least I won my title fight without breaking my back," Leandro says.

"At least I didn't cheat in mine," Théo snaps back, but they're still smiling.

"Don't act like you don't believe in the curse," Leandro says. "Dad was some brother from New York, swoops in and learns all the secrets, grabs the Professor's daughter, and makes out like a bandit. That's how you get cursed."

"Oh, knock it off," Brooklyn says. "She's going to think you're serious."

"I am serious. You have it too."

"Dad loves Ernesto, and he spent all his time in the gym busting his ass to help out. Of course he met and fell in love with Mom. And he did not make out like a bandit. He stayed out there and opened a school. It took them years to come back to the States, and he credits Grandpa Ramalho all the time."

"You've awakened daddy's girl," Théo says.

"Oh, shut the fuck up."

Théo turns to me now with a twinkle of mischief in his eyes. "She's Dad's favorite, hands down. You'd think a macho man like him would be all about his sons, but she had his heart from day one."

"You were the favorite before her, you know?" Leandro says to Théo.

"Nah, not like her. Why do you think she's the only one with a name like *Brooklyn*?"

"Oh, fuck off," Brooklyn says.

"What? It's true! Nicolau? Leandro? Théo? Mom's kids. Brooklyn? You're Dad's."

"You don't even make sense. Mom likes me better than you too."

All three of them burst out laughing so hard we don't notice Samson has snuck up until he slides into the seat next to Leandro.

"Scoot down, boy."

Leandro jumps to make more room for him. "Sorry, sir."

Samson settles in with his forearms on the table and his fingers interlaced. "Eden, I want to thank you for taking Brooklyn on. A lesser person wouldn't do it. We're happy with the Mendez fight."

"Brooklyn's an incredible martial artist."

"I hope that means you intend to continue coaching her?"

"Of course," I say. "I intend to coach careers, not fights."

"When do you see her getting another title shot?"

"Maybe a year." I figure that's about as ambitious an answer as he could hope for, but he looks disappointed.

"That long?"

"Hard to say. Depends how some other fights go. A year is aggressive, but reasonable."

"A match offer came in today," he says.

"What?" Brooklyn leans forward. "You didn't tell me?"

"I wanted to discuss it together."

"Who is it?" Brooklyn looks like she's going to come unglued.

"Karinov."

"That's awesome," Brooklyn says. "That'll be a huge win."

"If you win," Samson says.

"Of course, I will." I know her personality well enough to know she's offended even at the suggestion, but she doesn't show it.

"You're not undefeated anymore," he says.

"So?"

"So, you're not always right when you say that. I want to hear what your coach thinks."

I can't even look at her. I don't want to see the pain I know is there.

"It's not a great matchup for you," I say quietly.

"What? Eden!" She shoots to her feet.

"Coach," Samson snaps.

Brooklyn seems startled to realize she's exposed how close we are with her willingness to yell at me. She dials it back, but she's still seething. "*Coach.*"

"Sit down," Samson says.

"With respect," Théo says. "I think Brooklyn can win that fight, and it would be huge for her."

"You're not any better equipped to know that," Samson says. "You destroyed your career taking fights before you were ready, and you started Brooklyn down the same path. When I want your opinion, I'll ask for it." He glares at Théo for a long second as if to make sure he doesn't try to speak again before he turns back to me. "I'm sorry, my children don't seem to understand when it's time to shut their mouths. Please, go ahead."

I don't feel like I can handle looking at Brooklyn, but I make myself. "I'm sorry, but I don't think this is the best fight for you. It's a nightmare of a matchup. That's why they want it. Karinov is a big featherweight and she's a Jiu-Jitsu black belt. Everything you're about she has an answer for. She knows what she's doing on the ground, she's never been knocked out, and you won't be able to throw her around like you can with most people."

"You beat her," Brooklyn says.

"I had the same reach she does. You won't. And it took me five rounds of technical kickboxing and went to the judges. Nothing about that is your style."

"You don't think I can beat her?" She sounds more wounded than angry.

"That's not what I'm saying. I do think you can beat her, but I don't think it's the right move for you, especially if what you care about most is getting back to a title shot as fast as possible. I'd want to train you for four or five months, and even if you won, there's a good chance you'd get hurt and have to take time to recover. If you want this fight, I'll get you ready, but expect it to eat up your whole year."

"I'm not trying to dodge the hard fights."

"I know you're not, but these decisions shape your career one way or the other. I think you're better off building up your record right now. Take a fight like this when it's for the belt. Stay healthy as long as possible."

"Sounds like a pussy move to me."

Samson slams the table and gives her a glare I think may kill her. "Fifty, right now."

"You can't be—"

"Now."

Brooklyn's jaw clenches. I'm confused about what's happening until she drops to the ground and starts doing pushups. Even though his glare could kill, I swear I see pride mixed in. You can see she's his beloved just like they said. It feels like forever waiting for her to finish. I'm sure she hates me, which hurts, but it's too important a decision to just say what she wants to hear. When she finishes and sits back down, there's a sheen of sweat on her forehead, but she seems calmer.

I take a deep breath. "Théo's right. It would be a huge win. And yes, I think you could do it." I already said it once, but she can stand to hear it again. "*But* I think something better is going to come along. You're coming off a big win. You're going to get other offers. The title shot comes back around to you faster if you crank out four wins this year rather than one or two."

She stares at me for a long time before she finally sighs. "You really think something better is going to come fast?"

"I promise it will." Almost anything is better.

"Okay," she says it like she's been defeated.

My phone rings, and I smash the sides to silence it. I put my hand on Brooklyn's shoulder. "Start thinking of it as a privilege to compete with you. You don't have to just say yes to anyone."

She nods. "Okay, Coach."

Théo slaps the table to break the tension. "Refills anyone? Eden?"

"Sure, thank you." My phone buzzes with a voice mail, then immediately rings again. I glance at the screen and see it's Laila calling. She usually favors texting and almost never calls more than once. It wouldn't be unheard of for a student to be hurt, and it's the only thing I can imagine could be wrong.

"If you need to take a call go ahead," Samson says.

"I'm sorry, let me just make sure it's not important." I walk toward the empty part of the yard as I hold the phone to my ear.

"Hello?"

I hear a scramble against the speaker and her muffled, panicked voice in the background.

"Laila?" Something scrapes the speaker and her voice comes closer.

"Eden? Jin's in trouble, they're taking him to the ER. You need to get up here. I'm following the ambulance to Lebanon now."

"What?" I almost shout it. "What happened?"

"He was stung by a bee."

A moment passes as my brain tries to catch up. A tiny little insect does not send *Jin* to the hospital. "A bee?"

"He's allergic, I think. I don't fucking know. He told me he was fine, but then he couldn't breathe, and he passed out and was turning blue. It's not good, Eden. They may have to do CPR."

It feels like poison is creeping through my body, cold and crawling. "I'm on my way." I hang up and turn, realizing my body feels like some other entity. I don't quite have control over it. The Shaws are all staring, clearly aware something serious just happened.

"I have to go."

Brooklyn springs to her feet. "Are you okay?"

"Uh." I put my hand on my forehead. "No, not really. Jin is on his way to the ER. He's not breathing."

Brooklyn's eyes go wide. "Oh my God. What happened?"

"He's having an allergic reaction. I can't. I have to go."

"Are you okay to drive?"

Something about the way she says it tells me she won't be coming with. She's offering to call me a driver, not to be one. Part of me expected her to drop everything and come with me, but how could I think that would happen in the middle of a family affair? I don't have time to care.

"I'm fine." I bolt for the door.

The moment I'm in my car, my phone starts buzzing with messages from Brooklyn. I skim enough to catch that she's sorry and feels the need to explain herself, but just seeing the blocks of text is enough for me to know I can't deal with this right now.

CHAPTER TWENTY-ONE

I don't know what to make of seeing Laila by the automatic glass doors as I jog up. Does that mean everything is so fine she doesn't feel the need to be by him, or that it's so awful she wants to make sure she sees me first? I can't even imagine Jin not making it. Jin is my personal superhero. That he's even mortal seems far-fetched. Picturing him wheezing as his throat closed, falling to the ground, medics pounding his chest, I can't even deal with it. It makes *my* throat close and my vision speckle with black. Life without Jin would be worse than lonely. It would be empty. It would be dead.

"They revived him," Laila says even though I'm still twenty feet away. When I catch up to her, I wrap her in a tight hug. I don't have a clear picture of the whole event yet, but I can already tell Laila's presence likely kept him alive.

"Revived him?"

She nods gravely. "He didn't breathe for a long time. His heart stopped. But they got him back. He's on oxygen and an IV now. They're saying he should be fine."

"Should be?"

"You know how they are."

"Can we see him?"

She nods. "We *can*, but the stubborn ass said he didn't want us to see him like that."

"Oh, like hell." I march inside. Laila directs me to his room, staying behind in the hall as I go inside. It's strange how just being in a hospital bed makes you look small and weak. Jin's the same man he's always been, but it's impossible not to notice someone's mortality when they're in one of those gowns. His eyes fix on me, and I see the exact expression Laila likely saw just before he threw her out. Self-conscious, embarrassed. I cross the space and hug him before he can say anything.

"You scared me to fucking death," I say, hoping I can make him forget his own vulnerability by fixating on mine. He slowly wraps his arm around me and returns the hug. "What happened, you crazy man? You're deathly allergic to bees and you don't have an EpiPen somewhere?"

"I didn't know." He shrugs. "A bee has never dared to sting me before." A loaded moment passes, and we start laughing until it curls me over. Jin's laugh has a slight wheeze to it still, but he's beaming at his own humor.

"Is the little bastard dead at least?"

"Oh yes, he paid with his life," Jin says with a smile, then sighs. "Can you imagine? Taekwondo grandmaster dead from bee."

I shake my head. "Don't make me imagine. Nothing can kill you."

He doesn't argue, but it's impossible not to think about the fact that things could have gone differently. Just like that, I could've lost him. And what the hell would I do if that did happen? Jin is my family. My only family. He's the only person I can say with any confidence loves me. I still feel raw inside even as I hold his hand and see that he's okay.

It takes hours for them to release him, unsurprisingly. Laila takes off once Jin finally lets her say good-bye. He tries to send me away too, but it's a weak effort. Even Jin knows I won't be leaving him to find his own way home after a near death experience. It's after midnight when we finally walk to my car and drive back to the dojang. When we park in back, I'm shocked to see Brooklyn sitting on the back step. She stands up when she recognizes my car, shoving her hands into her back pockets. I glance from her to Jin, checking for his reaction in a jerky and totally suspicious double take motion. My automatic reaction is to figure out how best to play this to make it look as normal as possible, but Jin would never buy anything fake from me even if I was willing to lie to him. My best bet is to just shut up and let him think whatever he thinks.

I turn off the car, pausing for a second to prepare. I don't know what to expect from Brooklyn. I haven't answered or even read her texts since I left her party. I could have made time to respond by now and admittedly credited myself with a free pass in the midst of what was happening. I can't help but feel abandoned by her, but I haven't mentally worked through whether or not I have ground to stand on there.

It all happened to settle well, but when I was leaving the BBQ, Jin wasn't breathing. My only family was possibly dying, and all she could do was ask if I could drive myself. I understand the whys, realize I knew what I was getting into with her, and still there are certain moments you expect to trump the rules. Tonight, I learned there are no trump moments with Brooklyn's family. No matter how awful it is, I may be alone when it counts.

When I finally open my car door, Jin does the same, and we step out into the cool night. Brooklyn looks uncomfortable but not panicked. She goes straight to Jin and tells him how glad she is he's okay. When she turns to me, her eyes are blatantly searching me. There's a thick layer of anxiety and insecurity all over her.

"Give me a minute to help him get settled, and I'll be back." I try to sound professional and am shocked just how convincingly businesslike it comes out.

I unlock and open the door for Jin, but he turns to me just inside the entryway. "I'm okay." He squeezes my arm. "Go." I look him over. He really is okay, and it will insult him to treat him as if he's frail. My desire to help him is for me. I pull him into a long, tight hug, and let him walk upstairs alone. When he's closed inside his apartment, I take a deep breath, turn, and go back outside to Brooklyn. Her head snaps up when she hears the door open, but she doesn't speak. She looks frozen. I can't believe she's willing to show up here now in the middle of the night after she was just too afraid to leave her family barbecue.

"What the hell are you doing here?" I scan the empty street.

"Eden, please don't be pissed. I'm sorry."

"It's almost one a.m."

"I know. I came the second I could, but you weren't here and weren't answering me."

"How long have you been here?"

"Maybe an hour."

"And how is it okay for you to sit on my doorstep for an hour in the middle of the night, but you can't be seen with me when I actually need you?"

"I couldn't just run off with you in front of my family," she says. "They would have gotten suspicious."

"If they're half as oblivious as you say, they would not. You act like it's unheard of to be a supportive friend. It's not like my goldfish died. The man who is a father to me wasn't breathing."

"You're not supposed to be my friend, Eden. You're my coach to them."

"We train together every day. You don't think they realize we're friends? Are you in that deep they can't even know you *like* a gay person?"

"That's not what I'm saying."

"Just go home, Brooklyn."

I've been dealing with life alone for as long as I can remember, and I've gotten good at it. I'm not *that* mad at her. I don't even particularly like people being there while I'm a mess. It just feels right to attack the outlook that results in me ranking so low in the priorities. That is, until her eyes start to shimmer. Then I just feel like a jerk. Nothing makes Brooklyn cry, not getting kicked in the head, not being called a failure by her father. It never occurred to me I have that power.

"I'm sorry, Eden. I didn't know what to do. I've been texting and calling you for hours. I'm here now. Please let me in."

She's wearing her stress everywhere. Does she think I'm breaking up with her? I want to just reassure her we're okay and send her away, but I can see she won't go easy, and she's been a champ about letting me chew her out more or less in public long enough. I step aside and wave her in. I close and lock us up in my room. She looks uncomfortable, like she's not sure if she should sit or not.

"Look, I get it," I say. "You were clear you wouldn't be taking chances, and I signed on. You didn't have to run over here. I'm just wired still. This was one of the scariest nights of my life."

"I understand." She reaches out to hug me. I let her, but I just can't relax into it. I need to count on her for these things or not. Realistically, not. It's not like me to want more, but of course I would from the one person who can't do it. I can live in the box she needs me to live in. I really can. But she can't come and go from that box as she pleases. I need to know exactly what the box is.

"You don't have to stay, Brooklyn. This has nothing to do with you. Jin is fine. I'm fine. I'm sorry I freaked you out."

"Eden, I *want* to stay. I want to be here for you."

"It's too late. It's over, and you weren't."

"I'm right here."

"But it's fine now. You saw him. They got his heart beating again. It's already over."

"I can see you're not okay. I know they got him back, but you thought you were losing him, and you're not done feeling it yet. You were strong for Jin. Let me be strong for you."

My eyes start to water, and I have to turn away from her. She comes up behind me and gently puts her palms on my back, kissing the side of my head.

"Don't tell me you're afraid to let me see you cry," she says quietly.

Somehow it makes the knot in my throat worse. My breath comes in a ragged shudder as I fight the tears.

"Come lie on the bed with me," she says. "Let me hold you."

I sigh and close my eyes, absorbing her touch. I don't want to need someone who may not be there. I don't want to need someone at all, but pretending it doesn't feel good to have her here is just asinine. She's right. The chemicals of hearing that Jin wasn't breathing are still encoded in my body, and now that he's taken care of, the reality not just of what happened, but what could have happened is descending again. I turn and look into her eyes as if they'll tell me if I can count on her. They unequivocally say that I can. I'm sure even she believes that. That doesn't make it true, but I don't have the strength to fight her.

I glance at the twin bed and can't help but laugh a little. Sex only works on it because we're on top of one another, and our hurried situation means cuddling never lasts long. I'm not sure how long we can make it work, but I lie down with her, and she pulls my head onto her shoulder and kisses the top of my head.

"You want to talk about it?"

I breathe her in, letting a long time pass before I speak. "I almost lost him."

She runs her hands through my hair. I keep waiting for it to end. Any second now she'll want to run off and get back to her supposed location, but it doesn't happen.

"He took me in. He's the only family I have."

"There's no one else?" she asks quietly, sounding mildly surprised. "What about your mom?"

"She was a hooker and a drunk and an addict who could barely remember my name until I had money."

Brooklyn doesn't answer at first, and I don't blame her. What the fuck do you say to something like that?

"How'd you end up with Jin?"

"He pulled me into class one day when I was hiding from some people in the entryway. I took classes for about a year before he invited me to move into a student room. He knew my home life was shit and just mentioned that I could if I wanted to. I jumped all over it. My mom was too drugged out to stop me. He saved me."

"You weren't sad leaving your mom? Or scared? Even though she was a mess?"

I laugh lightly. "She used to leave me home alone while she went out on binges and lost track of the days. She'd come back a week later like nothing happened. When she saw me, she'd jump like I was a stray pigeon that got inside."

"What about your dad?"

"Could be anyone. She was a hooker."

"Fuck."

"It's okay, I don't want to know. Not one of those freaks she brought home was worth a damn."

"She brought them around you?" I can hear her trying to subdue the horror in her voice.

"Yeah, I had to listen to them all the time. She'd get beat sometimes. They stole our shit sometimes. Once I got a little older they started making eyes at me. I spent most of my time in the streets to stay away from them, but that wasn't great either. Jin gave me somewhere to be. He's the only one who's ever given a shit about me."

"Fuck, Eden. I didn't know you grew up *that* hard. Why didn't you tell me?"

I shrug. "Everyone grows up hard here. You did too."

"Not like that."

"Hard is hard."

"Nah," she says. "I had more good times than bad."

It's impossible not to see that her family is responsible for that. She experienced a lot of the same things I did, went without food and heat and light, not to mention all the things I haven't like being biracial and moving to a new country. It's never felt right to cry about my past to her even though a huge part of her upbringing was also glitz and fame. The important difference was love. She has this beautiful family that adores her. Who am I to ever in a million years suggest she owes it to me to risk that? Just thinking about losing Jin, losing my family, has me deeply shaken.

Brooklyn's arms squeeze harder as if she knows whatever I'm thinking is pulling me apart. I squeeze back around her waist, sinking into her warmth. I got so good at living without this, but that person might already be gone.

CHAPTER TWENTY-TWO

I wake up to a quiet clang in the kitchen. I sit up and have to stare at her a while before I can comprehend it. I check my phone and see it's already nine.

"Hey," she says softly when she notices I'm up. She's in one of my T-shirts and her boy-shorts, looking cozy and natural. She comes over and puts a cup in my hand. "Coffee?"

"Did you spend the night?" She clearly did, but I can't quite believe it. She kisses me softly and puts her hand on my chest.

"Yes. And I'm making breakfast. I saw you had pancake mix. I hope that's okay?"

I can't remember the last time someone cooked for me, but before I can say anything, a knock at the back door pulls us apart.

"Who's that?" she asks.

"I have no idea."

We spring up and creep to the back door. I look through the peephole and turn to her, relieved.

"It's Mateo," I whisper, so low it barely makes a sound. She looks through the peephole, then back at me, then down at her bare legs. She could get dressed, of course, but that doesn't change that we're in my apartment alone together while the gym is clearly closed.

"He'll know," I say. I look back through the peephole to make sure he isn't leaving. I don't know what to do, but it can't be nothing. His clothes are a mess and he has tears running down his face. He knocks again, harder.

"Eden!"

"He's crying," I say. "I have to let him in."

"Of course," Brooklyn says.

"I can get you out the front if you want."

She pauses, then shakes her head. "No, I'm not leaving. Just give me a head start to change." I'm shocked, but we don't have time to talk about it. She jogs down the hall and into my room. I unlatch the door and slowly open it.

"Hey, Mateo," I say. "What's wrong, bud?"

He just launches at me and hugs me, tears flowing fresh. I hug him back, letting him stay there as long as he needs. When he does finally let go, I motion for him to follow me inside. When we get to my room and he sees Brooklyn cooking at the stove, surprise passes over his face, but it goes as easily as it came, and he just goes over to hug her too.

Brooklyn meets my eyes and smiles as she returns the hug.

"Well, hey, bro. You're just in time for breakfast. You two sit." She points at the tiny round table in the open space of the kitchen. I don't even have three seats, but I pull cardboard boxes from the supply closet, and Mateo's tickled to sit on one. Brooklyn gives him a glass of orange juice and me another coffee. I can't help but watch Brooklyn, dazzled by how soft she can be, how sure I was she was a pig-headed brute. I was so wrong.

Mateo's tears have dried, but his body language is still heavy. It feels like the obvious thing to ask him what happened, but I take Brooklyn's no pressure lead.

"My dad locked me out of the house. He says I can't go back unless I bring food."

Brooklyn meets my eyes again over his head, outrage all over her face.

"Has he been doing drugs again?" I ask. Mateo is shy about details, but he's forthcoming with yes or no questions. He nods.

"Let's give him some time to get himself together," I say. "Do you want me to talk to him?"

"No!" He looks terrified. I would have reacted the same way as a kid. I never know what to do with this type of thing. I can give him food to take home, which is something I want to do anyway, but I don't want to reinforce this kind of behavior from his father. Calling the police or social services never goes anywhere. I've tried. What I really want is to pluck Mateo right out of that awful home, but that's probably kidnapping.

"All right, just for you." Brooklyn sets down a big plate of chocolate chip pancakes in front of him, and his eyes light up.

"Chocolate chip?"

"Yep."

He attacks the pancakes while Brooklyn sets a plate in front of me and winks. Mine are topped with strawberries and bananas.

"Dang, Brooklyn," I say. "You didn't have to do all this."

She laughs. "Calm down, they're just pancakes."

"Thank you, Brooklyn," Mateo says.

"Any time, bud. So, we going to do another private lesson on the mat after breakfast?" she asks him. "I think it's time you add a baseball choke to your arsenal."

"Really? You mean it?"

"Yes, sir."

They chatter away about submissions, upcoming fights, Mateo's friends and enemies, and suddenly it's all so beautiful. Mateo and Brooklyn giggling over pancakes in my home feels so right, so perfect it can't even be real. The feeling of *home* is one I've never identified with. Having it surge through me now takes me off guard. No amount of training, no number of wins has ever made me feel safe like this. No amount of independence feels as good as trust. But then, it isn't real. Soon Brooklyn will have to pretend I'm nothing to her again, and Mateo will have to go back to a home he isn't sure he'll be able to get into. Is it all a delusion to think it will ever be different?

CHAPTER TWENTY-THREE

Brooklyn and I drop Mateo off back at home together and carry a full load of groceries to his apartment. I want the opportunity to get some kind of feel for the situation, but no one's home anymore. Mateo gets in by removing the window screen and prying the window open. The home is trashed. It looks like a WWE fight took place in the living room.

"You going to be okay?" I ask. What a dumb question. How do I expect him to answer that? But he promises he will be. I give him a hug and assure him he can come back to the gym anytime he wants to. Brooklyn hugs him too before we go. When we're back in her Escalade, we just sit for a minute.

"Is it wrong to just take him back to that?"

She shakes her head. "I don't know, but we sent him back better off than we found him."

"Doesn't feel like enough."

She grabs my hand. "He doesn't seem afraid, and he knows he can come to you. He'll be okay."

I nod. "Well, you want to go get in some training?"

"Just one stop first." She pulls out and starts down a series of side roads until she pulls into a giant vacant parking lot behind a shut down grocery store.

"What're we doing here?" I ask.

She takes off her seat belt and leans toward me, wrapping her hand around the back of my neck and kissing me, her lips parted.

She has a way of kissing me when I don't know it's coming that sends me tumbling through space. Her hands move over me with such hunger I want to give her everything, whatever she wants.

"Oh, I see," I whisper as I kiss her back.

"Théo's coming to training. I don't think I can behave around you unless I fuck you now."

"Mm, I'm warning you, it'll make it worse, thinking about how hard I just made you come."

"Go ahead and torture me."

"Yes, ma'am." I take off my seat belt and climb on top of her, straddling her in the driver's seat. She runs her hands up my thighs and pulls my hips against her tightly. My pulse picks up in a rush. I reach down to control her seat and lean her backwards a bit as I grind against her. She closes her eyes, gripping my hips and just letting me move on top of her.

Watching pleasure pass through her face makes my whole body light up, and my brain flips into a primal space. I ride her, losing myself and becoming wilder the longer I do it, the more she submits to me. Then her hands are moving again. She slips under my shirt and squeezes my nipples hard, riding the line between pleasure and pain expertly, and then she's unbuttoning my pants. I plunge my fingers into her thick curls and pull her head back, pinning her to the seat as her fingers brush over my clit. She looks in my eyes, letting me see all her lust and need, her brow creased and her lips parted as she breathes in ragged surges. I kiss her with all of me, crashing against her body and exploring her mouth with reckless heat until a gentle moan vibrates from her chest against mine. She slides her fingers inside me in a long, steady motion that sucks the strength out of me.

Her other hand moves to the back of my neck, and she tightens the grip to make me look in her eyes as she pushes into me again and pulls an unrestricted moan from me. I ride Brooklyn hard, fucking her fingers as I hold her to the back of the seat with one hand pressed into her chest and the other on her side like she may try to escape. She takes the pressure, tension and pleasure building and collecting in her face as she bites her lip.

"Yes, baby. I'm yours," she says. "Use me." And I do. I grab her hair, pull her shirt, sink my weight into her, and I'm hovering on the edge of orgasm.

"Fuck, Brooklyn. I'm going to come."

She sits up a little straighter so she can bite my neck, just hard enough to cross into pain without it becoming overwhelming. It sends a jolt of sensation through me, flooding me with chemicals that make me weak and energized at once. Her hand wraps around my throat and squeezes, gently at first until I react with a moan that rumbles against her hand, and she tightens her grip as I ride her harder.

"Come for me, baby."

I never expected I could in this position in an uncomfortable car in a parking lot, but when she squeezes my throat and sinks her fingers deep inside me, I come so hard it's fucking blinding. My hands tighten into fists as I bunch her shirt up until there's no extra fabric and the grip lends me complete control of her. I yank her closer violently as my body floods with pulsing ecstasy. When it subsides, she slowly removes her fingers and wraps her arms around me, holding me to her chest. I soak in her warm scent as her chest rises, floating me on the swell of her breath.

I kiss her gently, running my tongue across her lower lip on the edge of the kiss until she's leaning forward, chasing for more. Then I climb into the back and fold down the seats before leaning close to her ear.

"Get back here and take your clothes off."

Brooklyn smiles and looks out the window before she turns and climbs back. There's no one around, and even if there was, her windows are too dark to see through. Even the spacious Escalade feels very much like a car. Part of me can't believe the fooling around in parking lots part of my life isn't over, but the other part doesn't give a single flying fuck where we are as long as I'm with her.

Brooklyn's deep brown eyes lock on mine as she slowly pulls her shirt up and off, followed by her bra, obeying my command. We're on our knees with the warm skin of our stomachs touching. I loop my arms around her lower back and kiss her, our lips sure and soft and wet. She leans into me in the rhythm of our kiss, so subtle I'm not sure she realizes she's doing it. I slip my tongue into her mouth, slow and rhythmic too, pulling away, then falling into it.

I lower her to her back and pull off her pants, caressing her over her underwear so lightly she squirms beneath me. I don't actually know, but I can't imagine Brooklyn often gives up the reins this way, and having her trust like this makes me want to make her come harder than she ever has in her life. I tease her relentlessly, running my lips and tongue over the sensitive skin of her collarbone, her breasts, her hips, working my way down to her thighs, touching her with pressure light enough to always feel her rising into me for just a little more, then holding her down when she tries to rush.

"Fuck, Eden. I want you so bad." She's breathless. "I'm so ready for you."

I kiss between her hips, pressing my chest down against her center, letting her rise into me just enough she doesn't completely lose it. Then I feel her fingers in my hair, her palm against my cheek. I take her hand and nibble her fingertip, touching it with my tongue before I suck her finger. She trembles and whimpers. I trace my hands up her body and play with her nipples as she writhes beneath me. I can tell she could come like this if I keep it up, but I can't bear not to fuck her, so I finally push my fingers inside her, slow and deep. Her head falls back as she moans, loud. The sound travels through my skin to my core.

"Jesus Christ, Eden," she says as her hand balls into a tight grip in my hair. I move down and suck her clit as I fuck her and she cries out in pleasure, her nails digging into my back now. It doesn't take long before her whole body is tightening around me so hard it hurts, her nails dragging up my back. She holds me against her hard as she comes. I can feel her clit pulsing against my tongue and her pussy tightening around my fingers as she moans with each wave of her climax.

She's still breathing hard after her body finally relaxes, and I feel stupefied by the beauty of her glistening skin, the flawlessness of her body, and the power of the fact that she lets me touch her this way. I trace my fingers over her body, following every curve and valley. We lie there for the most perfect minutes of my life, and then she rolls onto her side and kisses me.

Tears inexplicably stab at my throat as we just look at one another. The realization materializes from nothing, the words blaring into my mind followed by a calm sense of truth. I am completely in love with Brooklyn.

"You okay?" she asks.

I smile and touch her face. "Yes." She's not ready to hear it, and I'm not ready to say it. I kiss her and break the spell. "I guess we better get to the gym."

She laughs. "You were right. It's going to be painful not to touch you."

"Tell me about it." I wink, and we climb back into the front seat as Brooklyn pulls her clothes back on. Brooklyn pulls onto the street and starts toward the gym.

"Maybe Théo will take the night off."

"Yeah, right," I say. "Don't count on it."

"I know," she says. "He loves being up my ass making sure I'm working."

"You really don't think you could tell Théo at least? You two are so close."

She looks over, a little stiff, then sighs. "You don't understand, Eden. I don't even want to explain to you how anti-gay they are."

"They all know I'm gay and act normal. I don't think they're as far gone as you think."

"That's just how important winning is to them. You win. And you helped me win. And they do like you, but they also think you're going to hell."

"Seriously? This is all a religious thing?" I know the Shaws are devout, Brooklyn included, but it doesn't seem to trouble her, so I didn't think that was the source of their hang-up.

"There's a healthy dose of just thinking it's gross, but yes, it's also religious."

I glance at the tattoo on her right shoulder, a portrait of Mary, and the cross on her left forearm. "Is that a problem for you?"

"I've made my peace with it. I could never convince them though."

"But maybe you could, Brooklyn."

She shakes her head. "Look, I know they're nice to you, and that's confusing, but they can tell themselves you're not their business. If it was me, the fucking sky would fall. I'd never see or talk to them again. They can never know, Eden. I thought you understood that."

I nod and drop it before I push her too far. I knew this was going to be hard, but I haven't accepted that it could be forever.

When we arrive at the gym, we park on the street. There's the buzz of a gathering by the front.

"What the fuck is this?" Brooklyn asks.

As we walk up, a guy with short spikey black hair comes at us holding out a microphone.

"Brooklyn, when are we going to see you fight again?"

Brooklyn looks thrown as two more people beeline toward us, armed with microphones. "After your last victory, is it safe to say the problem was your brother wasn't a qualified coach? Can you give us a few words on why Miss Bauer is better?" Shock and anger flash over her face.

I step forward before she clocks the guy. "Théo Shaw is a gifted coach and still part of this team. You guys know better than to just show up here. You know the process to schedule an interview."

A woman with chestnut hair wearing an awful brown blazer stretches her mic toward me. "Can you confirm rumors that you two have become an item?"

"What?"

"Can you—"

"What the fuck are you even talking about?" I'm afraid to hesitate even a little. I have no idea how Brooklyn will react. The woman holds out a couple of pictures of me and Brooklyn from New Mexico, one of me checking out her cut eyebrow, one of us leaving the club together. They're fairly tender photos, but not even close to being something you could call evidence.

"There's been talk," she goes on, a little sheepishly. "And it looks like you just arrived together."

Brooklyn starts to walk toward the woman, stiff and ready to rip her a new one. I stretch my arm in front of her as subtly as possible.

"This is a close-knit team," I say. "We train at least four hours a day plus sauna, ice baths, trail runs, you name it. Of course, we're together a lot. You print some bullshit clickbait you can forget ever getting an interview again. If you want to do this properly, I suggest you leave now and call to set up an appointment like everyone else."

I walk past them without waiting for an answer. Brooklyn follows, and I lock the door behind us with them on the other side of the glass looking crestfallen.

"Do *not* let them in," I snap as I pass Laila. Brooklyn and I don't even look at each other until we're in the training room in back, which only has windows around the top foot of the left wall, a space only meant to light the room that offers no view. I face Brooklyn and find every ounce of panic I expected to see.

"Don't freak out."

"How the fuck can I not freak out?" she says. "What does she mean there's been talk? Who did you tell?"

"She made that up. They've got nothing."

"How do you know?"

"Because if she had something, she would have printed it. She's fishing."

"Who knows about us?" Brooklyn asks, not calming down at all.

"No one."

"Oh, come on, who'd you tell?" Brooklyn's eyes flash with anger. "One of your buddies sold you out."

"Brooklyn," I snap. "No one fucking knows. I haven't told a soul. I swear."

"This is too dangerous." Her hands fly to her head as she paces.

"Brooklyn, I'm out, and you look gay. I'm sorry, but you're an easy read. They're just taking a stab that the two lesbians who work together also hook up. Think about it. They've asked you shit like this before. You're just letting this one get in your head because they happen to be right."

She finally starts to slow down. "Really?"

"Yes," I say with confidence. "Blow this off like you always do. Don't act weird or they really will know."

"What are those idiots doing here?"

Brooklyn and I each leap about two feet when Théo waltzes into the room.

"Whoa, sorry." He laughs.

"How did you get in?" I ask.

"Laila. Are you two okay? You look weird."

"Fine," Brooklyn says.

He sets down his gym bag and starts fishing through it. "Okay, well, get it together. We've got training to do."

Brooklyn and I hold tenuous eye contact, neither of us ready to stop talking, but shackled.

"Don't worry." I answer him, but I'm looking at Brooklyn. "We're good."

CHAPTER TWENTY-FOUR

The car jumps forward, then rocks back to a stop. The rumble of the engine feels good to my nerves even though traffic is relentlessly slow. I'm not usually the road rage type, but I'm not quite back to normal after the reporter issue from yesterday, or to put it more directly, Brooklyn's not back to normal.

Our entire training session was lackluster, her mind clearly gone and mine not much better. Théo wouldn't so much as go to the bathroom, so we never got to talk it out. Her texts after she left were calm and agreeable, but distant.

"You're nervous," Jin says. I glance over and nod. Today is hopefully my last appointment for my neck, a full evaluation on how it's healed. It's reason enough to be nervous, but that isn't it. I force myself to ease up on the aggressive driving.

"Brooklyn will do right by you," Jin says.

I whip around to stare at him. "What did you say?"

He chuckles and looks out the window before he meets my eyes, still wearing a knowing, affectionate smile.

"How?" I throw my hands up. "How can you possibly know? I just swore up and down no one knows, and here you are, knowing." The night she came over after his hospital visit flashes through my mind, but it wasn't so obvious he should be *this* confident, was it?

"You're my family," he says. "We live in the same building, and I've seen you every day for more than half of your life. You think I don't see when something changes?"

I sigh and shake my head. "What did you see?"

He shrugs. "I saw nothing, and I saw everything."

I shake my head, but I'm relieved he knows, even if his conclusion is characteristically vague. She'll do right by me. What does that mean? Or is that the point? She'll leave or she'll stay, and either way will be right.

"I wish her family could just see like that," I say. "Preferably a decade ago."

"The pieces will move without your interference."

I pull into the hospital parking lot and swoop into an empty space, then turn in my seat to face him.

"She won't risk her family for me. When the pieces start moving too much, she's going to break my heart." It hurts just thinking about it.

"She's a fool if she does."

I shake my head. "She just loves them."

"She knows you aren't the problem. Have faith in her."

God, I want to, but that sounds like emotional suicide. It'll be hard enough to lose Brooklyn if I see it coming. If I let myself believe she'll stand by me it will obliterate me.

He puts his hand on my knee. "She will rise if you believe in her."

Jin has a beautiful way of seeing the world, but the child in me remembers how fruitless it was to have faith in my mom, to wait and starve when I should have found a way out of that house and helped my damn self. That's what I'm good at. Helping myself. Helping others, too, but not waiting. Not trusting. What is there to trust? She's made no promises.

"Let's get inside."

He sits in the waiting room while they do their scans and measurements. Once they're done, they let him in to wait with me for the results. Six months of recovery. It feels like a lifetime, and like nothing at all. I feel better than I ever expected to, but I can also believe a nasty punch in the wrong spot could still take it all away. That's what they've been saying, which isn't comforting as a professional martial artist's coach and main sparring partner. Brooklyn has grown exponentially in her control and care. She doesn't take stupid risks anymore, for herself or me, but that doesn't change the fact that it's a contact sport. Am I tempting fate? The door finally opens as the doctor knocks.

"Well, Eden, let's take a look," he says. Dr. Crowe is a thousand times more positive than the ER doctor who promised me the worst, but he hasn't been a barrel of sunshine either. "You've healed beautifully. Phenomenally, really. I'm sure that's thanks to you being so healthy."

"So, I can coach full time?" I ask. "I can spar?" I'm already doing both, but he doesn't know that.

"It's as safe for you as the next person. I'll clear you to get back to competition."

Jin and I lock eyes. Dr. Crowe doesn't seem to realize competing isn't something I had on the table for myself.

"I can compete?" I ask. "Like, full contact?"

"Yep. You healed properly, have your muscle strength back, posture looks good. I see no reason to keep you from what you do. Send over the papers any time. I'm happy to sign."

I walk back to the car in silence. It's like I'm walking through space, floating and falling at once. I don't know what to make of this lack of emotion, or maybe it's every emotion, which makes them all meaningless. I'm relieved, but also afraid. A piece of me isn't quite buying all this.

It's one thing saying you don't want to compete when you can't anyway. It's another doing it now. Part of me feels the need to rise, to overcome, but I'm suspicious that has more to do with concern over the way people see me than what I really want.

I've built a new life already, one I love. If my first doctor hadn't been so negative, would I have done this differently? Would I have done it at all? Brooklyn and I certainly wouldn't be what we are, and as much as I miss the action, the heat, the thrill of finding out how deep your will runs, I've done all that, and I wouldn't give up what I have now for it.

"I'm not going back," I say once Jin closes his door. "I can't. I'm Brooklyn's coach. I promised her. We talked about this before we started. I can't do that to her."

He nods. "What do you feel?"

"I…" I stare out across the parking lot at the deep gray asphalt against the deep blue sky, a string of pigeons parting directions. "I'm fine. I already made peace with not competing. I like coaching."

"It's rewarding," he agrees. "You have an excellent mind for it." Jin knows this transition as well as I do. He went through it himself.

"I'm not going to tell anyone about this," I say. "They'll try to make me come back. I'm sending over my retirement. It's time to make it official."

"Be sure," he says.

"What do you mean?"

"You won't be able to compete forever, Eden. Imagine it every way it can go and make sure your heart isn't heavy with regret. There's no worse feeling."

If I stay out for Brooklyn and she leaves me, will I wish I'd gone back? That's the scenario I imagine he means. It would complicate my feelings. I can't pretend it wouldn't, but I want something richer than glory now, deeper than fame or gold or achievement. I want the look of joy on Mateo's face when Brooklyn made him chocolate chip pancakes. I want training sessions that go deep into the night and turn into horseplay and belly laughs. I want the bond of talking my martial artists through the fire when they're afraid they're not enough. I want to watch my students feel strong for the first time in their lives. I went pro to represent Emerald Tiger, to honor Jin. I've done that. Now I want to come home.

CHAPTER TWENTY-FIVE

The entryway of the dojang where students take off their shoes is packed with seven- and eight-year-olds, probably the most challenging age group, but also one of the most fun.

"One minute!" I warn them, and they all spring onto the mat. Just as I'm about to call them to attention, the front door swings open so hard it slams into the bench next to it, and I cringe, half expecting it to break. The bells rattle and a breeze rushes in. Brooklyn is standing in the frame with white-hot fury in her eyes. She steps toward the mat. I can't imagine she intends to scream at me in front of my class, but that's exactly what it looks like.

"Laila," I say. She reads the situation with wide eyes and takes my place as I step off the mat to meet Brooklyn before she gets any farther.

"You're coming back to defend the belt? Are you fucking kidding me?"

"Brooklyn!" I flash my attention to the kids just ten feet away.

"You're unbelie—"

"Not here," I say between my teeth and walk out the front door. If she wants to do this, she'll have to follow me. I walk around the building, then in the back door to the backmost, vacant student room. I turn in and close the door before I finally face her.

"Have you lost your mind? You can't act like that around them."

"That's all you have to say to me?"

"I don't even know what you're talking about. You just come in here freaking out?"

"You said you wouldn't do this shit. We talked about this. This is exactly what I was worried about. Everyone thought you were above it, but here you are. You spend months figuring me out, seeing everything there is to know, changing everything about the way I work, and then suddenly your neck is all better? Just in time to rematch me for the belt and make me look like a complete jackass? Fuck you, Eden."

It's like getting sucked up into a tornado and whipped through a house. Just as I was getting my bearings, the "fuck you" rips away my equilibrium.

"Fuck me?"

"What'd you think it was going to be, Eden?"

"I *thought* you would know me better than this by now, or that maybe you'd ask me if it's true before you flip the fuck out. Where'd you read this shit, TMZ? Is that what we're doing?"

"I know it's true, Eden. I have a fight offer sitting in my email right now. Is this what you meant when you said a better fight was going to come along soon? *This* is why you wouldn't let me sign with Karinov?"

"Wh—" I stop myself to rub my eyes and gather myself. "Brooklyn, please, for the love of God, listen to me." I pause to see if she's paying attention at all, and she is. I speak slowly and deliberately. "I have no idea what the fuck you are talking about."

Now she's the one who looks spun as she examines me. "I got a fight offer this morning for the title. Against you."

"Did you bother to check for my signature? Because it's not there." If it went anything like her last fight offer, she probably hasn't even seen it. Samson manages her, and I can't help but wonder if he created this conflict on purpose. Did he get word the reporters were asking about Brooklyn and me? Did he want to blow up the arrangement? Brooklyn's stunned face confirms she hasn't seen it herself.

"You're telling me you had nothing whatsoever to do with this?"

"Zero," I say. "I didn't offer you that fight, Brooklyn, and I would never take it. The matchmakers just want to see it. My manager probably agreed to float it by me and they put together an offer, but it means nothing. I say no and this goes away. I would have done it already, but I had an early class and haven't touched base with Taylor yet."

She's much calmer, but her body is still taut with tension. "Why would the matchmakers randomly think you're coming back?"

I sigh. "I went to a follow-up doctor's appointment yesterday. They said I can fight if I want." Her face lights up to respond, but I power on before she can. "*But* I'm not coming back. Not to fight you or anyone else. I didn't even want anyone to know. I don't even understand how they do. I should sue the shit out of that hospital for giving out my information."

"You're serious, aren't you?" Brooklyn's face finally softens.

"Yes."

"Jesus." She takes a breath. "You probably signed something allowing the hospital to release your shit to the UFC so they can cover the bill. That's how they found out you're cleared."

She's right, and I should have seen it coming, but I'm too rattled to switch to casual talk so abruptly. She picks up on it and steps closer, taking my hand in hers.

"I'm sorry," she says. "I should've asked you. I just thought you were screwing with me this whole time, and I kind of lost it."

"You thought I had some scheme all along? What, to spy on you? Teach you bad moves? Mess with your heart?"

"Believe me, I realize how stupid that sounds now."

"Brooklyn, I would never do something like that to you."

She looks down. "I know. I'm sorry."

"I don't think you do know. I *love* you, Brooklyn." It comes out so naturally it takes me a second to realize what I just did. Brooklyn freezes. My stomach drops as the silence builds. I don't need to hear it back. I barely even meant to say it, but it's true, and it's too late.

"You can't love me, Eden." Of all the things she could've said, I didn't expect that. "I can't tell my family about you."

"I didn't ask you to."

"Not just now, but you have, and you will again. You ask me every time you look in my eyes." She touches my cheek.

The tenderness of the gesture mixed with what she's saying is so confusing I have to pull away to hear her.

"Come on, Eden. You need that. I can see that you need it. And I am so sorry, but I can't give it to you. I shouldn't have let this go so far."

Even when she burst through the door in a rage, I never guessed this conversation would end up anywhere near here. I knew it may happen someday at either of our hands, but not so soon. It's like she's knocked the wind out of me. I can't even speak. She shouldn't have let it go so far? What was *supposed* to happen? She just wanted to work me out of her system?

"You should just forget retirement," she says. "Maybe we should do the fight after all."

"Are you fucking crazy?" I snap. "I'm not going to fight you."

"It's just business, Eden. You deserve your career back. You don't owe it to me to stay retired."

"You were just screaming at me about this and now you want me to do it?"

"I was screaming because I thought you lied to me. I'm not mad at the idea. I don't want to hold you back. I've been sick for months about hurting you and screwing up your life. Now we can make it right. I'm not going to mess it up for you again. I can't let you give this up for me. Please just come back."

"I don't want to come back, Brooklyn. I want what I have now." Had half an hour ago anyway.

"Of course you want to come back."

"Do I seem like the kind of person who doesn't know what she wants to you?"

"You're a champion, Eden. That doesn't just go away. It's still your belt. No one could take it from you, and you can still defend it."

"Fuck the belt. What is it with you and the stupid belt? There's more to life, Brooklyn."

"Yeah, easy for someone who has it to say."

"Believe me, I wish I didn't." I turn away, raging with the question of whether or not she would even like me if I wasn't a champion. Does she measure people the same way her father does? "Do you really want to punch me in the face, Brooklyn?"

She rolls her eyes. "Of course not."

"Then what are we talking about? Think about this."

"It's not real, Eden. It's just competition. It's just our sport. We do it in training all the time."

"Not even close to the same." It's not just that we don't go full contact in training, sometimes we do come close. But in training, when someone's hurt, you back off. In competition, that's your cue to go harder. I can't do that to her anymore. But more importantly, in training I'm not trying to pry her dreams from her fingertips.

"It just makes sense, Eden," she says. "It'd be the fight of both our careers."

"Oh my God."

"What?"

"Oh, Jesus, I just got it." I feel sick. "*You* want the fight. You don't want me to have my career back. You don't want it for me, you want it for you. You want your loss back."

"I do want it for you."

"No, you want to win the belt, and you want to win it from me for your stupid legacy."

"Eden…"

I can barely look at her. I'm on the edge of breaking down, and I can't stand to let her see it. I turn back abruptly.

"You want the fight, Brooklyn, you can have it, but don't think winning is going to make you feel good enough for them. You're still going to know in your heart they don't accept you."

I leave her standing there. Hot tears roll down my face as I blast outside and down the street, putting as much distance between us as I can with each stride.

CHAPTER TWENTY-SIX

Taylor and the matchmakers all apologize when I chew them out for mentioning a potential fight to an opponent before even feeling out if I wanted to come back first, particularly since they know Brooklyn and I work together now. It's true Taylor wouldn't be much of a manager if he shut down a fight this huge without at least trying to talk me into it, but there was no reason to send it out to Brooklyn before I'd shown viable interest. They do say they're sorry, scramble to toss the blame around, hit all the notes of a good apology, but they clearly don't grasp how much it's messed with my life.

It goes a lot like our conversation about my first match with Brooklyn. It's what everyone wants to see. The sales will be enormous. It'll be the fight of the year. Only now the numbers will be that much bigger after our first encounter and my quasi-retirement.

I give up the idea that anyone will understand. My world is one of elite competition with absolute studs. Not one of them can wrap their head around the idea that this is anything other than a dream for me. Any one of them would kill for a rivalry that brings in half the attention Brooklyn and I seem to. It strikes a little doubt. It's not like me to lead with the heart, and it's not like Brooklyn to lead with cold hard numbers. Maybe that means she's right.

I pull up the fight contract that's been in my email for three days. Brooklyn's signature showed up yesterday. I wish I could take comfort that she hesitated, but I suspect it was only for my benefit.

Brooklyn cares about her career first through ninety-ninth, then whatever's left. How can I be so surprised?

I have the power to take away an opportunity that means everything to her. She can not only be the champion, but go on to be the best ever, something she thinks is impossible so long as her loss to me is unanswered. She can defeat "the best." I can't bear to think of myself that way, but that's what they'll say if she does it, which seems likely since she's already shattered me. No one can make you fight, but I can't take this from her.

I click to fill in my signature boxes and finalize the document. It's real now. Just days ago, Brooklyn and I were wrapped in each other's arms sharing all of ourselves. Now I suspect the next time I see her, it will be with gloves on, trying to stop her from getting everything I want her to have.

I send a text to Jin and Laila to meet in the MMA room in ten minutes. I don't have to say it's urgent. I never talk to them like that. When I go to meet them ten minutes later, they're waiting for me with concerned faces. I'm sure they've heard the buzz, but I haven't talked about it.

"Brooklyn and I are fighting for the belt in three months. I need your help."

Laila's eyes go wide. "I thought those were just rumors."

"So did I."

"She really wants to do this? Who's going to coach her?"

"I'm sure Théo will. And it's a title shot. Of course, she wants it."

"But after all you've done for her?"

"I haven't done her any favors," I say. "This was all business to help her career. This is the best thing for her career now."

Laila looks equal parts concerned and confused. If I didn't know better, I'd say she knows about me and Brooklyn too. Secrets are never as secret as you think. "So, *you* want this?" she asks.

I keep my voice dead and measured. "I'm ready to move on from competition. This will be my last fight. It's just as well it's a massive one. It'll be a payday that means the gym never worries about money again. We can run it exactly how we want, take care of our kids. We could even expand it, make enough room for a full facility, redo the student housing and scholarship them out to people in need. Like Mateo."

Jin squeezes my shoulder. "And Brooklyn?"

"She made her choice. We're competitors again. We won't see her here anymore, and yes, it sucks, but I can't have her breaking my neck again. We're going to train hard. You'll be my corner?"

"Of course," Laila says.

Jin doesn't answer. He's deep in thought, and he somehow looks closer to no than yes. I can't imagine training without Jin, nor can I imagine him turning me away.

"Jin?"

"If we train, we train to win, not to survive. If you fight without heart, you'll get hurt. I won't take part in that."

He doesn't trust me to really go after Brooklyn, and he doesn't trust her not to really come after me. I know exactly how he feels.

"I understand," I say.

"And?"

"We fight to win."

He studies me, looking skeptical.

"If she'd rather fight me than work with me, that's exactly what we'll do." I know he switches out "work with" with "be with" easily enough.

He nods. "When it hurts, we train harder. I'll make the schedule. Today, ten rounds on the bag with a mile run after each. You have two and a half hours."

It's an aggressive first exercise, but I never got back to competition shape since my neck. I'm fit, very fit even, but not nearly fit enough. He's right to hit hard. His time window allows for ten-minute miles between five-minute rounds, not a particularly fast pace, but by round four it'll feel like it is.

I'm already in sweatpants and a hoodie, so I move to complete his task without ceremony. I wrap my hands and put on gloves while he sets up a timer, then step up to the heavy bag and hit it with a hard, crisp combo that rattles the chain. It's not good practice to just start wailing on the bag without loosening up first, but damn does it feel good. I throw a kick and receive a thunderous smack that fills the room as a reward. My body reacts with a shot of energy, elation even. I go after that bag as hard as I can and let Brooklyn pass in and out of my mind as she pleases. It hurts, but every twinge of pain also makes me feel stronger. I know this person. She's lonely and hurt and a little battered, but she's a fucking savage. She's the person I made when people let me down, and I need her now.

CHAPTER TWENTY-SEVEN

I throw myself into training in a way even I never have. Everyone takes notice, the students, Laila, Jin, the guys at both my Muay Thai and Jiu-Jitsu gyms as I've started spending two hours at each every day on top of everything else. Training with Brooklyn has made me exceptionally better at Brazilian Jiu-Jitsu. I can throw around people who used to have their way with me. Soon the reporters are finding creative ways to get pictures. I've always been private about my training, haven't wanted others to know how prepared I am and for what, but I don't care if Brooklyn sees. I want her to know I'm not still some injured little bird.

The speculation runs wild, that we hate each other again, that I want revenge, that Brooklyn betrayed me by leaving my school, that I betrayed her by coming back to fight, that Théo and I couldn't get along, that I'm training so hard because I'm afraid, that Brooklyn needs to be afraid because she doesn't understand how hard I'm training, and yes, even that we're secretly lovers with theories both that we're together still and that we've split. All the buzz means we're on track for the kind of viewership everyone wanted. I wonder how Brooklyn is handling people poking their noses so close to the truth, but the nice part is I don't have to care. It'd be a lie to say I don't, but I find moments where I can file it under "not my problem," and it feels good when they come.

I'm not pushing so hard because I'm afraid, though I am a little, or because I'm mad at her, though that's there too. I spend all my time training because when you can get deep enough, when you can work so hard your body descends through pain and into something else, your mind peels back and a vast sky of peace settles on you like falling snow. It doesn't hurt anymore. My heart feels mended because there is no Eden Bauer, and every time she comes back, I'm off for more.

In just a couple of weeks, my body transforms. I'm stronger and faster and can go not just longer, but harder than I ever have, and my real fight camp hasn't even started yet.

I trot to a stop in front of Emerald Tiger, just shy of fifteen miles after spending all morning running. I'm about to go around the block to round it off, but I notice Mateo sitting on the mats inside, alone, and open the door instead.

"Mateo?" It's two in the afternoon, an exceptionally dead time of day with no classes scheduled soon. "You okay?"

He nods but looks sad. Finally, I piece together that it's Thursday. He's here for his Jiu-Jitsu lesson with Brooklyn, who isn't going to show. His disappointed face is crushing. I walk over and sit next to him.

"I'm so sorry, Mateo. I forgot to tell you—"

Rattling bells cut me off, and Brooklyn is standing in the doorway in shorts and a sleeveless shirt, looking a little breathless and infuriatingly gorgeous. The shock of seeing her makes it impossible to come up with anything to say.

"I'm so sorry," Brooklyn finally says. "I wasn't sure if I should—"

"You should." I stand and back away, remembering I'm absolutely soaked in sweat from my run and too flustered to trust myself with conversation. "Have a good class."

"Eden."

I'm already almost to the door to the back even though I'm covering the distance mostly by way of awkward, stumbling backward steps. I wave her off, gesturing between her and Mateo, trying to force her attention to him where it belongs, but she keeps chasing me across the mats and catches me at the door.

"I'm sorry," she says again. "I didn't mean to just drop in on you. I tried calling like six times to ask what you want me to do."

"I wasn't here. I went on a run."

"I see that." Her eyes move over me, taking in my sweaty racerback tank top and tracing over my chest and arms, wandering like she just can't control herself. It sends a maddening lightning bolt of stimulation through me, but I push it violently from my mind.

"Wow," Brooklyn finally says. "You look good."

This isn't the tone I expected from our first conversation since splitting up. It's almost like it didn't happen. She's just here, being thoughtful with Mateo and looking at me like her clothes are going to burn off of her skin, and damn it, are those my weaknesses. That doesn't mean I forgot the last weeks.

"Your body, I mean," she says, then scrunches her face at her own comment. "Your abs. Arms. Muscle. Fuck, you know what I mean."

I want to laugh or say something flirtatious, but I can't. Brooklyn isn't mine. It's only painful to play at it.

"Thanks." She looks good too, but that's nothing new. Even when I didn't know her as anything other than the woman who talked shit about me all the time, her body demanded notice.

"You must be hitting it really hard, huh?" she asks.

I shrug. "Of course. You didn't expect me not to, did you?"

"No," she says quickly. "No, I know Eden Bauer, record holding champ, doesn't play around."

She's obviously trying to be nice, but it just reminds me of what's important to Brooklyn, and my anger flares. "Just go enjoy your session." I turn to walk away, but she speaks again in a hurried string of words like she's using them to lasso me before I can escape.

"Can we be friends?" she asks. "This fight doesn't mean I want to hurt you or that I don't care about you. It's just bus—"

"It's not just business, Brooklyn. We're competing, but this isn't fucking tennis. We get in a cage and try our hardest to hurt the other person badly enough they can't continue. That's what we just signed on for, and it's not a joke. It's not a game."

She looks a little stunned and somber. "I've never heard you talk about it that way before. You're everything that's beautiful about martial arts. What's all this cage and blood stuff?"

"It's reality." She's right. I've always known the dangers, but I've never seen this as malicious or barbaric. I don't know if it was getting hurt so badly or falling for Brooklyn that's made it all so different.

"But you've fought people you knew before. Friends, training partners. Right?" she asks.

"Yes."

"Why do we have to be so different?"

"You know why."

"Even people you didn't know or like, you were always respectful at least." Something vulnerable floods her eyes.

"I respect you, Brooklyn."

"But you don't want to be my friend." She says it flat, with no question in her voice.

"You know what I want." It comes out with more snap than I intended. I feel so naked letting her have the benefit of the present tense. Of course, I *want* to be her friend, but you can't remotely describe my feelings for her with that word.

"You know I wish things were different," she says.

I try to dissect what that means, exactly, before deciding it doesn't actually mean anything. It means in a perfect world that gives her anything she wants, I'd be somewhere on the list, but in a real world that requires choices and action, I don't make the cut.

"Mateo is setting a record for the most patient kid ever," I say. "Go do your lesson."

"Eden." Frustration bubbles up in her voice as I turn for the door again. I look back, exasperated because I can't keep this up much longer. There's a pained look in her eyes that makes it feel like I'm breathing broken glass, and I want to make it stop, but I can't. We're already doing it her way. What does she want from me? She can't possibly think trying to be friends is going to make it easier or that it won't end with us right back in bed.

"What, Brooklyn?" My voice comes out quiet and soft, the only way I can keep it from shaking. I hold her gaze even though it's burning me up inside. All of our closeness is right there showing in her raw eyes, and at the same time, she's across the ocean and drifting farther away every day. The silence is agonizing, but I wait. She has nothing to say, not really. No plan, just a feeling.

"I'm sorry," she finally says.

I just sigh, exhausted. "Do what you gotta do, Brooklyn."

This time she lets me go. I can still feel her on the other side of the door as I stand there in the dark. A few minutes later, I hear Mateo's musical laugh.

CHAPTER TWENTY-EIGHT

Mateo doesn't live far, but I opt to drive. It feels unprofessional not to. Brooklyn's visit rattled me in a way only she seems to be capable of, but if there's anything that can shove her out of my mind, it's this. Mateo's father's name is Eddy, and after weeks of trying, I finally got him to agree to meet with me. Even when I assured him Mateo was far from in trouble, he seemed convinced I couldn't possibly have good news.

Everything I know about Eddy makes me picture something in the realm of my own childhood, but I try to hold out the possibility he could be a better guy than it seems. My stomach knots when I pull up outside. He could be offended by my proposal. What if he doesn't even want Mateo coming back to Emerald Tiger after this and I just make everything worse?

I walk up and knock with my heart in my throat. The door swings open and a thin, shirtless man answers with a cigarette in his mouth. He looks like he's in his fifties, but I suspect it's a result of the way he lives more than real age.

"You're the instructor?" His voice sounds like an engine chewing something up.

"Yes, my name is Eden. It's nice to meet you, Mr. Perez."

He squints before he turns and walks back inside. "Come on."

The house is still a mess, but that's no shock in a home with boys. He shoves clothes off the couch to make room to sit. It feels a little strange to sit beside him, but there aren't any other chairs.

"He break something?" Eddy asks, a repeat question from our talk on the phone.

"No, Mateo is very well behaved."

He chuckles and taps his cigarette on a plastic white ashtray that looks like it was stolen from a restaurant. I can't remember the last time I was even in a room that smelled so strongly of stale smoke.

"Then what's this about?"

"I'm not sure how much Mateo has told you about the school, but we teach Taekwondo and mixed martial arts. It used to be fairly common for schools to have living facilities for their most dedicated students, a little like dorm rooms."

I expect him to pick up on where this is going and react, but he doesn't.

"You don't see it much anymore," I go on. "But we do have four rooms like that at Emerald Tiger, and we're beginning a renovation soon to make them nicer. We're planning to offer three of them to some of our students we think would be good candidates. I wanted to talk to you about the possibility of Mateo being one of them."

"So, like a boarding school for Karate?"

I smile, relieved his first reaction isn't that I'm insane. "Yes, that's a great way to put it. I know it would be difficult not to have him here, but we're just up the road."

"I don't have money for something like that."

"Oh, no," I say. "It wouldn't cost you anything. It's more like a scholarship. We would provide his meals and room. He would be expected to help out, but they'd be tasks similar to standard chores. As he gets a little older and more advanced, he'd start helping teach the beginner classes."

"So, what? You think Mateo is going to be the next Mike Tyson or something?" His raised eyebrow and curled lip communicate how far-fetched he thinks that is. He's right that the arrangement I'm proposing is more generous than the traditional ones, and such offers usually go to the phenoms.

"I think he could be a talented martial artist and patient instructor. He has character."

"You'll feed him?"

"Yes."

"And he sleeps there?"

"As often as he wants. We can arrange for him to come home on weekends or something similar if you like."

"No, take him."

It's so abrupt it takes me a second to process. "The renovations are scheduled to be finished in three months. If you'd like a tour—"

He starts laughing a breathy, silent laugh. "Is it going to be worse than this?" He motions around the apartment.

That's an awkward question to answer, but I just power through it. "No."

"I didn't even know he did Taekwondo, but if you want him, take him."

It's jarring to hear him say it that way. Take him. Like he's an object. Even though I knew it was unlikely, I hoped to find a loving family just on hard times here, but Eddy doesn't care at all. Mateo is a burden, and the relief is all over his face. It makes me angry on Mateo's behalf, but I'm not going to argue when I've just gotten my way.

"I'll let you know when it's in order for him to move in."

As I leave, it hits me just how much this will turn my life upside down. I knew it was a big commitment, but this makes me all but a parent, and I haven't looked at it quite like that. I'm responsible for him now. That's scary, but Mateo deserves it. I can finally *really* help him. That's more important than any win in the octagon. This is Jin's legacy.

I'm so happy on the drive home it feels like sunlight is exploding out of me. As much as I've always wanted to duplicate what Jin did for me, a part of me always felt like we were a fluke. It's hard to imagine someone letting their kid go live at a Taekwondo dojang with someone they've never met. My mother only did it because she was strung out and couldn't stop me. Or maybe she did know and did care how dangerous our situation was. I've never entertained giving her any credit for letting me go.

I'm still riding high on my image of the future starting to become real, and I don't want to lose the momentum. I pick up my phone and dial Arlo. He answers on the first ring, a pleasant surprise given most people are afraid of the phone these days.

"Motherfuckin' Bauer," he says. "How the shit are you? Please tell me you're calling for tips on how to crush Shaw, because I've got them."

Just her name is enough to put a damper on my mood. That we would talk about the fight didn't even occur to me. How silly. I want to tell him no, but that's equally stupid. I need everything I can get to defeat Brooklyn, even though I don't love the idea of *defeating* her. I've taught her everything I know for months. Her early fears that I would hold information back or limit her in some way were beyond false. I gave her all I had, and she learned well. If she was a millimeter from beating me before, how the hell do I expect to even be competitive now?

"Not exactly, but do tell," I say.

"Kicks all day, girl. She's going to be terrified of them after last time."

My stomach turns thinking of kicking Brooklyn in the head again. It hit me with a nasty dose of dread the first time I knocked her out with a kick, and I didn't love her then. I didn't even like her.

"Fancy kicks," he says.

"Fancy?" Taekwondo is full of fancy kicks because their tournament rules forbid punches to the head, meaning people had to master the use of their legs, so I can do fancy, but you mostly only see the basics in MMA.

"Yeah, remember how she used to always talk shit about how you were so technical and in your head like it was a bad thing?" he says. "You're fancy. When you fight it's beautiful. It's over her head, and it scares her. If you go in there and throw a few wicked fast, high level techniques, she's going to remember you're the elite of the elite, and she's a brawler. She'll start backing up."

I remember Brooklyn calling herself "a brawler" at Emerald Tiger and telling her she's more just seconds before our first kiss. Even the memory of it makes a shiver crawl over me. Arlo's right. That is how she thinks of herself, and she's insecure about it. If I can make her feel that way, it'll give me an edge, but the idea of intentionally making Brooklyn feel less-than makes me sick. Her soft spots that I found out about in intimate moments can't be fair game. Then again, Arlo figured it out easily enough, so maybe it is.

"Thanks."

He laughs. "What, have a million people already told you that?"

"No, why?"

"Because you're so clearly not into it. It's gold, I swear."

"Sorry, Arlo, I know it is. It's just weird for me. I'm still getting used to the idea of competing with her again."

"Roger that. You'll get used to it real fast when she's trying to take your head off in there. Don't forget what I said, huh? And don't let her get her hands on you. Don't clinch with her."

"Thanks, Arlo. I hear you."

"So, if you're not calling for my wisdom, what can I do for you? You just miss me?"

I wish he was here so I could hug him. "I do miss you. And I did call for your wisdom. I'm expanding and renovating Emerald Tiger. I'm buying the space next to us so we can have a full MMA side."

He whistles. "Look at you finally spending some money."

"Yes, sir, a lot of it. I'm calling because I want to offer a full MMA curriculum. People don't want to have to go to more than one gym. I need a Jiu-Jitsu coach. A good one."

"And you're looking for recommendations?"

"I'm looking for you," I say, my pulse picking up. "I know you have a life out there and your own coach and all that, but you're always talking about wanting to come back to the States. You were an incredible coach to me for my fight with Brooklyn, and we get along. What do you think? I do the striking. You do the grappling?"

It feels like the silence goes on in an endless expanse. I even look at my phone to make sure he's still connected.

"Not so much, huh?" I don't want to let him off the hook so easily, but it seems like the decent thing to do.

"I'm sorry, Eden," he finally says. I roll my eyes and sigh. "I love you to death, girl, and I'm beyond honored. I'm just running out of time to get a title. I'm close right now, but if I screw up, it's over. I can't afford to switch teams or be distracted right now."

Jesus, what a familiar sentiment. "Okay," I say. "I get it."

"I'm sorry."

He sounds so upset I force myself to be more upbeat when I answer him. "No, don't be. The gym isn't going anywhere. Maybe later."

"I'd love that."

"All right, I have to run." The end of the call is abrupt, but he doesn't fight it. I hit the end button and lean back in my seat. I'm already parked at the gym, but I can't bring myself to move yet. I try to turn my attention back to the huge win I just had with Mateo's dad, but this still stings. I need a Brazilian Jiu-Jitsu coach, and I had myself convinced Arlo would do it, that the whole picture was going to magically fall into place just because of how perfect it looked to me. But then, Arlo isn't the perfect picture, is he? Letting myself imagine it makes my entire being ache for what I can't have, but it's a truth that's screaming in my face. My Brazilian Jiu-Jitsu coach should so clearly be Brooklyn.

CHAPTER TWENTY-NINE

Jin has a demeanor that is both hard and soft. He's kind and nurturing but also demanding and intolerant of weakness, especially weakness of will, and I've run his patience dry. It's been a long time since I've been on the wrong end of Jin's skills, but he's using them now to take me to task in a most unforgiving way.

The sharp, hard ridge of his shin slips under my elbow and impacts my ribs so hard it racks my entire body and folds me nearly in half before I can recover and stand up straight. I wheeze in a flaming breath, aware the grimace I can't control won't do me any favors. His right fist is already on the way, and I get my hand up so late I don't get a strong enough frame to stop him. My block folds, and I end up punching myself in the face.

I try to circle out, but he's a master of footwork. He cuts off my angle by switching his stance and spears me with a front kick to the solar plexus that puts me on the mat. Even as I gasp for air that won't come, I expect him to jump on top of me and shower me with head shots, but he finally stops, not out of mercy, but anger. It's all over his face. He circles the mat with tension all through his rigid body. When he turns back and sees that I'm still down, he looks even angrier.

"Breathe," he demands. Like I'm not trying. Finally, my diaphragm calms down enough I can suck in a gulp of air and force myself back to my feet. My arms feel like they weigh a thousand pounds. Just holding them up takes every ounce of effort in my body, but fear of the next shot I'll take if I don't is enough that I can fight through it. Jin makes a swatting motion through the air and shakes his head.

"It's no use with you right now," he says. Laila tentatively approaches with a water bottle when she sees we're stopping, but I can't bring myself to take it. You have to earn water, and I haven't.

"I can continue," I say, even as my body screams.

"For what?" he snaps. "You're not here."

"I am here, Sah Boo Nim."

The affectionate term translates to "teaching father," and it softens him up just a little. He walks up to me until he's very close, making me aware of how tall he is, as tall as I am, and fit as a man in his twenties.

"Your problem is in here." He puts his palm over my heart. "I warned you that you should not do this unless you were ready to win."

"I am ready," I say, even as tears start to tickle my eyes, but he shakes his head.

"We're done here." He walks away.

"Jin." My voice cracks. Jesus, Eden, don't fucking *cry*. It's a cardinal sin in the gym. But we're just a week from the fight and my coach, my father, the man who made me everything I am is so disappointed he's walking away at the eleventh hour. "Jin!" I yell in a rage as he leaves the room without even looking back. I turn and kick the bag as hard as I can, sinking into it so solidly even the sturdy heavy bag indents and swings away like it's light. Pain rips through my side where Jin hit me with the same kick, burning through me hot enough I wonder if he cracked some ribs. The pain says yes, but Jin is a master. He doesn't break you unless he means to, and no matter how angry he is with me, he'd never break me a week from a fight.

I pace as I fume and kick the bag with everything I have again, ignoring the pain, then punch it with equal effort. I don't care about form. I wind up like I'm in a batting cage. All I'm after is the satisfaction of causing damage. Laila slips next to me between blows and wraps her arms around my shoulders, pinning my arms to my sides gently but firmly. I'm just exhausted enough to let her.

"You're going to hurt yourself," she says.

"I don't care."

"I know you don't," she says. "You need a break."

"Fuck a break."

"Please take a break with me," she says. "Then I'll train with you all night if you want."

When I finally look at her face and see all the compassion in her light brown eyes, a lump forms in my throat again, and I realize how fragile and fake this anger is. I nod, defeated, and she pulls me into a hug before she takes my hands and starts to free me of my gloves. She tosses them on the mat and I unravel my wraps, letting them fall in a pile instead of winding them back up properly. She takes my wrist and pulls me across the gym and to my room.

Laila's only been in here for a minute or two at a time, but it feels good and right that she's with me now. With Brooklyn and Jin both gone, she's all I have, but it doesn't feel like a stretch that she's filling this role. We've run this gym together for years now, seen each other at our best and worst, in our moments of glory and crumpled into a pale pile of failure. She's family. My students and my fighters are family. We go to battle together, and there's nothing stronger.

"Sit down." She gestures at the couch while she walks to my kitchen. I obey, and only in doing so do I realize how sore I am. My quads protest as I lift my feet onto the small wooden coffee table. Laila fishes around in my freezer and returns with ice packs, pressing them against my ribs and neck.

"Water." She nods at the water bottle I still haven't touched. After the first sip, I realize how badly I need it and chug most of it.

"Jin will be back," she says.

I shrug. "I don't know. I guess."

"Come on, now. You know better than to think he's just abandoning you."

"Awful close to the fight to be playing these games," I say.

"He's just worried about you, Eden. He doesn't want to see you hurt again. He was a mess when you were in the hospital after the last fight."

"Jin was a mess?" I raise an eyebrow at her.

She nods and pulls at her hair like she's afraid her spikes have flattened. "We all were. Even Brooklyn looked like a ghost."

"What?" I hiss. "Brooklyn?"

Laila looks like she's been caught. "Yeah. She was there for a while. You knew that, didn't you?"

I sigh. "No." I go to the kitchen, taking the ice packs with me, and pour myself a glass of Patrón. I hold the bottle up at Laila.

She smiles but hesitates, then finally makes a what the hell expression. "All right, Bauer. You're on." I pour her a glass and bring it out to the couch, sinking in beside her. Relaxation floods through my muscles with my first sip of tequila.

"You want to watch the fights?" I ask. There's a fight night programmed tonight, a smaller, non pay-per-view event. I've been training so much I've missed a lot of the recent events, but if we're pulling the plug on training, we may as well.

"Fuck yeah," she says. I open up my membership that allows me access, but before I can scroll to the fight, featured right at the top of the screen is an interview with Brooklyn with the header, "Shaw Speaks on Bauer Rematch." I cringe. It's probably been out for weeks. I've been avoiding media like the plague.

"Jesus."

Laila takes a sip of her tequila. The way she's leaned way back on the couch, lazily putting her weight on her upper back makes her look like she's a mile long. "Have you not seen it?"

I shake my head. "Is it awful?"

She shrugs. "No, but…"

"But what?"

"I don't know. I'm just not sure if it's a good idea for you to watch her."

I can't argue with that. "She call my first win a lucky shot?"

"No."

"Say I'm weak and broken?"

"No."

"That I'm—"

"You know what, go ahead and watch it," she says. I'm terrified of what Brooklyn might've said and what it'll do to my stitched together heart, but I click the interview before either of us can change our minds.

The screen opens straight to Brooklyn sitting in a tall folding chair with a giant print of our event poster behind her and a reporter with black hair and a fitted suit in a chair to her right. She looks incredible. I almost want to say better than ever, but that's probably my imagination. She's always been a showstopper with confidence that sets the room on fire.

"Brooklyn, I'm so glad to have a chance to talk to you about your upcoming bout with Eden Bauer. There are so many things we all want to know, so I'm going to just jump straight in and ask what it's like for you going up against Eden a second time and what you think makes this time different?"

Brooklyn lets a long second pass before she answers. Her demeanor is already so different, serene. "Pretty much everything is different," she says. "But I guess the biggest thing is that this time I know what I've gotten myself into."

"Are you saying you underestimated her last time?"

She nods. "Definitely. I took her seriously then too, but you just don't understand how good she really is until you're in there with her."

"There's been a lot of speculation about whether or not she'll be returning as the same caliber martial artist we all remember. She's coming off a serious injury, and you'll be her first fight in almost a year. Do you think that's going to be in her head or have an effect on her performance?"

"I don't see how it could not be on her mind, but I expect her to be better than ever."

Better than ever. Guess I'll be falling short there. I slam the rest of my glass of tequila and get up to refill it as Brooklyn goes on.

"Eden never comes unprepared. She's a brilliant strategist. She never gets tired. She hits you with shots you didn't know were there. She's tough as nails. I mean, she won with a broken neck. She always finds a way to win. And now she's fought me before and trained me. This is hands down going to be the hardest fight of my life."

"I'm glad you mentioned that, Brooklyn. For our viewers who aren't aware, Bauer coached you for around five months before she decided to return. I think we were all shocked to see you two working together after how much you hated each other. You seemed to work well together, but now you're rivals again. Can you settle for us once and for all if you two are on good terms or not?"

"Nothing but respect," Brooklyn says. "She's still the champion. She's never lost. You're not the best until you beat Eden Bauer. That's what this is all about."

"Nothing but respect," I mutter.

"Who do you think gains the advantage from you two having worked together?" the interviewer asks. I notice Laila watching me, attempting and failing to be discreet as she examines my reactions.

"That's hard to say," Brooklyn says. "She taught me much more than I taught her. So, I have the advantage there. But she knows how I think and move and work. In the hands of someone with a fight IQ like Eden's, that's a massive weapon."

"All right, Brooklyn, we're almost out of time here, so I have to wrap it up with the most important question. How do you win this? And how do you see it ending?"

I sit up and study her face like it's going to reveal some essential truth. How are you going to beat me, Brooklyn?

"I have to be perfect," she says. "Pick my shots. Save my energy. I burned myself out last time trying things that were never going to work, and you just can't do that against her without paying for it. She's a master of making you play her game. You have to find a way to fight your own fight."

"And your prediction?"

"I think I get the submission in round three."

"All right, there you have it everyone. Thanks for joining us. Brooklyn, we can't wait to see you in the octagon, March twenty-ninth in Philadelphia."

The video ends abruptly, and we're back on the main screen. I scroll down and click into the fights without saying a word, but even as the event fills the screen, the air is heavy, and I take another sip of tequila.

"Not bad, right?" Laila asks, her voice unsure.

"All very…" I search for the word. "Polite."

"Is that bad?"

"No."

"Aren't you glad she didn't come in swinging and flexing and all that shit?"

"Mhm." I am glad. I'm just also watching Brooklyn turn into a stranger. I'm becoming a person she respects from a distance, a girl her dad told her to train with once upon a time, and it fits better than I thought it would. Our connection was so powerful I thought it was unbreakable, but it was also fleeting. I wasn't even her coach long enough to claim to have much to do with whatever she goes on to be. I told Brooklyn I loved her, but she never said it back. Am I just a fling who helped her figure out her left hook? She knew we were never going to be permanent. Maybe that afforded her the presence of mind not to fall the way I did. It's a little easier thinking of it that way. If I'm stuck in this thing solo, I need the fuck out, pronto.

I stand to get another drink and realize I've picked up a buzz. "Whoa, hello."

Laila chuckles. "Feeling a little better?"

"You know what? Yes," I say. "I think I am."

"Thank Jesus. Come watch the fights."

I bring the bottle with me this time and sit close to Laila, leaning against her. She wraps her arm around me and squeezes me in a half hug as we watch the first fight.

"You know it's going to be okay, right?" Laila says.

"I guess so. I just wish Jin hadn't ended training like that. What's he trying to do? Make me think I don't stand a chance?"

"Of course not."

I remember his disenchanted face. "Do you not think I can win?"

"Of course, I think you can win, Eden." She faces me, looking at me intensely as if it's very important I believe this. "So does he. It was just a little tough love."

"He acts like I quit on him or something. I'm giving it everything every day. I'm in the best shape of my life, and I was no slouch before. He's out there hitting me with shit that would send most people to the hospital. I don't bitch about it. I don't cry about it. What else does he want?"

"We all know you have the skills. And you're right, you're training around the clock. You're overtraining if anything. He's worried about your heart. He told you that."

Laila never pussyfoots, but it still catches me a little off guard. "You agree with him, don't you?"

She cringes.

"Go on, I'm not going to freak out." I rattle my tequila glass at her.

She laughs. "Okay, look, I don't know what's going on, but yes, you're different. I wish you'd tell me why, but you've made it pretty clear it's not up for discussion."

"What's so different? I'm doing everything I've always done."

"Yeah," she says. "But…" She grabs the bottle of tequila off the table and holds it up. "Okay, this. This would never have happened a week from the fight before."

I stare at her, stuck. "Yeah, okay."

"And you're distant. You're nice. You teach your classes. But you practically run off the floor at the end of class. You used to hang out. And your training is great, but it's also kind of obsessive."

"Obsessive?"

"I was driving home Saturday night and saw the lights on in the MMA room at three in the morning. You should have been getting your sleep and recovering. And you run all the time. It's like you can't stop. You do know this isn't a fucking marathon, right? You're obviously going through something. He's concerned about it. And yes, I am too. Are you afraid? Do you think you're going to get hurt again?"

I sigh and stare at the floor. I don't want to lie to Laila, and shit, could I use a good talk about it with a girl, but I can't. I can't break my word to Brooklyn, even though I'm not with her. I can't risk that Laila will tell her close friend who will tell their close friend who will sell it to a magazine. I do trust Laila, but if I don't have the self-control to shut up, how can I expect her to?

That leaves me with no idea how to answer her. I don't want to be distant. I don't want to deal with this alone, but I can't even tell her I can't tell her without risking she'll figure it out. It's not that big of a jump. I give her the best truth I can.

"I just don't have this in me anymore. I want to coach. I wanted to be Brooklyn's coach. I wanted to help her get the belt, not fight her for it. I liked things the way they were."

Laila spins and crosses her legs on the couch to face me completely, looking excited to finally have something to work with. "Then why the fuck *are* you doing this? Why are you changing everything if you liked the way it was?"

I shake my head. "Because Brooklyn wants to fight me, and changing everything is the only way I can squeeze some good out of it." God, I hope this isn't too much information. This could all be true in a universe in which we've never been more than friends, right? "I'm her only loss, and a rematch with me is the only way she gets another title shot this fast. Giving her this fight is more than I could ever give as her coach."

"I don't think that's true," Laila says. "And even if it were, what are you planning to do? Lay down for her so all her dreams come true?"

"Of course not. I'm giving her the opportunity. The win is on her."

"Part of you wants to lose, though, doesn't it?"

"No," I say firmly, and Laila's face floods with relief. She's not crazy to think it. I asked myself the same thing. I do want Brooklyn to win the title, but not from me, and there's no way in hell I'm putting my body through what Brooklyn would do with a freebie.

"I'm one fight away from retiring undefeated and being set for life," I say. "I'm not laying down. I still represent this gym, and Jin, and you, and my students, and myself. Brooklyn would never want it handed to her anyway. She'd be furious, actually. I'm going in there to win. I just wish what we could have achieved together meant more than one stupid loss to her."

"Easy for a person with no losses to say." Laila's sly smile hits just the right note to make us both break into laughter, and God, does that feel good.

"She said that too, but fuck you both." I laugh. "If I had one loss and it was to Jin I wouldn't care in the least."

"I hear you, but I don't know what you're so damn sad about." She downs the rest of her drink. "She wanted it, and it's your ticket out in one measly fight. It's a win-win. And once you crush her and retire, she'll come asking for your help just like she did the first time."

She's not going to come back, but Laila's point stands. For the first time, I can kind of wrap my head around that idea, that it's a win-win. The fight benefits us both, and the relationship was going to crash at some point anyway. We're not exchanging a future together for a fight. We never had a future. It's what Brooklyn suggested already, but I couldn't hear it.

"You're right," I say. "I shouldn't feel like shit about this. It was her idea."

"She wanted it, she's going to get it." Laila slaps my chest, a little rowdy from the tequila. I laugh and pour her another but cut myself off. She's right that getting drunk in training, especially this close to the end of it is not something I'd normally be okay with. If I stop now, I'll be able to look myself in the mirror tomorrow and still get after it one last time before weight cuts.

"Hey, where's your belt?"

I shake my head and laugh. "Oh God, why?"

"Just answer the question."

"In the display case in the MMA room."

"No, that's a replica for display. Where's *yours*?" I'm a little impressed she knows that, and I reward her by pointing at the closet. She yanks open the door and stands on her tiptoes to pull it down from the highest shelf. "Jesus, Bauer, in the fucking closet getting dusty? You're a mess."

She brushes it off, moves everything except our glasses off the table and sets it down in front of me. "I want this in your line of sight until the fight. You got it? You earned it, and you don't owe that to anybody."

"That's really not necessary."

"Don't push me, Eden. I swear to God I'll make you wear it."

"Okay, okay. Plain sight."

She sits next to me just as the fighters on the screen start lighting each other up in a staggering exchange.

"Oh shit!" We both lean forward, barely even on the couch. The young guy in red lands a hook that finally puts his opponent's lights out, and Laila and I are both yelling at the screen just as a knock sounds on the door. We lock eyes, confused and surprised. It's at my actual room door, not the building door, which means it must be Jin telling us to shut the hell up. Laila does that math at the same time and we both fall into silent giggles. Or maybe he's coming to make peace. That'll be short-lived if he sees I'm drinking.

"Hide that," I whisper as I point at the bottle. Laila scrambles to do it while I walk to the door. Once she's shoved it all into a cabinet, I open the door. But it isn't Jin.

CHAPTER THIRTY

Not even the smallest fraction of me is ready to see her there. Brooklyn, in all her devastating sexiness, in my doorway. At twelve o'clock at night. It short-circuits my brain, and I can't seem to make a sound come out of my frozen mouth. Her eyes bounce between me and Laila half a dozen times, and she looks just as paralyzed. I'm guessing Laila is too, because she's not saying a damn word either.

"What're you doing here?" I finally manage.

Brooklyn's gaze is still jumping around the room, from me to Laila to the belt on the table to the fights on the television, and she's not saying a word. Laila finally appears at my side, and I'm just glad someone has recovered the ability to move.

"Hey, Brooklyn," she says. "It's good to see you."

Brooklyn's eyes switch from being glued to Laila, to repelled by her, and she locks on to me. "I want to talk about the fight."

I thought I would become a normal, functioning person again once she spoke, but I was wrong. It's like the entire room is in the vacuum of space being sucked into the timelessness of a black hole.

"I'll just take off and let you two talk," Laila says. I finally come out of my trance enough to turn to her.

"You're not driving, are you?"

"Yeah, but I'm not far at all. I'll be okay."

"No way," I say. "Nuh-uh."

"Really, I'm fi—"

"Laila," I say sternly.

"Okay, okay. I'll walk."

"Nope."

She groans. "Fine, I'll get a Lyft, okay? Don't worry about it. You two just…" She gestures between us. "Whatever, talk."

"Promise," I say.

She raises her right hand in an overly animated gesture. "I solemnly swear to get a Lyft home."

"Thank you."

"Yep. See you tomorrow." She kisses me on the cheek. "Night, Brooklyn." Laila squeezes past Brooklyn in the space Brooklyn makes for her, a space not quite big enough to qualify as polite. Once she passes through the second doorway into the main gym space, I motion for Brooklyn to come inside. Brooklyn holds eye contact for a second that feels extra heavy, then comes in. I almost ask her how she got in, but remember how training ended and realize we never so much as turned the lights off, let alone locked up.

"You want to talk about the fight?"

"What did I just walk in on?" She maintains a normal volume, but there's anger simmering through it.

"What do you mean?"

"You know what I mean."

I scoff, cross my arms, and look away from her, an automatic reaction popping with attitude I can't seem to control. "What do you care? I'm single. Remember?"

"Yeah, I remember." Brooklyn scratches the back of her head, drawing my attention to her hair. Her curls are starting to grow out a little more to create a kind of shaggy look while the sides are freshly shaved despite her wearing that a little longer too. She's wearing a sleeveless hoodie, a look that's always inexplicably made me crazy. The way it's showing off her tattoos isn't helping matters. "So, what? Are you two just playing around or are you a thing?"

Once the accusatory tone leaves her voice, I hear pain, and as much as I want to tell her my personal life is none of her fucking business anymore, I know it won't feel as good as it seems like it will.

"Look, it's not what it looks like," I say.

"You're in your place you never let anyone see with a beautiful woman getting drunk in the middle of the night, but there's nothing going on?"

"Two friends watching the fights and having a few drinks at the end of a long and fucked up day of training."

"She kisses you on the cheek now, huh?"

"What are you doing here, Brooklyn?"

"I just wanted to…" She paces around the room, suddenly having a hard time with eye contact. Then she turns back abruptly. "I knew you two were hot for each other. Didn't I say it?"

"Brooklyn," I say sternly. "I don't owe you an explanation, but I gave you one. Don't call me a liar."

"You're right." She raises her hands. "Sorry. I just didn't expect you to have company."

I probably wouldn't do much better if I saw Brooklyn with another woman, but Brooklyn isn't in the same place I am, so what is this? Some kind of bruised ego at the mere notion I could move on from her?

"What about the fight, Brook—"

"I don't want to do it." She spits it out like it's a parasite she has to get rid of.

"You…" I pause and touch my forehead. "You what?"

"I don't want to do it. I don't think I can."

"You can't be serious."

"I am."

It feels like there are actual moving parts in my brain and they're all breaking down at once. It's such a mindfuck I start to laugh, but it's not funny. Whatever it is, it's not funny.

"You're the one who wanted to do this."

"I know, Eden."

"I asked you not to do this. I told you I couldn't. I told you it would be too hard, but you needed to win. You needed your legacy."

She stares at the floor. I pause to let her respond, but she doesn't.

"What's the game here?" I ask. "You trying to confuse me to death?"

She steps closer. "No. I fucked up, Eden. You were right. I don't want to fight you. I don't ever want to hurt you."

"What happened to 'it's just business'?"

"I'm an idiot."

I dip my head to the side, surprised and amused despite myself. "Kind of." I smirk at her. When she smiles back, the pressure in the room releases and I catch a full breath, but this is a mess. "It's a week away, Brooklyn. It's too late."

"I could fake an injury or something."

It sounds like an idea for a second, but it would get out. Speculatively at the very least, which could still hit hard. "It'd have to be documented."

"How hard can it be to break something?"

"You're a professional athlete," I say. "We're not breaking your bones on purpose."

"Well, I'll just eat the fallout and back out then," she says. I don't know how seriously to take her or how the hell she'd explain such a thing.

"They think it's going to be one of their biggest fights ever. It's too late to change your mind unless you want to seriously fuck your career, and I know you don't want to do that."

"Of course I don't want to do that," she says. "I want to go back in time and undo that whole shitty conversation and change it so that when you tell me it's an awful idea, I *don't* destroy everything, but that's not where we are. We're here, and I don't know what else to do. I can't handle you thinking I don't give a shit about you. I don't need to beat you. I thought I did, but I don't."

I sigh. "You're seriously thinking about backing out? You understand what that would mean for you?"

"It means I may have a shot at you not hating me forever," she says. "You don't know how much I've missed you."

"Oh, Brooklyn, what are you doing to me." I turn away and take a deep breath. "I can't let you do that. It'll kill your career." I turn back to her. "I know you care, okay? I know I meant something to you, and I don't hate you. I can handle it. Just do the fight. Go back to thinking of it as us doing our jobs."

"I can do that, but I need you to understand something." She steps forward, closer than I expected, within a casual boundary. The urge to back away is automatic, but my feet don't move. She has me under a spell, a familiar whirlwind feeling that leaves me floating and a little dizzy. There's a palpable heat of energy hovering over her warm skin. It's like the space between us is humming more and more violently the closer we get until it's screaming at us to touch. And then there's her steady, intense eyes. It's like she won't stop until she's sucked out every ounce of my strength.

"What, Brooklyn?" I whisper.

"It's not, 'you meant something to me,' and it's not, 'I care about you.'" She touches my face. "It's more than that. I love you too, Eden. I should have said it back." She leans in slowly. I have all day to stop her, but I can't. She kisses me, her lips landing sure and hot, sweet and sensual at once. A shock of desire floods my body, and I open my mouth to her without thinking. Her arms wrap around me, her hands on my back pulling me tight to her body, fitting me against her. It feels like it's been so long, but also no time at all. Her tongue slides between my lips, and I can't stop the soft moan that sounds in my chest. She holds me to her tightly as the kiss takes over. Her palms move up my stomach, and I smile at the shudder that runs through her arms.

She steps forward, pushing me gently toward the bed, and finally my brain starts to function again, if in a fog.

"Brooklyn, wait," I say, breathless.

"Please no," she whispers.

"What about your family?"

She exhales long and slow. "It's the same." Her voice is so heavy. I'd give anything to take that sound out of it.

"What are you going to do?"

There's a sheen of tears across her eyes, but it never grows, never spills over. "I still can't tell them, Eden. It would kill them."

"What about you? Don't you want to be free?"

"Of course, I do," she says, a little agitated.

"Don't you want to be able to answer your phone without panicking they'll hear me? Or go to a restaurant without wondering if anyone's taking pictures? Or live together one day?"

"Yes, I want all of that," she says. "But I'd rather live without that than them."

I touch her face, trying to make her look at me. "I love your family, but this will strangle you, Brooklyn."

"It's not *that* bad. You're exaggerating. We saw each other every day. You said you weren't asking me to come out. You said—"

"I know what I said, and I meant it. I don't need you to come out right now. It doesn't even have to be soon. I just need to know you're going to one day. What kind of life can we have if you don't?"

"I can't promise that." She says it strong and flat. Final.

"Never?"

"I'm sorry, Eden."

I close my eyes to try to keep the tears at bay. "I'm sorry too."

"Why can't we just have this?"

"Because we'll go crazy, Brooklyn. The best-case scenario is that we live separately forever, you smile while your dad calls me a dyke behind my back, we see each other in the gaps, I spend birthdays and Christmas and funerals alone, and you spend yours without me. That's the version where things go to plan. The way the press is talking about us, it's more likely we eventually get caught. Part of me wants to let that happen so I can have you, but I can't do that to you if it's not what you want."

She pulls away and faces the other direction, putting her hands on her head. I feel like I can see her adding it all up, considering our fame, how close by her family always seems to be, scanning my assessment and getting angrier as she does.

"Jesus, so that's it?" she says.

"That's up to you."

"No, it isn't," she snaps. "I can't fucking tell them." She punctuates each word, overflowing with anger that I'm not grasping it. "This is the price to be with you? I can't fight for the title *and* I have to turn my back on my family? It's too fucking much, Eden."

"No, Brooklyn. I committed everything to helping you get the title, and we would have. Then I agreed to come back for *you*. So *you* could have your shot because it meant so much to *you*. And I will still do it. I'll do whatever you want. I'll fight you for it next week or I'll back out right now and take all the heat. And get this straight, I am *not* asking you to turn your back on anyone. I'm asking you to love yourself enough to be who you are. You don't even know what will happen. You could end up with everything you want. But if they do turn their backs, that will be their doing. Not mine. Not yours."

"But they will turn their backs. They will." Her voice breaks. "I can't do it. I fucking want you, Eden, but I can't do that. It's never going to happen."

I nod slowly, feeling the swell of emotions rise and fall, words failing to gather. She paces back and forth burning off frustration.

"I understand, Brooklyn."

She finally stops, turns to me, and holds her arms up to her sides in a defeated gesture.

"That's really it then. I'll just see you in the octagon?" She scoffs as if she's been blindsided by her own decision. She spins and rips the door open, primed to slam it.

"Brooklyn," I say sharply. She stops, and I grab her arm, spinning her back to me. "Not like that." I kiss her, hard and angry because that's what she needs, and because I can't let her go without kissing her. She balls my shirt in her fists and pulls me roughly against her so the edges of the neck and sleeve slash against my skin. I shove her into the door as she grabs my ass. She pulls me harshly against her as she returns my forceful kiss, drowning me in the heat of it. When we part, we share a second of breathless eye contact, and then she's gone.

CHAPTER THIRTY-ONE

The soft scraping sound of my feet sliding over the mats is the only noise in the entire building. It's so quiet I can hear my own heartbeat in my ear and my breathing as I slide my right foot in a semicircle behind me, turning my stance ninety degrees and cutting the air with a left hook. I'm wearing sixteen-ounce gloves even though I'm staying off the bag today just for the added weight. Shadowboxing isn't anyone's favorite way to drill, but it's important. It's more exhausting to miss than to connect. People who only do pad and bag work aren't prepared for that and run out of energy once they're actually fighting.

My hangover from the tequila is mild, thankfully. It wouldn't even be detectible if I had a nine to five kind of job, but once you start exercising, you feel it. The silence feels right. The sound of my lungs and heart working reminds me I'm alive. I duck, jab, slip, hook, step, roundhouse, fighting an imaginary enemy.

I picture Brooklyn in front of me, pressing forward with her overhand right that will put me to sleep if I forget it even for a second. I visualize ducking under it as I return the exact same punch. It doesn't feel surreal anymore. There's no more time to wrestle with it.

Having Laila help me finally cross into a headspace where I can actually do this last night, only to have Brooklyn show up seconds later and turn it all upside down again was a shock I thought would knock me permanently off the tracks, but I'm strangely calm.

We've said all there is to say. There's a cavernous rip in my chest that feels like it will never close, but there are no more questions, just a wound, and I can perform with wounds. I can accept what we are now. We're adversaries. We're teammates. We're friends, lovers, and exes. We're warriors. We're angry and desperate and prideful. We're unbreakable and broken. We can give each other everything, and nothing. We're in love, and we're impossible.

All this time I thought Brooklyn was the emotional fighter and I was the cool head, but she was the one to call it business. She was the one to call me weak and fake and still look confused when it hurt because none of it ever meant anything. She was the one ready to bury our rivalry on a dime. It's a game. It's a sport. It's a business. It's a show. While I bow and meditate. While I search and scream and cry and wage war with myself. I was the one to court emotions. From the second I first saw her, she had a grip on me that squeezed tighter until it brought me to my knees. But it's time to stand up.

I have to stand up. For Jin. For Laila. For Mateo. For every Highbridge kid I'm going to take off the streets. For myself. Even for Brooklyn. I have to be Eden Bauer again.

My breath evens out as my focus centers, and I rip a spinning back kick that whistles through the air. I'm sinking through time to the first moment I stepped into the dojang, when Jin was a tall, mysterious, yet comforting stranger who appeared at my side like a savior when I was sure I was going to be dragged into an alley and beaten. I can feel my dobok snapping again with every punch, the crack of thick fabric. Jin's patience meeting mine as he stretched my leg into the correct position while saying words I didn't understand. My spirit salvaged from a smoky drug house, the sounds of my mother pretending to come in the next room, the terror of unwanted eyes, of watching someone decide whether or not to hurt you. And sudden peace. Tranquility and discipline and structure. Incense and pine. Sweat and blood and breath.

I move over the mats, savoring the dance my body knows how to do, the way it glides and lunges, strikes and flows. I carry my past, all my years with Jin, the love and the battles, all deep in the memory of my muscles. It's woven through my entire being.

I feel Jin in the room and slowly lower my high kick from well over my head to the ground and turn to find him standing in the doorway watching. I bow, slow and silent. He steps into the room and approaches, his eyes soft and quiet, until he's right in front of me. He doesn't say a word, just looks at me. And then he reaches out and hugs me. He pulls me tight, holding the back of my head and wrapping me in his arms.

I feel his fear for me, his helplessness watching me struggle, his pride witnessing my roots hold me when the winds of heartbreak tried to rip them out. I know I am as much his daughter as he is my father. I feel loved. I feel ready.

CHAPTER THIRTY-TWO

Having just Laila and Jin as my team is the barest setup I've ever seen, but I wouldn't have it any other way. I feel stripped to my essence. Only the most important pieces get to ride. Getting from the Bronx to Philadelphia is only a two-and-a-half-hour drive. Not having to deal with time, climate, or altitude changes makes the entire fight preparation smoother.

We show up at the Wells Fargo Center early. I've been locked in and focused for hours, settling into my pre-bout mindset. I don't make idle chitchat or look at my phone. I stay clear of TV screens. I don't need to know what they're saying about me. I've never been the most invested in it, but I've never cared less than I do now. I go through drills with Laila at an easy but crisp pace.

Other martial artists poke their heads in as they see me and tell me they're glad to have me back. Brooklyn and I are the co-main event, which means we're at the end of the night. At this point I want to just do it already.

"Don't blow it out too hard, Bauer," someone shouts as they pass by. It's a deep male voice and almost certainly someone I know, but he doesn't pause long enough for me to catch a good look at him, and I don't care. There are only two fights to go, and the crowd is absolutely lit. I need to be loose. Laila and I work hard until I'm coated with sweat.

It isn't until I see Brooklyn in the opening of the doorway that anything can command my attention. She's just passing through, but someone stops to talk to her in just the right place, and we catch each other's eyes. Théo, Leandro, and even Samson are at her sides, fielding whatever question the young man in a black button-down is hurling at her.

I feel her eyes moving over me, taking me in, and yes, sizing me up. She looks uneasy, an expression that's out of place on her face. I wish I could hear her thoughts, have any clue whatsoever what's putting that look in her eyes. Is it emotional? Or am I seeing real, legitimate concern about her ability to win? Is this the face of Brooklyn realizing she's been outworked? I was afraid I wouldn't be able to show up my best self, but I never worried about her figuring it out. I still can't quite imagine that's true.

"Yo, Brooklyn!"

The Shaws all stop and look over. I've never felt so in control of such a group of alphas' attentions before. Brooklyn, especially, is fixed on me with intensity that feels like a physical force. I raise my arms out to my sides the way I did the first night I saw her fight, when she dominated and circled the octagon to point at me with such furious confidence. When she was positive she could not only beat me, but dwarf me. When the only thing on her mind was ripping the belt from my waist and putting it in her father's hands. Be that person again, Brooklyn. You don't have to give anything up for me.

"I'm ready."

She slowly smirks, then turns and points at me. "Good, because I'm coming for you."

I slowly smile back, and she nods in such a small motion I can barely see it.

The fights before us feel like they take eight months to end, but finally they do and someone shouts "five minutes." I get the bolt of adrenaline I've been staving off. It hits so hard my heart pounds in my throat, and I'm suddenly thinking way too hard about how to breathe. Brooklyn's intro song blasts through the arena. The crowd screams so loud I feel the air shake. This is typically the part where Jin says something wise, but he doesn't, just squeezes my shoulder.

When they signal us, I shake out my arms and jump in place trying to expel the nervous energy. My song starts playing, and they wave me down the aisle. I'm surrounded by the standard entourage, my team and a fleet of security and cameras in my face. The crowd explodes.

When I pass through the opening, I catch a glimpse of myself on the screen. The emerald lights glow bright over the octagon in the black sea of the arena spotted with twinkling phone lights. The octagon looks like it's a mile away. Every seat in the house is full and the crowd is deafening, shaking the floors. Metallica's "Fuel" blares and mixes with their energy, spilling into me. All the heaviness of this night lifts for a second as I finally honor the fact that this is the last time I'll make this walk. I soak in the feel of twenty thousand voices, of all their energy focused on me.

I make it cageside and pull off my hoodie and sweatpants, handing them off to Laila. I hug Jin hard but quick, slapping him on the back before moving on to Laila and doing the same. I pop in my mouth guard and let the staff go through their routine to make sure I'm ready. When they clear me to step into the octagon, I bow at the steps and launch inside. The crowd erupts again as I sprint from one side of the octagon to the other, changing direction in a few quick motions that give each side of the arena a little love before I settle into my corner across from Brooklyn.

I barely process the intros. I'm fixated on Brooklyn on the other side of the octagon. Her body is in her typical fight shape, which should not be mistaken for mediocre just because it's her normal. Her arms and abs are so well defined she should be a sculpture. She's holding eye contact, and though there's an inherent predatory fierceness to her face, I also still see that same quality from the locker room. Uncertainty.

"Ready?" the ref screams at me. There's no time to figure Brooklyn out. I nod and get ready. "All right, let's do it. Fight!"

He pulls his hand back and the crowd erupts. I watch for her to come flying across the octagon with an early blitz, but she only moves to the middle. I meet her there, make eye contact, and touch her outstretched glove before I pull my hands back to a fairly low guard that looks aggressive in its confidence, but lends me a better chance to stop takedown attempts. Brooklyn hangs back, moving her head and showing some angles, and I can't fucking believe this is real. It's happening, right here and now. I'm in the octagon with Brooklyn, and she's as dangerous as they come. I can't hesitate or shy away or try not to hurt her unless I want to go straight back to the hospital.

I can already tell her strategy is exactly what she said it was. She wants to hunt the perfect shot and either end it or put me on the ground in one go, keeping herself covered the rest of the time to limit my ability to pick her apart. If I allow the counterstriking, she'll have a good chance of finding that shot. If I get frustrated by it and become overeager, she'll look for the takedown. It's a solid game plan. But then, so is mine.

I throw out a couple of jabs, good, crisp punches to see how she moves. She slips with a small move of her head, a beautiful and precise adjustment she and I worked on for hours. It feels like the crowd isn't here at all and we're just training in the gym. Doing this dance with her is so familiar, but it's an illusion. Brooklyn will go out of her way not to be the same fighter I've grown to know.

I stay active, not throwing anything particularly aggressive, but keeping her off balance and reacting to me. I feel looser than I ever have, flowing and free because everything Brooklyn's taught me about Brazilian Jiu-Jitsu means I'm not chained by fear of the ground anymore. I'm still no match for Brooklyn on the ground, but it's not so dire anymore that it has to control me.

I lean in to threaten her space and see if I can lure her away from her plan. She takes the bait and launches forward. I lean away from the jab and cross, but she rips a hook in my right ribs so fast and hard I can't get out of the way, the price you pay for daring Brooklyn to come forward. The pain sprawls across my ribcage like a Tesla coil, but the combo opens her up. I bob under the cross she follows with, coming up on the far side and ripping a hook into her body, returning her gift. She swings back, and we're already in an up close, dangerous exchange.

She lands something to my temple. I don't even know what it was. I just feel a glove smashing into my head and my brain blink. I swallow down the automatic jolt of fear I've felt so many times and keep my wits level, covering my head and fixing my eyes center mass so I can see when and how her shoulders move. When she winds up, I come up the middle with an uppercut that connects with her chin and sends her stumbling back.

Brooklyn strains to regain her footing, and I know I rocked her. It wasn't the hardest punch, but it hit the right spot. Both of our corners are screaming at us, but I can't make out any of it. I'm sure mine must be telling me to go in for the kill, but I hesitate, and within a second, she's upright again, her eyes locked on mine. I want the round to end. I want her to go recover and come back. That's insane. It isn't what someone who came to win thinks, but I'm not prepared to demolish her while she's compromised. I don't know how to knee her in the face while she has no equilibrium. I can't do it. Maybe she can, and maybe that will end me, but I don't have it in me.

She steps forward and launches a jab in her fabled style, high risk, high reward, hard and crazy. It's difficult to explain just how fast these strikes come from someone like Brooklyn. You can see it when you're supposed to and still not escape. I try to move, but she still rakes over my ear and against the side of my head. My hearing goes out and is replaced by a screaming ringing like my ear's wiring was just disconnected.

I push her backward before she can fire off another shot, just two hands on her chest and all the strength I have to literally push her away. I lift my left leg between us and push-kick her farther away. Her eyes fix on me as she moves her head while coming in again. I broke her plan. She's tasted success and she's chasing it, pressing forward in her high-pressure way. I'm not sure this is better for me now that I've done it. Being aggressive like Brooklyn always is isn't inherently wrong. In fact, it's incredibly difficult to deal with. It's sloppiness that makes her vulnerable, and even now as she slips back to her natural style, she isn't half as sloppy as she used to be.

I snap a leg kick into her thigh, keeping my posture and using my length so her counter can't reach me. She doesn't react to the kick, but it landed solid. I follow it up with another, then immediately step into another on the other side, and follow that with a spinning back kick. It doesn't land, but it does send her leaping a few steps back and off of me. The horn blares and ends round one.

It's like my body is tuned to the horn, and the moment it sounds, all the pain comes. My ribs and ear ache, but I walk calmly to my corner and sit. Laila puts ice on my back and Jin kneels in front of me.

"She can't keep up this pace," he says. "She's already tired."

I nod and take the water Laila's offering.

"Do not hesitate again," he says. "She isn't."

But she is. I can feel it. Neither of us are pulling punches by a long shot, but we're both missing that dose of animal that made us what we are. The break ends, and I jump back to my feet. The round starts, and I come in hot. I take it to her, kicking her leg again, but using it as an entry to follow with a cross that catches her in the jaw. She moves back to circle out, but I follow her and back her up to the cage. I land three shots to her body before she manages to cover up, then rack her in the head once her hands go down. Everything is landing. I watch for something devastating to come back my way, but it doesn't. I slowly realize I've got her on the cage, and I'm teeing off on her. It isn't an exchange. She's just covering up the way people do when they're overwhelmed and accepting a loss. The crowd is freaking out. Théo and Leandro are screaming at her to clinch up, but she's not moving to do it. I thought coming in hot would make her loosen up, force her to shake off whatever reservations are holding her back, but it's not happening. She's clamming up more, and I can't win like this.

I hook behind her neck with both hands and drag her into a clinch, a stupid horrible decision as far as strategy goes, but I don't care. I put the side of my head against hers, holding her tight in the vice of my forearms. My back is turtled, and my chin tucked so we're hidden in a cage of arms.

"What're you doing?" I snap into her ear. "Fight me."

"I am, Eden. You're better. And fuck you."

"Bullshit. You're quitting." I throw a knee to keep the ref from separating us, but hit on the outside where her elbow is blocking. Brooklyn's body fills with life again, and she snakes her arm between my forearms to take control of the clinch, then drops down and wraps her arms around my legs. I switch the function of my forearms from holding her to pushing her down and drop my weight onto her back. It's a good, hard sprawl that would flatten most people, but she bears my weight and keeps her grip on my legs. She steps forward and swoops me up. I feel the entire arena hold its breath as she lifts me into position to slam me.

I expected this moment to horrify and paralyze me, but I feel a strange sense of peace as Brooklyn uses her freakish strength to hold me nearly over her fucking head. I track her movement and predict the throw. Once she's positioned and smashing me down, I shift my weight and manage to land flat. It doesn't feel good, but I'm fine, and the crowd roars. Brooklyn postures up and throws a series of punches at my head.

The round must be winding down for her not to work on a submission. I cover up, but Brooklyn's so fucking strong she can make my head hit canvas even when I block. She leans down and smothers me. She's in mount, a high one, which means she's sitting on my chest and I can barely do a fucking thing. Careful what you ask for, I guess.

She rips an elbow that tears my eyebrow open on impact, and warm blood spills down my face and onto the canvas. I feel the ref close to my right, watching intently, ready to stop the fight. I'm bleeding so badly my shoulder is sliding on the canvas. I reach out to pull Brooklyn against me and stop her strikes. We're locked in a battle, me trying to pull her close, her trying to pry free when the horn ends round two.

She gets off of me, her hand lingering just a second on my ribcage as she does. I go to my corner and the cutman goes to work to control the bleeding. Brow cuts are a crowd pleaser. They bleed like crazy and make us look like savages, but they're not serious and won't end a fight. The worst part is getting blood in your eye.

"You done fucking around yet?" Jin snaps.

He's genuinely pissed, but I'm smiling and trying not to laugh that I've actually driven him to cuss at me. "Yes, sir." She's here now.

"Keep her on her heels," he says. "Push the pace. Double your strikes. She's running out of gas."

I nod and look to Laila, who's on the other side of the fence, to see if she has anything, but she shrugs. "Watch the right." She echoes the instruction I always gave her before she trained with Brooklyn. She's smiling now too. I'm surprised, but I love it.

Rounds three and four are rough and long. We give it everything. The bridge of Brooklyn's nose is bleeding now and her cheek is raw and red. Her thighs are minced from my leg kicks and my shins have lumps where she's checked a couple of them. My ribs are almost certainly cracked, and my neck and shoulders knotted into solid slabs from fighting off her clinch attempts. We've taken each other to the edge of defeat, but we're still here, and I don't know who's winning.

Round five is about to descend, and I'm exhausted and hurt and exhilarated all at once. I see the same spark in her eyes. I'm not afraid anymore. Not to win or to lose or to get hurt. For five more minutes, Brooklyn and I are in a universe of our own, one no one else can ever understand or be part of. We're stripped down to instinct and will. There are no lies in the octagon. Nothing superficial survives in here. You can't fake this. No weapons, no friends, no distractions, no outs, barely even any clothes. We're naked and vulnerable, staring at one another from the edge of our capabilities with nothing to help us but ourselves. Somewhere in the middle this stopped feeling like a battle with Brooklyn and more of a journey with her. My heart hammers in my chest. Sweat drips from her face. And the ref signals us to fight.

We walk to the center to the loudest cheers I've ever heard in my life. Brooklyn and I smile at each other and bump gloves again before we take our stances for the last stretch. Brooklyn has held up extraordinarily well, but Jin's right, she's had no energy for two rounds now and has been running on adrenaline and stubbornness. The price of having so much muscle is that it requires a lot of oxygen, which makes you tired faster.

I cash in my obsessive cardio training and push it, maintaining a blistering pace. I throw most everything with only sixty percent of my power so I can keep it up back to back to back. Brooklyn's mouth is open as she heaves for air, too slow now to get out of the way of most of it. We're so deep into the fight, if nothing has stopped her by now, it's not likely to, but we're going to throw down until the last second.

I snap up a head kick I expect her to back away from, but she shoots in instead and scoops my legs out from under me so seamlessly I'm on the ground before I even realize what happened. Genius timing.

"Take the arm!" Théo screams at Brooklyn. Working with Théo for the last five months has tuned my ears to him. Brooklyn's leg swings over my face, her hamstring pinning me flat across my chest and face in preparation to pry my wrist toward her so my elbow is braced and overextended against her hip. I can feel the crowd stand, their intense focus. I feel Jin and Laila stop breathing. It's like I'm out of my body as Brooklyn's arms hug my wrist to her chest and she starts to lean back to lock up the submission.

I launch my free arm at the one she's attacking and latch on to my bicep with the hand she's ripping away less than a second before it'll be too far out of reach, hooking the other hand under Brooklyn's leg to create a grip that will save me for the moment, but it's not a solution. She leans forward to break the grip, but I use the small space that makes under her knees to scoot down and walk my feet toward her head. I curl toward her, lifting my back shoulder off the ground and release my grip so I can slide my arm out. It's a risky maneuver that could end in her snapping up my arm again and breaking it if she beats me to it, but I move fast and turn my palm to protect the angle of my joint. Almost to my own surprise, my arm slides free.

She doesn't waste time trying to salvage it, just moves straight into the next submission, taking advantage of my low head position by trying to slam on a triangle choke, but I see it coming and pull my head back. My arm and neck are both free, and we scramble for position. Maybe I'm so high on survival chemicals I'm in fantasy world, but I swear to God she smiles at the escape. I think I have side control, but she swivels and locks her legs around me in a movement that looks small and easy, and just like that, I'm in her guard, not a place you want to be with someone like Brooklyn.

Breaking out of it in the next three and a half minutes doesn't seem likely, but I have to try. I round my back to put pressure on her interlocked ankles so they're primed to pop apart and start dropping punches on her. She eats the punches, trying to swipe up an arm to attack again rather than block. Each punch is a dangerous game for both of us as she absorbs the impact and I try to pull my arms back to safety before she can constrict around them.

She sees an opportunity and slings her leg across my upper back, gripping my wrist and trying to pull it tight. Her weight threatens to drag me down where she'll do what she likes with me, but I get my feet under me and use all my strength to stand, picking her up right along with me. She lets go of her attempted submission before I slam her, and I'm able to spring back and out of her grip, on my feet again. I glance at the clock. Two minutes to go. Brooklyn stands, a little slow but not stalling and waves at me to bring it on with a smirk.

I go at her with a flying knee. I don't expect it to land, but it's pretty and closes the distance. She has to lunge out of the way to avoid it, and I follow it with a spinning back kick. I finally catch her with a reaching front kick and follow it with a cross. She locks up with me, throws a knee, and steps out, but I still catch her with a jab on the exit.

Someone shouts that we have thirty seconds left, and we let loose every second of it. My arms are fucking lead and every move she makes is like she's overhand throwing a bowling ball. I can't even tell if she's hitting me anymore. She has to be. I know I'm hitting her. But we're both so tired and in so deep none of it registers, and finally the last horn sounds. Brooklyn and I drop our arms, practically falling into one another. I wrap my arms around her and hug her.

"You're a legend," I say. The words just happen. It's like they come from somewhere else. She hugs me back tight. I let her go sooner than I want to. It's not strange at all to embrace after a battle like that, but I know it won't be long before she worries what people think.

I can see she wants to say something back, but it's like the volume in the arena comes back on, and it's deafening. Our world, our universe of two, suddenly has twenty thousand people in it. Then the octagon is full too. Staff and cameras and both our corners flood inside. I have no idea if I won, and I don't care. Jin pulls me into a hug, and I squeeze him tight.

When I turn to see Brooklyn again, she's still beaming. They start to wave us over for the decision, urging us to stand by the referee for the announcement. It takes a second for us to do it. I don't know about Brooklyn, but I almost like this moment better, when we don't know who won and we're both champions as far as the crowd is concerned.

I play back the fight in my mind at top speed like a flipbook and try to take a mental tally. I think I got it, but it was so close, and you always give a little more weight to the shots you land than the ones you take. You're predisposed to think you won. I won't be shocked or upset if Brooklyn took it. I could never be upset at something that would make her that happy.

I finally let the referee grab my wrist and wrangle me next to him. He grabs Brooklyn and guides her to his other side. My stomach drops as Buffer starts reading the results.

"Ladies and gentlemen, after five rounds we go to the judges' scorecards for a decision. Jonathan Brunson scores the contest 48-47 Shaw. Kyle Silver scores it 48-47, Bauer. Donovan Jones scores the contest 48-47, for the winner by split decision…"

Buffer pauses for a loaded second. We're not waiting for a name. The words that will tell us who won will either be, "And new," or "And still." *Still* if I keep the belt, *new* if Brooklyn takes it.

"Aaaaaaaand…"

I can't fucking breathe.

"Stiiiiiilllll!" He screams the word with every bit of fervor he would an actual name. The ref lifts my hand, and Jin and Laila yell and celebrate to my side. A bizarre mixture of pride and joy and grief swirl in my chest as Buffer finishes the announcement. "The undisputed UFC featherweight champion of the world, Eden Bauer!" I don't notice Dana White right behind me until he's fastening the belt around my waist. I look down at it, feeling a thousand miles from the moment. All I can think is that if I didn't lose Brooklyn before, I certainly have now. I'll always be the person who took her dream. I'm terrified to do it, but I summon the courage to face her.

Her gaze is already there waiting for me. I step around the ref with no clue whatsoever what I can say to her to make this moment easier, but she doesn't look mad. She's not crying, not protesting the decision. She's smiling at me, her warm brown eyes glimmering with affection. She pulls her arm free of the ref's grip, then steps close, just a couple inches from me in a swift and confident motion. I expect a hug, but as her arms loop around the back of my neck, her lips press to mine in a sweet but definitely romantic kiss.

My mind goes blank and reality melts. The crowd roars louder than I thought was possible, and suddenly I'm absolutely positive this is some kind of dream or death experience. She must have broken my neck again and done me in this time. It's a coma trip at best, right? But her lips are still touching mine, warm and soft and real, and my hands are linked behind her back, holding her too. When her lips leave mine, I slowly open my eyes, and the world comes back. We're in front of thousands of people, millions more on television, and still, Brooklyn, the same woman who was terror-stricken at the mere thought of coming out, is standing in front of me like all this doesn't weigh a thing.

"What are you doing?" I ask, equally happy and confused.

"I told you I was coming for you," she says. "I don't want to live without you, Eden. And I don't want you halfway. I want you back. I want you forever."

"That's good," I say. "Because you already have me."

CHAPTER THIRTY-THREE

W hat the fuck do you think you're doing?" Samson's voice sounds through the locker room, bouncing off the metal and concrete and reverberating so loud it sounds like it could fill the whole arena. Brooklyn and I have barely walked in when he screams it, and the sheer fury and lack of restraint sends a shiver tingling through me. Théo and Leandro are sitting on the bench to the right of him. Leandro is rigid, the entirety of his hulking mass tense and flexed. Théo's forearms are propped on his knees as his gaze shifts between Brooklyn and the floor.

"Are you out of your fucking mind?" Samson screams.

Brooklyn squeezes my hand, indicating for me to stay put. She walks farther into the locker room, closer to Samson, who seems to have lost all semblance of self-control. I stay where I am, close to the doorway, but in the room. I don't want to leave her, but I don't feel the right to be involved, either. Samson stares Brooklyn down with his body knife-edged toward her, leading with his left leg and shoulder forward like the only reason he's not lunging at her is some invisible force holding him back.

"Speak up!" he yells. "What do you have to say for yourself?"

"I didn't mean to hurt you," she says. "I never wanted that."

"Horseshit. You knew what you were doing," Samson snaps. He's a tall, strong, fit man, but he's never looked half as big as he looks now towering over Brooklyn. His handsome face is twisted in a snarl. Even when he isn't speaking, it's molded and setting in rage.

"Why would you do that on international television?" Leandro says from the bench. "On the biggest night of your career? Why would you ruin it like that?" He puts his hands to his forehead like he just can't fathom it.

"Yeah, the biggest night of your career," Samson echoes sarcastically. "You lost. And then you make a public spectacle of yourself? What kind of decision is that? What are you so upset about that you would do that to us?"

"It has nothing to do with you, Dad."

"Nuh-uh, don't you Dad me right now, Brooklyn, I swear to God." Samson puts his fist to his mouth and paces, tapping his fist into his own face as he fumes. "You know you just ruined the Shaw name, don't you? You do get that?"

She doesn't answer.

"Generations, Brooklyn. Your brothers, your cousins, your parents, your grandparents, all of us slaved to make the Shaw name mean something, and in one night you tear it all down? For what!" He's screaming at the top of his voice again by the end of his sentence. His volume is inherently scary.

"I'm sure it's not what it looks like," Théo mumbles. Samson's attention snaps to him, and Théo looks up. "Give her a chance." Samson turns his furious stare back on Brooklyn.

"Well?" he says. "Your brother's speaking for you, Brooklyn. What do you have to say to him?"

From my angle I can't see Brooklyn's face, but I'm certain she's trying not to cry. Her whole family is everything to her, but Théo is special. Théo is her heart, and she's his.

"Explain yourself!" Samson yells.

"It is what it looks like, Théo," Brooklyn says. Her voice is quiet, but not a whisper. "I love her."

Théo just stares back down at the floor with a quick shift of attention like he can't look at her.

"You what?" Leandro asks.

"I love her."

"She's a woman." He gestures at me while he says it, breaking my sense of invisibility.

"I know that," Brooklyn says.

"What are you, a child?" Samson says. "You can't love her. You're a woman. You're going to love a man. This is fucking ridiculous. What's the matter with you? You haven't been hit in the head that many times." He shifts his attention to me, his eyes locking on to mine with paralyzing focus. "And you. What part of your coaching contract did you interpret to mean you were being paid to debase my daughter? You're paying every penny back. I will fucking ruin you, do you hear me? You're done."

"Dad, stop it," Brooklyn snaps. "This is not her fault. I'm never going to love a man."

"Kiss your gym good-bye," he says, still tracked on me.

"Dad, look at me," Brooklyn says, louder now. "I'm a lesbian. I always have been."

"Just shut your mouth, Brooklyn," Théo says.

"I can't."

Samson leans over her. "I didn't raise a fucking dyke. You were fine until her." It's the first time he speaks without screaming, but the disgust is just as loud.

"I'm the one who kissed her. Tonight, and the first time. And she wasn't the first, either."

Samson lunges at her and forces her to back up into the lockers. He slams his fist beside her head. Brooklyn jolts at the crash of fist and metal by her face, and I about leap out of my skin, stepping forward until I realize he didn't hit her. Even when I put it together, I'm a second from intervening. I know it's not my family and not my place, but enough is enough.

"What did I do?" he says, low and close to her face. "We didn't have everything in the beginning, but all I had was yours. Why this?"

"It's who I am."

He grabs her shirt and twists it in a tight fist. "Take that back."

Brooklyn looks down at his fist and back up at him, but she doesn't say anything.

"You're a Shaw!" he screams in her face, just an inch away. "That's who you are!"

Brooklyn uses both hands to peel his fist off her shirt in a stern but far from combative motion. He holds the grip for a long second before he lets her go. She slides out from between him and the lockers and turns away from all three of them, walking back toward me.

"Where are you going?" Samson snaps.

"I have to go," she says. "I can't do this anymore. Not right now."

"We'll fix this, Brooklyn," he says. "Come home with your mom and me right now and we'll figure out how to fix it."

She doesn't turn around when she answers. "You can't fix me."

"We can always fix it, Brooklyn. Your family is here for you, but you can't have both."

She turns back to him and long, loaded seconds tick by. My pulse picks up, and I think I may die if she goes with them. It'd be worse than if she never came out, the idea of them locking her in a tower and trying to make her straight. Just when I think I'm going to implode, she walks the rest of the way to my side. She turns back one more time.

"I hope you change your mind," she says. "I don't want to lose you."

It's late, and the reality of our physical condition slowly creeps back to the forefront of my mind as I try to move my body. I was in a haze as staff physicians looked at us, and from the look of her, Brooklyn was even more absent as they checked our vitals and poked and pulled at us. I don't want to go to the hospital. I just want to be alone with Brooklyn. After a fight like we just had, they'll never okay that, but I do get them to agree we'll survive the car ride back to New York so we can go to our own hospital and be close to home when they let us out. It all sounds like a piece of cake until I try to walk.

Holding my gym bag is a task that threatens to double me over. Brooklyn can't feel any better, but the pain in our bones is a far-off silhouette next to the pain of what just happened in the locker room. The warmth and weight of her hand in mine is a comfort, and all I can think about is being a steady railing to hold in the cavern of grief I know she's walking through. I want to say so many things, but I can feel her trembling, and I know any one of them could break her before she's ready.

Jin and Laila have been waiting at the car. They step forward when they see us hobbling out together. Jin rushes forward and takes our bags.

"Are you okay?" Laila asks. It's clear on her face she doesn't mean the physical. Everyone within a quarter-mile knows Samson lost his mind on Brooklyn, and Laila is looking directly at her now. Brooklyn shakes her head but doesn't say anything. Laila just folds her into a careful hug.

"I rearranged the back for you," Jin says and guides us around the silver SUV. The back is open and the seats are folded flat to make extra space. Several plush blankets and pillows line the back.

"That may be the most beautiful thing I've ever seen," Brooklyn says, and Jin smiles. She crawls into the back and lies down, patting beside her for me to join. I crawl next to her and lie down. Jin closes the tailgate, and every muscle in my body slowly melts into the blankets. Everything hurts. I'm certain at least a couple of things are fractured, but none of it is dangerous, and all I care about right now is Brooklyn. We're each on our side, facing one another. I carefully wrap my arm around her.

"I'm so sorry."

A tear rolls down her face, but she squeezes my hand. "Had to happen."

"You were so brave."

"You were right. He knew. I had to do something he couldn't ignore. Something I can't take back."

I pull her hand to my lips and kiss her fingers. She touches my face, brushing her thumb over my eyebrow. "I love you so much." The tears are flowing down her face now, controlled but constant. The words don't really come out, but I can read her lips.

"I love you too, Brooklyn."

Laila and Jin finish tying our bags to the roof and jump inside. Jin turns the ignition, and the gentle rocking of his driving, the easy music Laila puts on, and their concerned glances over their shoulders turn the SUV into a little bubble of love and safety. I just hope Brooklyn can feel it too even though she's raw inside. I think she does, because her arm, draped across my side, pulls me a little closer, and she closes her eyes for the two-and-a-half-hour drive back to New York.

CHAPTER THIRTY-FOUR

Brooklyn takes a little longer to be released from the ER than I do, but not by much. By three in the morning, she comes through the giant swinging double doors, limping on legs that look locked, but walking under her own power. She smiles when she sees me in the waiting room.

"Hey, killer." She leans in to kiss me, a slow and careful motion. My chest lights up like a firework show at the newness of her being affectionate in public.

"What's the verdict?"

"Free," she says. "Nothing serious."

That's a phrase that doesn't mean much from someone as tough as Brooklyn, but they're releasing her, so it must be mostly true.

"You?" she asks.

I have some broken ribs, stitches in my eyebrow, and damage in my elbow at a minimum. I turned down every test they'd let me turn down. Everything hurts so much right now we'd be here for a week if I asked them to look at every little ache, and I just want to go home with Brooklyn. I'll see in a week or two what feels better and what feels worse. If I need to come back, I will.

"Same," I say.

"Thank God," she says. "Jin and Laila around here somewhere?"

"Napping in the car. I tried to send them home, but they wouldn't go. They want to make sure we're settled."

Brooklyn smiles. "You've got some good ones there, Eden."

"You have them too."

She kisses my hand. "Can I talk you into coming back to my place? I have a really fucking big bed."

"Try and stop me," I say.

"Never again."

When we get to the car, Laila is napping against the window. I smile and gently tap the glass, but she springs to life and leaps out like I was slamming it.

"Oh, thank God," she says. "You're both okay, then? Here, sit down. Shit, let me help you."

"Just need the door unlocked, Laila." I laugh. "We're fine."

Jin hits the automatic locks, but Laila helps us into the back anyway. We give them both the same vague but reassuring medical update, and neither presses for details.

"Where to?" Jin asks. Brooklyn tells him her address, and he swings out of the parking lot in a slow and smooth motion. Even though it's only a ten-minute drive, I'm drifting off by the time he stops in front of Brooklyn's high-rise.

"Is that..." Laila trails off. Brooklyn and I struggle to sit up and follow her gaze. The entrance to Brooklyn's building has long, shallow steps with two sets of massive pillars supporting an elegant overhang. The building looks like it was plucked out of Rome and placed here. The hunched over figure in the middle of the stairs wearing a black hoodie with the hood up looks incredibly out of place, but familiar. He has a recognizable build, even huddled up the way he is. Brooklyn looks over at me for confirmation, and I smile and nod.

"It's Théo."

She looks from him to me a couple of times, stunned and frozen.

"He came back." I squeeze her hand.

"You really think?"

"Yes. I really do." I kiss her forehead. "These two can take me back to the gym if you want to talk to him."

"No," she says quickly. "No, come in." The look in her eyes is sure and confident as she holds my arm.

"Are you sure? I don't want to make this harder, Brooklyn. You can take care of your family if you need to. I'll be waiting when you're ready."

"You are my family."

I glance at Théo on the steps. He's staring at the SUV, clearly aware it's us even though it's a rental, probably from our bags on the roof.

"Okay," I say. "Let's go." I reach into the front seat and Laila and Jin each grasp my hand and squeeze. "I'll call you tomorrow," I say to each of them and they nod, a touch of concern in their eyes blending with love.

When we open the back, Théo shoots to his feet and rushes over, extending his forearm for Brooklyn to hold on to as she struggles to her feet. He holds her until he's certain she's steady, then unties and pulls down the two bags from the roof and closes the back. I watch him in astonishment. I didn't think he'd driven over here just to say things that have already been said, but I didn't imagine he would be so helpful and sensitive either. We stare at one another in the dark of three a.m. March for some of the longest seconds of my life.

"Can I come in?" he finally asks Brooklyn.

She nods. "Yeah. Come on."

He shoulders both of our bags and leads the way so he can open the doors. He unlocks her door and swings it open to reveal her immaculate, luxurious loft. The floor to ceiling windows display a breathtaking view of the city as it twinkles in the night.

"I'll just go get some air on the balcony and let you two talk," I say.

"You don't have to do that," Théo says. Brooklyn and I both look over at him in surprise.

"What? I'm not an animal," he says with a brutish shrug. "You're hurt. You don't need to freeze on an iron chair outside. And this one's going to tell you everything anyway." He gestures at Brooklyn.

I barely catch her sly smile, but it's there and completely irresistible. She looks at me and nudges her head at the couch. We go straight for it and collapse onto it. Théo comes over, more reserved, looking awkward until he finally sits down in the chair across from us, scrutinizing us over the lavish rug.

He seems comfortable looking at me so long as it isn't my eyes, and he's scraping over Brooklyn with an even finer toothed comb. Finally, he takes a deep breath.

"That was a hell of a show, ladies."

There's a beat of silence, and then the sheer unexpectedness of the comment makes me laugh. My mouth tugs into a smile and I'm actually laughing, which hurts, but also feels so good. When I look over at Brooklyn, she's laughing too, even harder than I am, but silently as she tries to control it so the contractions don't shred her body. Théo looks surprised at our reaction at first, but then he shakes his head and laughs too.

When we quiet back down, Théo finally meets my eyes, and there's no hatred there, no anger, no disgust, just confusion, or...is it curiosity? He looks at the floor again.

"I'm sorry, Brooklyn," he says. "I should've spoken up. I should've spoken better. I just...I didn't kn..." He looks up at her, and it's like seeing her punches him in the chest. "There's no excuse."

"It's okay, Théo," she says. "It was my battle."

"It shouldn't have been with me, though."

"Is it with you?"

"No," he says quickly. "No, Brooklyn, never. I'm confused..." He glances at me, then snaps away like it's just too damn hard. "But you're my baby sister. I still love you."

"I didn't mean to hurt you," she says. "You know that right?"

"It's always been this way?"

She nods. "As long as I can remember."

"And you never told me?" He looks deeply and genuinely wounded, and though I feel his pain, I can't imagine he doesn't understand why.

"I wanted to," Brooklyn says. "I wasn't strong enough."

"Strong enough for what?"

"To break your heart. To lose you. To see you look at me like—" Her voice chokes off. Théo gets up and sits on the other side of Brooklyn, wrapping his arm around her shoulder and squeezing.

"I just feel like I don't know you," he says. "And I'm worried about you. I don't understand it. I feel stupid. But you're not losing me. You can't lose me, Brooklyn."

She wraps her arms around him and hugs him. She's never said as much, but I can't imagine crying was an acceptable act in the Shaw house, and it shows in the way she tries to hide her tears against his shoulder.

"Hey." He shakes her gently. "Come on, Brook, don't cry."

She sniffs and sits up straight again, swiping at her eyes with the sleeve of her hoodie.

"Did he tell Mom?" Tears spill down her face as fast as she can mop them up. Théo just nods, and Brooklyn cries harder.

"What did she say?"

"She's praying," Théo says, direct and simple.

"Fuck."

"No, it's for the best. You know how Mom is. She burns hot but fast. She'll be okay. I think I can help Leandro calm down too."

I want to squeeze Théo, this beautiful man. I always thought they were unbreakable. Brooklyn and Théo Shaw are so close their names sound more right together than apart. It was still far from a guarantee, and I love him for coming through.

"And Dad? Did he calm down at all?"

Théo shakes his head gravely. The boys always said it with levity, but there's a heavy dose of truth that Brooklyn is a daddy's girl. Every hope Samson ever had for his children cascaded down the fountain of his family tree and stacked on Brooklyn's shoulders. She was his pride, his last, his chosen, his beloved, and she built her life in devotion to his dreams. That can't just vanish, can it?

Brooklyn nods, but she sees me and Théo looking at her and shakes her head. "I didn't expect any different."

Théo sits forward and pats Brooklyn's knee. "You should get some sleep." He leans forward to peer around Brooklyn at me, then looks back to Brooklyn again. He points back and forth between us. "So, this is it?"

Brooklyn smiles and wraps her arm around my shoulder, pulling me close. "This is it."

"I don't really know how to give this speech to a girl," he says. "But that's my baby sister. Don't you ever let me catch you treating her wrong."

I smile and pull him into a tight hug right over Brooklyn. He stiffens, surprised, but I just squeeze him. I don't care that he can't look at me normally yet. I don't care that he has reservations. He's talking to me like her girlfriend, and it's so much more than I expected. After a couple of seconds, just when I'm about to let him go, he hugs me back. He actually hugs me back. When we separate, he hugs Brooklyn one more time before he gets up.

"Go to sleep," he says. "You two are going to be a hot mess tomorrow."

"Love you, Théo," Brooklyn says.

"Love you too, Brook." He waves and lets himself out. We sit in silence for a long second before we look at each other. Alone. Finally.

"Bed," she says. I nod and we move to her room, climbing her waist-high bed like it's Everest and finally collapsing into the plush mattress. It swallows me like a cloud. We each roll to face each other. It's not the most comfortable position, but staring into Brooklyn's eyes is more than worth it. I run my fingertips across her brow and down her cheek. Her deep brown eyes are swimming with a thousand emotions.

"What are you thinking?" I ask.

"I'm thinking I can't believe I almost let you get away," she says. "That would have been the biggest mistake of my life."

I gather her hands in mine and kiss her fingertips. "You don't regret doing this?"

Her brow furrows and her eyes are infinitely tender. She leans close. Her lips brush over mine so light I can barely feel it. "No," she whispers. The heat of her so close courses into me. Every cell of my body is reaching for her, crying out for her to touch me, and she does. Her mouth lands on mine. I taste her wet lips as they press into mine. Her hand moves around my back and pulls me gently against her, and I'm aching for her, hyper aware of all the places our bodies are touching, our arms, stomachs, thighs. I slip my tongue between her parted lips, and a low, longing sound hums in her chest and unravels me. She pulls me closer, but a blaze of pain shoots through my broken ribs under her hand. I want her so bad I'm prepared to ignore it, but she feels me tremble and remembers, pulling her hand away and resituating it on my hip.

"I'm sorry," she says in a voice that sounds so concerned.

"It's okay," I say. "I can take it if you're careful."

She raises her eyebrow at me playfully, and the adorable expression makes me break into a smile.

"What?" I say. "Just watch out for the ribs. And my right thigh. And knee. And probably the left one too. And—"

She laughs and lowers her lips to my neck, kissing under my jaw. "It's okay, Eden," she whispers. "We have the rest of our lives for that. And the next time I touch you, believe me, it will be everywhere."

No one has ever looked at me the way Brooklyn does, with such intensity, such endless warmth and acceptance and passion and calm all at once.

"The rest of our lives?" I whisper back.

"That's the plan, isn't it?" I watch her lips as she says it, low and dreamy and without a hint of doubt.

"Yes," I say. "Forever."

She kisses me again, and I melt into the confidence of her touch, the softness of her skin.

"I love you, Eden."

Her arms are wrapped around me, holding me close and sheltered, and I'm sinking into her, perched on the edge of sleep, holding on to this dream that is somehow real.

"I love you too, Brooklyn. With everything I am."

EPILOGUE

F ifteen seconds!" I yell into the octagon at Brooklyn as the
second round winds down, gripping the clean towel and
stool I have ready and glancing at the bucket Théo's holding to
check he has ice and water ready. The horn sounds, and we jump
into the cage. I slap down the stool and Brooklyn sits. I kneel in
front of her and wipe away the blood and sweat. She looks fresh, if
a little frazzled, breathing hard but not gasping.

"You're beating her on the jab every time," I say. She's beating
Karinov on most things, really. Brooklyn has never looked quite this
good. If the fight ended right now, she'd finally have it for sure. She'd
win the title. But everything could change with one shot. Karinov is
hurt but not out, tired but still capable of ripping Brooklyn's dreams
away again with one well-placed punch. The look in Brooklyn's
eyes says she knows it, which means the punches coming at her
must have plenty on them still.

"He's here," Brooklyn says, something so far from anything I
expected to come out of her mouth it takes me a second to follow
her gaze and see Samson Shaw watching from the first row of the
audience.

Mixed emotions surge through me. It only took Théo about a
month to start acting totally normal around us, another to graduate
to a more comfortable relationship than I imagined possible where
he comes over with beer and Chinese food to watch the fights and
talks to me like a member of the family. Leandro isn't there yet, but
he did start awkwardly showing his face now and then three months

after the blowout in the locker room. Brooklyn's mom won't see her, only talk to her on the phone, and every conversation is a fight, but it's better than silence. It turns out the most accepting of them all is Nicolau, who found out while watching our fight from prison. He called Brooklyn the next day to tell her to keep her chin up after the loss, not mentioning the kiss at all until Brooklyn did, then bursting into laughter with a direct but easy, "Duh."

But Samson? No, not a word from Samson in an entire year. He publicly renounced Brooklyn and refuses to let the boys mention her in his presence.

Having him show up now, on the most important night of her career is a glimmer of hope, a dream come true, really, but also a freight train of a distraction.

"I have to win," Brooklyn says, almost frantic.

"You are winning. Look at me."

She looks back, her attention flooding to me.

"You have her," I say. "She'll go down swinging, but you have her. Go put your jab in her mouth five or six times, right down the middle. When she sets her weight to throw hers, you drop the fucking cannon on her." I grab her right wrist and look her in the eye as confusion passes through her face. I've never said this to her before. She's never needed help going big. My instructions are almost always about control, but there's a place for Brooklyn to unleash, and it's now. She fights smart now. She has vision, and I trust she can look for the bomb without taking one herself.

"Drop it, drop it?"

I nod. "End it."

She nods as the break ends, and Théo and I leave the octagon. Brooklyn stands and waits for the ref to wave them into round three.

"You sure about this?" Théo whispers.

"She knows what she's doing."

The round starts and Brooklyn closes in on Karinov, pushing her back into the cage as she powers through Karinov's punches like she's folding over flowers. She sticks a jab, and Karinov's face changes. She knows she's in trouble right away, and Brooklyn does just what I said, sticking it again and again. She keeps slipping through even as Karinov tries to cover up.

She hits with patience, throwing more than the five or six I thought she'd need. Karinov finally opens up, pushing Brooklyn back, desperate for space, and tries to throw a jab back, opening up her left side. Brooklyn is already chambered for the punch. She sees the opening before it's there, and the second Karinov's hand extends away from her face, Brooklyn cracks her with a clean, devastating cross, and Karinov drops to the ground unconscious.

It's such a clean knockout, Brooklyn turns and puts her hands up as the ref lunges to call the fight off. She yells in victory with her eyes closed.

It slowly comes to me that Théo and I are screaming too. When they let us in the octagon, she pummels into me and wraps her arms around my neck with tears in her eyes, holding me so tight I can't move.

I don't want to let her go until I notice Dana White entering the octagon holding her belt. I squeeze her and let go, pointing her toward the moment she's wanted so badly for so long. He fastens the belt around her waist as Buffer's voice booms through the arena to insane applause.

"Ladies and gentlemen, the referee has called a stop to this contest at thirty-four seconds of the third round, declaring the winner by knockout, and your new undisputed UFC featherweight champion of the world, Brutalllll Brooklynnnnn Shawwww!"

She looks like she may cry, but before she does it turns to smiles as she looks around the arena. I feel like I can see her cementing it all into her memory.

Joe Rogan comes up with a microphone, beaming too. "I'm here with the winner and your new champion, Brooklyn Shaw. Brooklyn, how does this feel?"

She grabs the mic, still a little breathless. "It feels so amazing. There's nothing I could even say."

"It's was a beautiful fight. You were able to impose your will. Did you stick to your game plan tonight?"

"Mostly, yes," Brooklyn says. "And I didn't do this alone. I owe this to all the people who believed in me all my life. My brothers, Théo, Leandro, Nicolau, the best coach I could ever have and love of my life, Eden Bauer—" She's clearly not finished, but the crowd cuts her off when they explode in cheers. They scream so loud she can't continue for several seconds, but she doesn't look irritated. In fact, she breaks into a huge smile and looks at me while they cheer. All this time she worried about what coming out would do to her career, and they absolutely love her. They finally settle down enough that Brooklyn pulls the mic back to her face.

"Most of all, I owe this to the absolute legend sitting right over there." She points at her father, and the crowd cheers again. "We fucking did it, Dad!" She yells it with such passion a shiver goes through me. She hands back the mic and climbs over the fence, heading straight for Samson. The cameras try to stick with her and put Brooklyn and Samson on the big screen just as Brooklyn gets to her father.

An almost comical series of emotions pass over Samson's face, surprise, anger, confusion, and pride, definitely pride no matter how many other things accompany it. She stops in front of him and slowly unfastens her belt, holds it across both hands, and extends it to him. Her motions are so slow and precise it looks like a ceremony.

I squeeze Théo's arm involuntarily. He feels like marble, and I'm positive he's not breathing either as we wait for Samson to do something. Samson has spent a whole year publicly and ruthlessly attacking Brooklyn, yet she's standing in front of him like it never happened. He's unreadable.

"He's not going to do it," Théo says.

"Yes, he is."

The whole arena is still applauding in spite of the painful seconds passing. Finally, still stone-faced, he reaches out and accepts the belt from her. Without pause or hesitation, Brooklyn hugs him, tight and hard. He lets the belt drop to one hand and wraps his arms around her. The energy of the roaring crowd is incredible, and the next thing I know, Théo pulls me into a hug too. Life is more right than it's ever been.

❖

We cancel classes to have a blowout party for Brooklyn at the newly renovated Emerald Tiger. All the students and their families show up. Brooklyn isn't only the star of the gym, she's also been teaching Jiu-Jitsu classes when she isn't in camp, so they know the sweet, patient heart underneath the badass they've seen on television, and they show up in droves to celebrate her.

Even the Shaws show up, a fact that seems to be balancing on a razor's edge, but they're here. Zaira and Samson don't speak to me. I do my best not to even be in their line of sight so they stand a chance of not getting worked up. All that matters right now is that they let Brooklyn back in. They don't have to have a relationship with me.

Brooklyn is off with them now, sitting together in the Taekwondo half of the gym while I mingle on the MMA side. I'm dying to know how it's going, excited about what their presence could mean for the future, but I don't delude myself. Right now, they're far from over it.

When I turn, I see Mateo is standing at the glass case that holds Brooklyn's belt. Brooklyn insisted we set it up in the gym next to mine even though between having the replica here and giving the real deal to Samson, she doesn't have one for herself. She said it should be next to mine for all to see, and it's a display that gets plenty of attention. Even I can't help but stop and look at it sometimes, blown away by the fact that it's real, that we did exactly what we set out to do.

I cross the open floor and stand at Mateo's side, looking at the gold face of the belt, the UFC logo across the center, the leather belt studded with gold buttons, the glittering stones and tiny flags around the outside.

"You think I can ever win one?"

I look down at him, but his eyes are glued to the belt. Mateo has gotten much more serious about martial arts since he moved into the completed student housing. I expected that, to an extent, but he's surpassed even what I guessed might happen. He's put on muscle too, a lot of it, the result of regular meals meeting ample training meeting a natural growth spurt. He's not small and skinny anymore. I'm still trying to help him stop seeing himself that way. As devoted as he's become, he's never talked like this before.

"Is that what you want?"

He looks at me with big round eyes. It takes some measure of self-belief to admit you even *want* to be champion. It's such a big goal, and people don't stop laughing at it until you've damn near done it, but Mateo looks me dead in the eye and nods.

"Yes."

"How much?"

"More than anything."

I tilt my head and nod. "Then you can do it."

"You'll coach me?"

"Uh, yeah," I say. "Why, you got another coach in mind? 'Cause I'll kick their ass, whoever it is."

He giggles. "No, I want you to do it."

"Good. But first, we have a party to enjoy. I suggest you eat some cake now, because in training there's no cake." He beams and beelines for the food table, nearly taking out Brooklyn as she heads my way. She turns to watch him go, smiling at his excitement.

"We running out of cake?"

"He is," I say. "He just told me he wants me to train him to go pro."

Brooklyn raises her eyebrow. "Wow, how about that? Already moving on from me to the next champ, huh?" she teases me as she steps into a hug.

"Hey, he's half your champ. Don't you let him get choked."

She laughs. "You got it. And you don't let him get knocked out."

"Deal. How are your parents?"

She tilts her head side to side. "They're trying."

"I think so too."

"You don't mind that they're hiding from you?"

"Not at all. They'll like me eventually," I say. "I'm irresistible."

She smiles and shakes her head, then leans in and kisses me. Her lips are warm and sweet and completely intoxicating even after a year of head-spinning kisses. "You really are," she says. "They're a tough case, though. It may take a long time."

"You have all of my time, Brooklyn."

"And you have mine."

She kisses me again, wrapping her arms around me and crushing me against her, and there's nothing missing. It's everything I could ever need.

About the Author

Nicole is a lifelong storyteller who loves exploring the hidden corners of life. She has a passion for stories that dive into the emotional and the unseen. She lives in Denver, Colorado, where she is a collector of jobs that inspire her writing and has worked as a 911 operator, police and EMS dispatcher, and martial arts instructor.

Books Available from Bold Strokes Books

His Brother's Viscount by Stephanie Lake. Hector Somerville wants to rekindle his illicit love affair with Viscount Wentworth, but he must overcome one problem: Wentworth still loves Hector's brother. (978-1-63555-805-0)

Journey to Cash by Ashley Bartlett. Cash Braddock thought everything was great, but it looks like her history is about to become her right now. Which is a real bummer. (978-1-63555-464-9)

Liberty Bay by Karis Walsh. Wren Lindley's life is mired in tradition and untouched by trends until social media star Gina Strickland introduces an irresistible electricity into her off-the-grid world. (978-1-63555-816-6)

Scent by Kris Bryant. Nico Marshall has been burned by women in the past wanting her for her money. This time, she's determined to win Sophia Sweet over with her charm. (978-1-63555-780-0)

Shadows of Steel by Suzie Clarke. As their worlds collide and their choices come back to haunt them, Rachel and Claire must figure out how to stay together and most of all, stay alive. (978-1-63555-810-4)

The Clinch by Nicole Disney. Eden Bauer overcame a difficult past to become a world champion mixed martial artist, but now rising star and dreamy bad girl Brooklyn Shaw is a threat both to Eden's title and her heart. (978-1-63555-820-3)

The Last First Kiss by Julie Cannon. Kelly Newsome is so ready for a tropical island vacation, but she never expects to meet the woman who could give her her last first kiss. (978-1-63555-768-8)

The Mandolin Lunch by Missouri Vaun. Despite their immediate attraction, everything about Garet Allen says short-term, and Tess Hill refuses to consider anything less than forever. (978-1-63555-566-0)

Thor: Daughter of Asgard by Genevieve McCluer. When Hannah Olsen finds out she's the reincarnation of Thor, she's thrown into a world of magic and intrigue, unexpected attraction, and a mystery she's got to unravel. (978-1-63555-814-2)

Veterinary Technician by Nancy Wheelton. When a stable of horses is threatened Val and Ronnie must work together against the odds to save them, and maybe even themselves along the way. (978-1-63555-839-5)

16 Steps to Forever by Georgia Beers. Can Brooke Sullivan and Macy Carr find themselves by finding each other? (978-1-63555-762-6)

All I Want for Christmas by Georgia Beers, Maggie Cummings, Fiona Riley. The Christmas season sparks passion and love in these stories by award winning authors Georgia Beers, Maggie Cummings, and Fiona Riley. (978-1-63555-764-0)

From the Woods by Charlotte Greene. When Fiona goes backpacking in a protected wilderness, the last thing she expects is to be fighting for her life. (978-1-63555-793-0)

Heart of the Storm by Nicole Stiling. For Juliet Mitchell and Sienna Bennett a forbidden attraction definitely isn't worth upending the life they've worked so hard for. Is it? (978-1-63555-789-3)

If You Dare by Sandy Lowe. For Lauren West and Emma Prescott, following their passions is easy. Following their hearts, though? That's almost impossible. (978-1-63555-654-4)

Love Changes Everything by Jaime Maddox. For Samantha Brooks and Kirby Fielding, no matter how careful their plans, love will change everything. (978-1-63555-835-7)

Not This Time by MA Binfield. Flung back into each other's lives, can former bandmates Sophia and Madison have a second chance at romance? (978-1-63555-798-5)

The Dubious Gift of Dragon Blood by J. Marshall Freeman. One day Crispin is a lonely high school student—the next he is fighting a war in a land ruled by dragons, his otherworldly boyfriend at his side. (978-1-63555-725-1)

The Found Jar by Jaycie Morrison. Fear keeps Emily Harris trapped in her emotionally vacant life; can she find the courage to let Beck Reynolds guide her toward love? (978-1-63555-825-8)

Aurora by Emma L McGeown. After a traumatic accident, Elena Ricci is stricken with amnesia leaving her with no recollection of the last eight years, including her wife and son. (978-1-63555-824-1)

Avenging Avery by Sheri Lewis Wohl. Revenge against a vengeful vampire unites Isa Meyer and Jeni Denton, but it's love that heals them. (978-1-63555-622-3)

Bulletproof by Maggie Cummings. For Dylan Prescott and Briana Logan, the complicated NYC criminal justice system doesn't leave room for love, but where the heart is concerned, no one is bulletproof. (978-1-63555-771-8)

Her Lady to Love by Jane Walsh. A shy wallflower joins forces with the most popular woman in Regency London on a quest to catch a husband, only to discover a wild passion for each other that far eclipses their interest for the Marriage Mart. (978-1-63555-809-8)

No Regrets by Joy Argento. For Jodi and Beth, the possibility of losing their future will force them to decide what is really important. (978-1-63555-751-0)

The Holiday Treatment by Elle Spencer. Who doesn't want a gay Christmas movie? Holly Hudson asks herself that question and discovers that happy endings aren't only for the movies. (978-1-63555-660-5)

Too Good to be True by Leigh Hays. Can the promise of love survive the realities of life for Madison and Jen, or is it too good to be true? (978-1-63555-715-2)

Treacherous Seas by Radclyffe. When the choice comes down to the lives of her officers against the promise she made to her wife, Reese Conlon puts everything she cares about on the line. (978-1-63555-778-7)

Two to Tangle by Melissa Brayden. Ryan Jacks has been a player all her life, but the new chef at Tangle Valley Vineyard changes everything. If only she wasn't off the menu. (978-1-63555-747-3)

When Sparks Fly by Annie McDonald. Will the devastating incident that first brought Dr. Daniella Waveny and hockey coach Luca McCaffrey together on frozen ice now force them apart, or will their secrets and fears thaw enough for them to create sparks? (978-1-63555-782-4)

Best Practice by Carsen Taite. When attorney Grace Maldonado agrees to mentor her best friend's little sister, she's prepared to confront Perry's rebellious nature, but she isn't prepared to fall in love. Legal Affairs: one law firm, three best friends, three chances to fall in love. (978-1-63555-361-1)

Home by Kris Bryant. Natalie and Sarah discover that anything is possible when love takes the long way home. (978-1-63555-853-1)

Keeper by Sydney Quinne. With a new charge under her reluctant wing—feisty, highly intelligent math wizard Isabelle Templeton—Keeper Andy Bouchard has to prevent a murder or die trying. (978-1-63555-852-4)

One More Chance by Ali Vali. Harry Basantes planned a future with Desi Thompson until the day Desi disappeared without a word, only to walk back into her life sixteen years later. (978-1-63555-536-3)

Renegade's War by Gun Brooke. Freedom fighter Aurelia DeCallum regrets saving the woman called Blue. She fears it will jeopardize her mission, and secretly, Blue might end up breaking Aurelia's heart. (978-1-63555-484-7)

The Other Women by Erin Zak. What happens in Vegas should stay in Vegas, but what do you do when the love you find in Vegas changes your life forever? (978-1-63555-741-1)

The Sea Within by Missouri Vaun. Time is running out for Dr. Elle Graham to convince Captain Jackson Drake that the only thing that can save future Earth resides in the past, and rescue her broken heart in the process. (978-1-63555-568-4)

To Sleep With Reindeer by Justine Saracen. In Norway under Nazi occupation, Maarit, an Indigenous woman; and Kirsten, a Norwegian resister, join forces to stop the development of an atomic weapon. (978-1-63555-735-0)

Twice Shy by Aurora Rey. Having an ex with benefits isn't all it's cracked up to be. Will Amanda Russo learn that lesson in time to take a chance on love with Quinn Sullivan? (978-1-63555-737-4)

Z-Town by Eden Darry. Forced to work together to stay alive, Meg and Lane must find the centuries-old treasure before the zombies find them first. (978-1-63555-743-5)

Bet Against Me by Fiona Riley. In the high stakes luxury real estate market, everything has a price, and as rival Realtors Trina Lee and Kendall Yates find out, that means their hearts and souls, too. (978-1-63555-729-9)

Broken Reign by Sam Ledel. Together on an epic journey in search of a mysterious cure, a princess and a village outcast must overcome life-threatening challenges and their own prejudice if they want to survive. (978-1-63555-739-8)

Just One Taste by CJ Birch. For Lauren, it only took one taste to start trusting in love again. (978-1-63555-772-5)

Lady of Stone by Barbara Ann Wright. Sparks fly as a magical emergency forces a noble embarrassed by her ability to submit to a low-born teacher who resents everything about her. (978-1-63555-607-0)

Last Resort by Angie Williams. Katie and Rhys are about to find out what happens when you meet the girl of your dreams but you aren't looking for a happily ever after. (978-1-63555-774-9)

Longing for You by Jenny Frame. When Debrek housekeeper Katie Brekman is attacked amid a burgeoning vampire-witch war, Alexis Villiers must go against everything her clan believes in to save her. (978-1-63555-658-2)

Money Creek by Anne Laughlin. Clare Lehane is a troubled lawyer from Chicago who tries to make her way in a rural town full of secrets and deceptions. (978-1-63555-795-4)

Passion's Sweet Surrender by Ronica Black. Cam and Blake are unable to deny their passion for each other, but surrendering to love is a whole different matter. (978-1-63555-703-9)

The Holiday Detour by Jane Kolven. It will take everything going wrong to make Dana and Charlie see how right they are for each other. (978-1-63555-720-6)

Too Hot to Ride by Andrews & Austin. World famous cutting horse champion and industry legend Jane Barrow is knockdown sexy in the way she moves, talks, and rides, and Rae Starr is determined not to get involved with this womanizing gambler. (978-1-63555-776-3)